NANCY WERLIN

AND THEN THERE WERE FOUR

Dial Books

Also by Nancy Werlin

Suspense:

The Killer's Cousin

Locked Inside

Black Mirror

Double Helix

The Rules of Survival

Contemporary:

Are You Alone on Purpose?

Fantasy:

Impossible

Extraordinary

Unthinkable

DIAL BOOKS
An imprint of Penguin Random House LLC
375 Hudson Street
New York, NY 10014

Copyright © 2017 by Nancy Werlin

Printed in the United States of America
ISBN 9780803740723
10 9 8 7 6 5 4 3 2 1

Design by Nancy R. Leo-Kelly
Text set in Adobe Garamond Pro

This is a work of fiction. Names, characters, places, and incidents either are the product of the author's imagination or are used fictitiously, and any resemblance to actual persons, living or dead, businesses, companies, events, or locales is entirely coincidental.

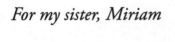

For my sister, Miriam

Chapter 1. **Caleb**

It is your new nightly ritual, as automatic as showering or brushing your teeth or thinking about her. You feed innocent paper into the teeth of the shredder. Then you put the scraps on the floor.

You shape them into a circle or a square or—you did this once, whimsically—a hand holding a cane. The pattern can be anything, as long as you position it in front of your dorm room door. That way, if you leave the room that night, in the morning you will know you did it.

Whatever *it* is.

The paper shreds have never been disturbed yet, not once, which is surprising and interesting. You're uncertain what to make of this.

One thing is true. You are not a little boy anymore. You are seventeen, and you don't believe in Mommy keeping you safe or in friends having your back or in anybody, including you, understanding the difference between good and evil.

You do, however, believe in the indifference of humanity and the absolute inevitability of your own destruction.

You never asked to be what you are. Why you? At this point, you rarely bother to ask that question. *Why* is a child's question, and there's never a good answer, not from him, not for you.

Because. That's the answer. His answer, and now also yours.

Because you are a monster.

Because you are too damn fucking tired.

One day soon, maybe tomorrow, you will stop fighting. You will go down. You will be done.

For tonight, though, you shape the hand and cane again, working the confetti to represent her small, determined fingers. You haven't bothered to learn her name, and you don't plan to. She's nothing to do with you.

But her world is a good place, you felt sure of that from the first time you saw her. You're glad for her, that she lives there and not where you do.

She's alive in the world. It is enough for you.

Chapter 2. **Saralinda**

I took the long way through campus in the storm on purpose, so I am certainly not lost. The Rockland Academy carriage house is somewhere ahead in the woods according to the map that was attached to my invitation. I'll get there but in the meantime I am dallying all I want. In the October rain, I lift Georgia and twirl in the middle of the path. I only revolve once but naturally I slosh puddle muck on myself. I do not fall, I stay balanced. So there.

Thunder rumbles somewhere in the distance.

For your information I don't lean on Georgia heavily when I walk anymore, I just press down gently. Some people assume she is an affectation. I like that in some ways, but in others it seems like an insult to Georgia, who despite her decorations is far from a fashion accessory.

My twirl throws my hood back and rain beats on my head which I like the feel of, it is real and I am glad to be alive and glad to be Saralinda de la Flor and glad to be outside in the most persistent storm in the New York area in

9

a dozen years. Sixteen is way too old to have never before been outside in a storm.

I turn my face upward to the sky which is opalescent (great word—you can almost taste it when you say it). Speaking of taste, the raindrops on my lips are earthy, not in a bad way.

I am late for the meeting so Georgia and I go faster (I don't limp much anymore except when my foot hurts or I am tired) and according to the campus map (I peeked at it again) the old carriage house is—

There.

With its gray stone covered by ivy, the carriage house merges with the woods like a fairy-tale cottage. It has arched eaves and gingerbread trim and it has a *turret* and it is adorable and I want it I want it I want it. Who would not want a home like that?

Although yes even in the rain I see the stone is crumbling, the paint is peeling, half the shutters are missing, and also there's a loose shutter banging with the wind against a window. I don't care however. The school might have thrown this place away but I know what it could be if someone such as me loved it. Geranium flowerboxes and colorful rag rugs and up in the turret, an armchair and a footstool and a tea cozy (I am not entirely sure what a tea cozy is, I will look it up if I remember) and also of course my books.

The turret could be my secret home which would be a big victory because once upon a time I couldn't have climbed its stairs. I am totally in love with this idea until I wonder if I would be lonely. But I don't know who I would invite to live with me and my books, except it would not be my mother.

I open the main carriage house door and discover a large empty garage with a cracked concrete floor and cobwebby lightbulbs hanging from the ceiling, it is not inspiring.

"Le sigh," I remark to Georgia. (I am taking first-year French.)

Okay I have been using any excuse to delay is the truth, which is why I am late. Why delay, you ask—well, it is because I am uncertain about this meeting. However I *was* invited I remind myself, so Georgia and I mount the metal spiral stairs (I can go up spiral stairs! I am extra careful as they are tricky) to the second-floor landing, and there I find a door which is closed.

Boldly I rap and speak. "Hello? Student Leaders Club?"

"Yeah, we're in here!"

It's *him*. I lean on Georgia then. He has rarely spoken to me but he smiles at me in the halls at school and he does it like he sees me. Antoine Dubois smiles at everyone, though. That's who he is.

As for me I am someone who when I reach for the doorknob and turn it and push, the door does not open.

Sometimes I think I've got a fairy godmother who believes that accessibility challenges are educational and fun and so she puts random freaky obstructions—above and beyond ordinary things like no elevator or ramp—between me and wherever I want to go.

I tuck Georgia into the crook of my elbow and try again to open the door, rattling the doorknob like mad until on the other side Antoine shouts with amusement, "Hey, whoever you are, are you pushing? The door opens *out*. Pull."

On the other hand maybe I should be less judge-y about my fairy godmother.

I pull and the door opens easily.

Before me is a big carpeted room furnished with chairs and a couple of old couches. There are four other kids inside: one girl standing, one girl pacing, a boy in my turret with his back to me, and another boy looking at me, who is Antoine Dubois.

Antoine.

He sits on the more hideous of the two couches with his long legs (he is tall and quite skinny) folded before him and his chin resting on one of his hands which are oversized. His skin matches his eyes which are deep brown, you could drown in them or I could. Okay I have the tiniest of crushes on Antoine and I even read the Wikipedia entry on Haiti which is where his parents emigrated from.

In Haiti they speak French and Haitian Creole (which is a language based on French it turns out), it might *possibly* be that this is one reason why I picked French and not Spanish to study. I'd burst into song, but singing is not my best route to impressing anyone (besides it would be odd). I have not figured out my best route to impressing people yet so instead I simply am glad I didn't stay out in the storm splashing in puddles and drinking rain and generally catching my death (to quote my mother, who thinks that Death is lurking 24/7 with a Saralinda-sized net).

Maybe because he hasn't fully grown into his legs and arms yet, there is something goofy about Antoine's looks, which is part of why I like him despite not knowing him. The thing is that when Antoine smiles, he is all dimples and unmistakable sincerity and in short he is not intimidating even though so tall.

He is the senior class president which is no wonder, I would have voted for him too if I were a senior.

"Hey," Antoine says to me. "You made it. Excellent. Welcome."

I am suddenly hyperaware of my saturated hair and face and hands and how stupid I was just now on the other side of the door. Still I manage to smile back at Antoine and I contribute to the conversation. I say:

"Hi."

Chapter 3. **Caleb**

You brace your hands on the rough-grained wood frame of the old turret window. Holding the frame allows your body to absorb the battering the window takes from the rain and the howling wind outside. The shaking feels good and clean and impersonal, as if you were one with the elements, and not a human being at all.

You put your palms on the cold glass. The wavy old window glass is thin. You could smash through it. You'd dive headfirst out the window and join your bleeding and broken body to the storm. You'd break free from yourself. You'd become a howl on the air.

Maybe the broken glass and the fall wouldn't be enough to kill you. But maybe it would, if you did it right.

Maybe it's time.

Chapter 4. **Saralinda**

I take my attention away from Antoine because (1) I have too much self-respect to stare at him like he's a new book that I am going to read under the covers when my mother thinks I've gone to sleep and (2) I do not want to be the kind of girl who totally ignores other girls in favor of a boy and (3) I am genuinely interested in who else is here. I realize listing (3) last makes it not so convincing but space-time requires that things be described in a chosen order even if your thoughts spurt out together. Also sometimes more important thoughts are buried deeper and arrive late. In short I believe sequencing is misleading at best and total crap at worst but I am stuck with it because like I said, space-time.

It turns out that I know one of the two girls in the room: Evangeline Song. Evangeline is texting so she doesn't immediately demand to know why I am there given that I am not exactly a school leader. She is one, but in a very weird way. I will explain.

I only know Evangeline by sight. And by rumor: She is rich (her father was Kevin Song Real Estate). She's also chic, she wears her hair in a chin-length bell that's somehow both ragged and artful, and today she has on a simple blue cotton sweater and leggings, which is not so different from what I'm wearing but *her* sweater has an asymmetric neckline and naturally her boots are not orthopedic, and she wears lipstick (I don't but I do use a touch of CoverGirl mascara which my mother does not know about). Oh but a girl shouldn't judge other girls by their appearance because then she is shallow. Okay so redirect: The main thing about Evangeline is that she is tough, in a take-no-prisoners way where if somebody says something she disagrees with she corrects them usually in a cutting voice. It's like she cannot let anything go, and she is usually right, and this is why though she is beautiful and smart and rich she is not popular, and yet she is powerful.

Evangeline has one friend though and it is Antoine. Is she more than a friend to him? That is my question but now I am again being shallow plus I am dragging a boy into it, what is wrong with me? Okay, I know what's wrong. I like boys, I notice them a lot. I even (briefly!) considered renaming Georgia to George, but I know better, that would be like dumping a faithful girlfriend (though a friend who is actually an oak cane with a crystal orb that I superglued on, the orb is beautiful although, I know, hobbit-juvenile) for a boy.

Evangeline seems to notice my presence with a flick of her eye but she's mostly focused on her phone (relief), and I look at the second girl, who I have never ever seen before. (Why is a new girl at Leaders Club?) She is a white girl, with *very* white skin unlike me, with blond hair cropped short on one side of her head, and dark eyeliner ringing her eyes so heavily that alongside her pallor it looks like she has trouble sleeping. She paces in small circles like a caged cat, not pausing though she does flap a hand toward me in what might be a greeting.

It then occurs to me that there are weirdly few of us at this Leaders Club meeting, only five. Are other kids still coming? Are they having trouble finding the carriage house?

I say five because there is still that other person in the room who is the other boy, the one who's standing in my turret (I recognize that being possessive of my turret is unfair, he might have a turret dream of his own to which he is absolutely entitled). He did not look toward me when I came in and he has not changed his mind so far. Without seeing his face, I am not sure if I know him. He is shorter than Antoine. (Most people are.) He has very straight very dark hair in a businesslike ponytail, tied with a green rubber band he might have swiped from a carry-out container at Whole Foods. Mentally, I refer him to Evangeline's stylist. (I do not have a hair stylist. My mother trims the ends every six weeks like she has ever since I can remember. I would hack my hair off at the neck so she couldn't anymore except that I love my hair as it is, medium brown and hanging to my waist and taking a curl if I try.)

Antoine gestures to the sofa beside him as if I am to sit there.

"You're a sophomore, right? Belinda, isn't it?"

He knows my name!

Sort of.

"Yes," I say. "Or wait. I mean, no. It's Saralinda." My hair feels matted and sticky. Was I entirely insane to get it wet? Yes, yes I was. It takes hours to dry. I long to be back on the other side of the door, where I could fish out my brush and groom. Shallow of me I know. Again.

"De la Flor, though, I have that part right?"

I beam a great big yes at him.

Antoine.

Antoine, whose jeans (speaking of style) are artfully split so as to expose his sports-playing knees. (Don't ask me which sports he plays. Sports are not my thing.)

Antoine is looking at me.

Maybe I can learn to appreciate sports.

Am I his type? (What type am I? I don't know for sure, I only know what I look like which is not exactly the same thing. What is a type really? Is it ethnicity or body type or personality or all of these? Or are we each unique individuals so the very idea of type is inherently false? Only I think Antoine is *my* type.)

Having sort of lost the conversational thread, I say lamely, "Saralinda de la Flor." I am grateful I don't add my social security number.

"I'm Antoine Dubois," he says. Which is polite because he has got to know I know who he is. I have meanwhile fixated on his bare knees and I make an attempt to meet his eyes but mine catch instead on his equally bare forearms and nobody could reasonably expect me to remain unmoved. I do manage to smile into his face at last.

He gestures at the sofa beside him which now I remember he did before. He wants me to sit next to him but I cannot focus on that because he is talking again. "This spot is dry, which I can't say for most of the chairs. The roof leaks." He points upward.

On the ceiling there is a big dark spot in which a drop of water visibly gathers, then plops to land splat in a puddle on a chair seat, making me reassess my building rehab plans to prioritize roofing.

"That's rotten," I say. I am obviously still somewhat intellectually impaired. Also I am leaning on Georgia. It might not be entirely that I am overcome by Antoine's presence, maybe I overstated the situation about not needing Georgia anymore.

The pacing new girl pauses for long enough to snarl over her shoulder.

19

"*Literally* rotten! I've counted at least five leaks. Building should be freaking condemned."

She doesn't appear to expect a reply which is good because I am entirely occupied in shrugging out of my raincoat. I put it on the back of the puddle chair and sit next to Antoine on the sofa, easing Georgia down unobtrusively on the floor.

"Evan and I were saying that we didn't know the school still used this building," Antoine says. He raises his voice. "Right, Evan?"

"Correct." Evangeline lifts her gaze from her phone and looks at me at last with steady eyes (and no smile) and after a few seconds I rate an unsmiling "Hello" which is more than I was hoping for. Then she goes back to whatever she's doing on her phone.

Antoine jokes, "Evan has tremendous multitasking powers but we're working on her social skills."

Evangeline glances up again to snap, "My stepmother keeps on texting me about my birthday. She wants to throw a party. I'm *trying* to be tactful."

"Really? That's new," says Antoine.

"Just following your advice."

"Also new."

Evangeline snorts.

I hope they are only friends.

I wonder if now is the right time to mention my suspicion that my invitation was a mistake. But *they* haven't said anything.

Instead I say, "So why are we meeting here, anyway? Is there something secret about Leaders Club? They wanted us to be somewhere nobody else would see so they wouldn't be hurt if they weren't invited?" I do not add: *If so, that's stupid because when you conceal things it hurts people worse. They always find out.* I think this however and I also think that I have given Antoine an opening to tell me (he would be gentle) that I do not belong.

But Antoine shakes his head. "Nothing like that. It's just another club, except that the faculty picks the members. I don't know why we're all the way out here in this rat-hole. Last year we met in the library."

I think about telling Antoine not to call my carriage house a rat-hole. Then I hear an exasperated sigh. It's the new girl, who stops pacing right in front of me.

"Leaders Club? Give me a break. This meeting is a total and complete waste of my time." She confronts me with a small, square palm. "I'm Kenyon."

Oh, I think. Oh! But I do not gape. I reach out and shake hands, which if it's a thing that girls do when they meet, I never experienced it before but then again I am sheltered. I also feel stupid because I should have figured it out. *This* is the famous senior transfer student. She *definitely* belongs at Leaders Club, even if she only arrived at Rockland Academy two minutes ago.

Martha (her true first name) McKenyon is maybe five inches taller than me, which is to say of medium height, and she wears a black tank top that exposes her arms. The short hair on one side of her head is trimmed so close that I can see pale scalp. She also has a tattoo in purple lettering which looks a little like bruising on her fair skin. The tattoo starts behind her ear and says WHY BE HAPPY WHEN—it runs down below her shirt so I can't read the rest (see previous mention of my creatively obstructionist fairy godmother).

I only have a second of frustration however since Kenyon immediately returns to pacing and also to grumbling.

"Everybody else better get here soon. At least the faculty sponsor. Because student leadership? Could I possibly care less? Listen, you guys. I will not be roped into it. I'm going to talk to whoever is in charge and make that absolutely clear."

She glares at Antoine and at me and at Evangeline and at the turret boy, who (if he hears) is no more interested in her speechifying than he was in my arrival. Evangeline is still working her phone with nimble thumbs, she doesn't acknowledge Kenyon's rant by even an inclination of her stylish head. Meanwhile the turret boy grips the window frame like prison bars and leans toward the glass as if he's going to smash his head against it.

"No worries, Kenyon," says Antoine peaceably.

Kenyon turns to him and me. Her eyes are very blue inside the rings of eyeliner.

"Sorry. I'm overreacting. It's just, here's the thing." Her fists clench. "I won't be Rockland Academy's token queer. I will not pose for photographs for the school website. I am not going to plan the prom or whatever it is this leadership club does. I am here to finish high school and get out. Low profile all the way. Nobody said my scholarship depended on anything like this. I'm just supposed to get A's. That's what I was told! Is that clear to everyone here?"

She is calm at first, but as she talks her voice tightens to match her fists, it's like she can't help herself.

I find myself leaning toward her.

"I'm sure nobody is going to make you do things you don't want to," I say. I think about adding that everybody knows about her tragedy but I don't say anything because maybe it would hurt her or remind her or something.

At the same time I am thinking that if there *is* prom planning to be done, I could do it for her. I would like to go to the Academy prom even if I am sitting behind the check-in desk with Georgia, handing out whatever.

Kenyon looks from me to Antoine. "So I've made my point?"

Antoine says again, "No worries." After a moment, during which another fat drop of water plops audibly down onto the wooden chair, he adds, "So what I think you're concerned about here, is that you might get used? No. Nobody is going to use you." He looks straight at her. "I promise."

If I were not sitting, I would swoon at his large sneakered feet. I totally have taste in boys do I not?

Kenyon reaches for the back of her neck. "Thanks. Thank you. I'm sorry. I appreciate that. It's just, I don't want extra responsibilities this year. I got a little scared and—and paranoid." Her eyes blink very fast.

Again I wonder about telling her that I understand about her mom's murder and all, but I haven't found the right way to say anything when Evangeline looks up from her phone and cuts in.

"If you ask me, *Martha*—which, I remind you, you did, you asked all of us—here's what I think. Since you don't care about helping make Rockland a good place for absolutely everyone, and you're only interested in yourself, then you *should* leave this meeting. The rest of us can explain to our faculty advisor why you're gone. In fact, I'd be happy to take that on personally, especially if it means we can be done with your drama. Deal?"

A fatter drop of water plops into the puddle in the center of the wooden chair and I think that Evangeline must not know about Kenyon's mother, although how can she not it was all over the news and everything—but if she knew she wouldn't be saying things like that.

Kenyon stiffens like a dog catching a bad scent. She swivels to face Evangeline. "No," she says distinctly. "No deal. I always speak for myself."

Evangeline's hair swings gently. "True. Quite a lot, I'm noticing."

I look at Antoine. He closes his eyes for a second and shakes his head, and then opens his eyes again, visibly trying to decide what to say and meanwhile for some reason I look over at the boy in the turret—

I get a squish-squish maybe-I'm-sick feeling.

I know exactly who the turret boy is. His hair is longer, the ponytail is new, and he is taller and broader than he was last year, but this is Caleb Colchester, and you should hear what they say about him. There's this one story about a suspicious fire in his dorm that I really find scary and frankly Georgia shall go nowhere near him. I decree it. Just to be safe.

We looked at each other once. Caleb and me, I mean. It wasn't just looking, I don't know how to explain it except that it was a *looook*.

It was last year not long after I started going to school here and I was puppy-smiley to everyone, although in kind of a cautious way by which I mean I didn't keep looking at people long enough afterward to see if they smiled back in case they didn't. (I am aware this is pathetic.)

But he wouldn't *let* me look away. Caleb. I cannot explain. I *had* to keep looking at him and in fact I was staring even though his face had all the expression of flat paint, which is to say he did not smile back, and our eyes locked and I felt my smile kind of dissolve but I kept looking at him and he kept looking at me. By the way he has very dark brown eyes not that I would notice such a thing and he has lashes which let me just say do not need CoverGirl mascara. Then (or maybe it was all happening at once) he noticed Georgia only not with a once-quick-and-away furtive glance like most people but instead he looked slowly, and my equally good foot started throbbing and I wondered about my blood sugar level and I had to lean on Georgia to make it down the corridor and around the corner to where I could rest. I sort of had a panicky feeling that he would follow me and to tell the truth I felt sure that he *would* follow me but he didn't and after a while I breathed again.

I didn't know then and I don't know now what that *was*. Am I his type? He is not *my* type. I like nice boys. Also he is Dr. Caleb Colchester's son. He's Caleb Colchester Jr. There are entirely too many students at Rockland with famous parents. (I am not one. Neither is Antoine, yay. Evangeline, yes. Kenyon is famous but for being herself which is awesome.) Anyway since then, whenever I see Caleb Colchester Jr. anywhere, I disappear however I can. He makes my insides jump.

But he's never glanced my way again as far as I can tell.

To repeat, I am not the kind of girl who goes for the bad boys. I have better sense. I like the good ones. Even in books and movies I disapprove of the bad boys, so there. I feel extremely strongly about this in case you can't tell. My point is that love should not be complicated if you can possibly help it, and I believe you *can* help it by picking out a good one from the start. How hard can that be, right?

Caleb keeps to his turret now, unaware that I have identified him, and I am glad glad glad and I think about leaving before he can turn and see me, which is crazy I know.

Meanwhile (and by the way that mental drama of mine took maybe five seconds) Kenyon takes a step toward Evangeline and looks her up and down and her lip curls. "I guess every school has its pretty little goody-goodies like you who care how things look, not how they are."

I blink because "goody-goody" is not what anybody would ever say about Evangeline.

Evangeline arches an eyebrow.

Antoine says, "Evan, no. Peace. Leave her alone. She's upset. She didn't mean it."

Kenyon glares at Antoine. "I don't need your protection. And I *did* mean it."

"Antoine?" says Evangeline sweetly. "She doesn't need your protection. Also, she did mean it."

Antoine drops his head into his hands, then looks over

at me and mutters, "Someday, someone is going to kill Evan. It might be a relief."

Evangeline drawls, "So, *Martha*? This little, er, goody-goody was looking forward to meeting you. I admired how you got those guys bragging on video. How you got justice for that girl. But now that I've met you, I know *your* kind. You wanted attention, not justice. That's why you did what you did."

I am appalled, I have to intervene. I blurt, "Evangeline, stop, listen, maybe you don't realize about Kenyon's—"

A tremendous crashing of thunder interrupts me and we all freeze listening to it and outside now the rain pelts down hard and the windows rattle and—

"I'm out of here," Kenyon says and walks to the door. More thunder blocks out whatever it is that Evangeline says as Kenyon grabs the knob and pulls. But the door does not open because she is making the same mistake I made before (maybe Kenyon has my same fairy godmother?).

Now she kicks the door and I grab Georgia and get to Kenyon as she kicks the door once again. I say, "Kenyon, we have to push, let me help," and she looks up just as I reach out—

Which is when from overhead there's this loud groaning crackling sound.

Which is not thunder.

Chapter 5. **Caleb**

Voices behind you force themselves into your consciousness. You don't want to look to see what's happening. You don't want to care or even be curious. But you turn anyway.

There are four other kids in the room now, not three. And . . . the newcomer is her.

That time you first noticed her, she smiled at you.

You don't know why the way she looked, the way she moved, got caught on a tape inside your head that plays and replays. All you know is that it did.

It does.

Her cane looks heavy. It is made of wood, and has a handle and a cloudy blue crystal ball on it, so it looks like something Gandalf the Grey would carry. As the son of a physician—because psychiatrists are physicians too, just ones that have chosen to screw around with people's brains with their medications and their questions—maybe you ought to disapprove because she'd be better off with something metallic and lightweight.

The Gandalf cane suits her, though.

You look at her cane so you won't look at her as she moves across the room toward the door, which the other girl has just kicked.

You know her name. You do. In a weak moment, you looked her up in the student directory—

A window shatters, and at the same moment there's an indescribable tearing, cracking, and crashing from the ceiling. More windows crash. Glass flies through the air. Gravel and plaster and tiles and thick, soaked tarpaper descend from above.

In the turret, you're semi-protected from the collapse of the main roof. Still, instinctively, you throw yourself to the floor and tuck your arms over your head. The crashing—the wind—the torrent of the rain—and the screams.

The screams.

Why it is that you can distinguish Saralinda's voice from the others, you don't know. You've never heard her speak before.

Still you know her voice.

But there is nothing you can do for her or for anyone, including yourself. Not now, not yet.

Your breath comes and goes. Your heart pounds. *I don't want to die,* you think, and your entire body jerks in surprise.

Beyond your crouched body, the wind howls. The

crashing goes on and on forever, though later you will calculate that it is all over in three minutes. At some point in the middle, the screams stop. Then the crashing ends. Mostly.

But now the wind and thunder are louder than ever.

Cautiously, you lower your arms.

The ceiling gapes open to the storm. Rain sheets into the room. Furniture is ripped into pieces. Shards and splinters of glass lie scattered everywhere, and heavy wooden support beams lie crashed amid the huge mounds of roofing material.

You cannot see or hear any sign of the other four kids.

You think of the shredded paper pattern on the floor of your room. Undisturbed this morning. Again.

I could not have done this, you think. *Could I?*

Unsteadily, unsure, you get to your feet. Did you maybe rig something? Somehow? On the roof? During the daytime? No, that's crazy. Also, you haven't had any intervals of blank time recently. But then again, you've never realized you've had an episode until you're confronted with proof. Such as—for example—the bloody, disemboweled body of a squirrel on your father's inlaid ivory-and-ebony chessboard.

Caleb, you're coming with me to give this poor animal a decent burial in Central Park. Then we will never speak of this again.

"I want Mama—"

No. No, you come back here. You're coming with me. It would destroy your mother if she knew you did things like this. Do you want to kill her? Do you?

What can you do when your enemy is yourself? Your internal evil twin?

You can't think about it now, though—you shove it aside.

Now.

Here.

The other kids are buried in the debris. Where?

You cup your hands around your mouth. "Where are you? Somebody answer! Somebody! Saralinda!" The howling wind tears your words away. Even you can hardly hear yourself over the storm.

Nobody answers.

You scan the room as your mind spits out questions. How much weight can the floor bear before it collapses? What about the main roof beam, looming in silhouette against the raging sky? Will it crack and fall next?

You shout for them again.

Nothing.

You'll search for them inch by inch.

Chapter 6. **Saralinda**

Tearing, cracking, crashing—

I scream. I scream and I'm on the floor flat on my back and there's something heavy on top of me I can't breathe I push upward with my shoulders against the weight the weight the weight but it won't move panic beats in me choking me my mother where is she she's always there whether I need her or not and now I do she's strong I'm weak she's right after all it's not safe for me my fingers try to tighten around Georgia who is not there either I lost her when I fell is she okay I try to breathe—

I gulp in air. There's air. There is air. Bad air, chalky somehow but I feel it in my lungs and it helps me push the panic a half inch away. I manage, and now I know what has happened and what to do. I will get out. I grit my teeth and push firmly upward with my hands and shoulders, because I am *not* going to suffocate to death in this rat-hole (Antoine was right) with its rotten roof which (Kenyon was right) should have been freaking condemned—

"No! Stop! Please stop moving. For the love of God, don't push at me!"

It's a whisper from directly above because it is not some*thing* on top of me, it is some*one*.

Someone who has saved me from being crushed, broken, and suffocated by the ceiling.

That is when I realize I am truly okay because (1) I know what pain is like and this is not it. This is fear and I can push it another half inch away and hold it there. Then (2) I can after all breathe, and finally (3) there is another living human being with me, physically with me. Which is a good thing, oh it is such a good thing hooray living human being.

"Kenyon?" If this were a romance novel it would be Antoine who saved me but it is Kenyon and ha! guess what, in real life that is utterly fine as far as I am concerned.

"Yeah," she whispers. "It's me. Don't move. Please don't ask me to move either. From what I can tell, we're buried under a mountain of stuff. There's an air hole, and I can see, but—I don't know—everything on my back feels unstable. I don't think we should even *talk* loudly. It might, uh, avalanche."

My chicken salad lunch shoots from my stomach toward my throat but I shut my mouth in time and swallow it back along with stomach acid which we are old friends when I am anxious. I breathe. Okay I am okay.

As reported before, I am lying on my back. I now see

that Kenyon is on top of me with her stomach to mine, and she is also sort of propped up on her forearms like a sphinx, which is what is giving me room to breathe.

The wind howls. It is no longer outside, it is inside, it is with us, it is on us.

I whisper to Kenyon, "You saved me."

"Yeah, don't give me too much credit. I don't know what I did. It's kind of a blur."

I squint to see what I can. Soaked ceiling material, I deduce. And gravel. All piled around us.

We are buried.

"So there's a pile of debris on your back," I say. "The same stuff that's all around us."

"Yeah." Kenyon pauses. "It's pretty heavy."

"You said there's an air hole. Can you see anything out of it?"

"It's only a small hole to the left of my face. I see rain."

"Okay, do you hear anybody? The—the others?"

"No."

My throat closes up for a second. Antoine. Evangeline. And Caleb Colchester. Hurt bleeding broken? Buried like us? Unconscious? Dead or dying?

Except wait. Caleb wasn't under the main roof. He was in the turret, which has its own roof, pointed and independent. Less likely to crash? Maybe so. Which means he could probably help, except—

Except he is Caleb Colchester Jr.

There are school stories about him.

I say, "Kenyon, listen. We can't wait for help because it might not come. We have to get ourselves out of this."

Kenyon's voice is dry. "Oh really? How? We can't move or we'll be buried. I'm the one with the crap on my back here, girlfriend. We need help from outside. Somebody's got to come eventually, right? Like, 911 people. We need to hold out. *I* need to hold out."

I hear something in her tone, at the end there. I say what I should have said at the start but I did not think of it then, because to be honest self-absorbed.

"Are you all right? Does anything hurt? What?"

Kenyon pauses for a fraction of a second too long. "I can hold on until help comes."

I have another bad moment but panic will do us no good, so I push it away. At which point I have an actual idea. "Do you have your phone on you?" Mine unfortunately is in the pocket of my backpack. (I don't always answer my mother which is easier when you accidentally leave your phone in things.)

"Yes! Yes, I do. My left back pocket." She hesitates, shifting slightly. "There's no way I can reach it."

Because her arms and hands are occupied in holding her sphinx position and incidentally that is what is also keeping me sheltered and safe.

"Maybe I can," I say.

"Try. But move very carefully?"

"Oh yes. I am not interested in an avalanche ruining our air hole," I say.

I edge one hand up alongside our bodies where her hips press into mine, trying to get to her rear pocket (and by the way there is nothing sexy-times about this believe me for either one of us). But the debris is so packed around us that it's like trying to force my hand slowly through a wall.

I try I try I try, sort of gently yet firmly.

"I'm sorry. I can't do it."

Kenyon exhales. "It's all right. Help will come."

If I were bigger. If I were stronger. "You were right," I offer. "This place *should* have been condemned."

She sounds resigned. "I'm right a lot. Guess what, it's always bad news. My whole life is bad news."

I choke back a hysterical laugh. "Mine too, pretty much."

"Really? What's your story?"

"You don't want to know."

"Tell me," she says. "What else do we have to do but talk?"

The thing is, I am not quite sure why I said what I said. I don't feel like my *whole* life is bad news. There's a lot of good in it. It's hard sometimes physically but the foot operations did work and I don't walk lopsided even and I don't know how to express this but getting used to pain can teach you things, which is not saying pain is good or worth it but something else happens. I told you I can't express it but I'm not sorry to be who I am—something like that. I have become tough in a peculiar way that doesn't show. And then many people have diabetes and it is not strange or odd, people get it. Basically, I am alive and there is my mother who did agree to let me go to school and live more normally, and I absolutely believe in counting your blessings.

Maybe I said my life was bad news to distract Kenyon, to be more one with her? Because she is in pain. You cannot be pressed up close against someone like we are and not feel what they feel, trust me.

But now I am stuck with having said it.

I say, "So I was a preemie and sort of sickly for a long time. Also, I was born with a birth defect called club foot."

"Is that why you have a cane?"

"Yes. I had operations to reposition my foot properly. It's still smaller than my other one which gets expensive for shoes. One foot is size five and the other one is six and a half. But it basically worked. The operation, I mean. I don't need Georg—my cane—very much anymore. I mean, sometimes I do." I trail off because I have messed up. "Okay so I call my cane Georgia," I add lamely (oh no, terrible pun unintended).

"Georgia is a pretty name," Kenyon says gently, like I

am four, and I think of punching her in the stomach for condescension (except maybe that should wait until after we're rescued and she is okay again, and also mentioning Georgia's name did make me sound pathetic probably) when she adds, "Saralinda is pretty too. I've never heard that name before."

"It's from an old book called *The Thirteen Clocks* that my mother loves."

I do not say the rest which is that I used to love it too until I realized that Princess Saralinda is one of those princesses who is beautiful but has very little character and also she is under a curse that stops her from speaking her mind (which troubles me though I understand the curse on Princess Saralinda is necessary for the plot). I like my name in any case and there are still things I like about the book but I can't love it anymore is my point.

However I'm reminded of Princess Saralinda every time I *don't* tell my mother what I think.

Kenyon says, "There're a lot of bones in the foot, right?"

"Yes," I say and I am not unhappy for the conversational topic to change to feet. She is right, there are twenty-six bones in the human foot and ankle. In fact, one-fourth of all the bones in the human body are located in the feet. All the bones are small obviously and interact in complicated ways which means that foot surgeons think very highly of themselves and charge a lot of money.

We should never be mad at our feet. They work hard and they are beautiful and I have taught myself never to say "my good foot" and "my bad foot" because they are both my feet equally. Thank you, feet. I also believe that it is a good idea to regularly say thank you to the rest of your body because really the whole system works hard on your behalf and is a miracle. So even if your pancreas doesn't work and you monitor your blood sugar and take insulin shots, you should not resent it but be grateful.

"Also, I have diabetes," I say. "Which *sucks*."

Not a word I normally say aloud even when I think it but it's not every day that a roof collapses on you and there's nothing you can do but wait and hope. (Which ought to give me more insight into Princess Saralinda's situation.) Still I am so surprised I said it—and it's true, diabetes does *suck* and don't tell me I could get an insulin pump instead of shooting up because I tried that and for me that was worse, I felt like I was part machine not in a good way and I would rather test all the time and worry all the time too. And yet I am glad I said it yet shocked yet ashamed yet (again) glad that I laugh, and then Kenyon laughs too. Then we are cackling like hysterical witches but trying to do it quietly so all the stuff on her back doesn't shake, and in the middle of it I gasp out:

"Plus! Guess what? I'm a huge burden to my mother. She's single, and deciding to have me basically ruined her life!"

At this point we are dying laughing.

Also I have shocked myself to the core. My mother has never said that and she would be devastated that I did which means in a way I just betrayed her. So I suck too but I don't care it feels so good to laugh.

To tell the truth aloud.

Finally I can talk and I say, "What about *your* family? Why is it all bad news?" Then too late I remember about her mother and I freeze for a second because I cannot *believe* I forgot, I do suck, and I start a stumbling apology but she cuts me off.

"Saralinda, it's okay. Right now it's that my grandfather hates me. I mean, *hates* me hates me."

Somehow this sets first her and then me off laughing like hyenas again. I don't know why. It's not even slightly funny.

Sometimes you laugh instead of crying I guess.

When we stop and she finally talks, her voice is quiet and thoughtful and sad. "So my grandfather is my guardian now, and he blames me for my mom's death and maybe I *am* to blame. Um. You know what happened? You heard about it?"

"Yes," I say quickly because I don't want to make her talk about it, it is so horrifying. Basically after the teenage boy rapists that Kenyon got on videotape were arrested, then this crazy man who didn't even *know* any of them went to Kenyon's house with a gun and hid there and then when Kenyon's mother came out, he shot her in the head. He thought she was Kenyon. This was a truly crazy person whose ex-wife had a restraining order out against him and he had no connection in real life to Kenyon or her mom, none.

But he had a gun.

So Kenyon's mom died just like that in the driveway with no head anymore.

"Also," Kenyon says in a voice with no expression, "my grandfather is kind of homophobic. So. There you go. He's got two good reasons to hate me."

"You have to live with him?"

"I live at school," she corrects me.

"Right," I say.

"A teacher at my old school helped me get this scholarship to Rockland Academy. It's just until I'm eighteen and then my grandfather won't be my guardian anymore. Maybe I'll never see him again after that. I think that's what he wants."

"What do you want?"

"Oh. I don't know . . . I guess for now, just to get the hell out."

I imagine all the details that she's not saying. I feel honored that she has told me what she has. "I am so sorry about your mother. It was not your fault. You were doing the right thing. You are not responsible for the choices of an insane person."

"I don't know about that. If I could go back—but I can't. You know what? I wish I *could* wish that he'd gotten me instead. That's what my grandfather wishes. But I'm not sorry to be alive. Which isn't the same thing as wanting my mother dead. It's—I can't explain."

"I think I understand anyway," I say.

"Thanks."

I want to confide more to Kenyon about myself, things that before this moment I didn't know—didn't let myself know—bother me. Like how my mother won't tell me anything about my father (who was a sperm donor but there is supposed to be at least some pictures and some other basic information and why can't I at least see them I won't love her less). Our last name isn't anything to do with me since it's the name of my white mother's ex-husband who wasn't my father, and because I am darkish and have the name de la Flor everyone assumes I am Latina but I don't know what I am. I would like to know, is that wrong? The thing is that I feel like I'm assembled out of spare parts, some of which are (to be honest) dysfunctional. I don't only mean my foot and my pancreas but something inside to do with my soul feels like it is not connected properly. It doesn't help that we have no other family but each other, I mean me and my mom.

But this feels extremely petty next to Kenyon's situation because at base my mother is alive and she loves me and wants the best for me.

I say, "I think you're amazing."

"And I think you are a sweetheart, Saralinda."

It is lovely to hear this.

We are both silent then. The wind roars and the rain slams.

It is very strange circumstances under which to make my first real friend.

"Kenyon?" I say.

"Yeah?"

"Let's not die today. Not even to make things easier for my mom and your grandfather."

She laughs. She has a wonderful laugh, it is like a trill.

"Do you have an idea?" she asks.

Yes. Yes, I do. Caleb Colchester was in the turret. That is a fact. He is out there and I believe he is unlikely to be injured.

Antoine.

Evangeline.

I pray they are okay too.

I say to Kenyon, "I'll shout for help, as loud as I can. If the others are okay, they'll be able to find us. If you can hold still while I yell, maybe the stuff on top of us will stay stable. Maybe it won't, you know, vibrate."

She thinks it over.

"Do it."

I am scared. It doesn't matter. I draw in a deep breath. Then I yell as loud as I can, over the wind and the pounding rain.

"It's Saralinda and Kenyon! We're buried! We need help! Help!"

Sharp gravel pours in beside my head. Kenyon's body shakes in reaction. Panic spikes through my heart, but then the gravel fall slows and I go again.

"Is anybody there? Help! *Help!*"

Nothing but the rain and howling wind and more gravel dribbling down alongside my face in a relentless stream. Above me Kenyon shakes.

"Help! Help us!" I yell.

The wind. The rain. More gravel pouring down on us, around us.

"Help! Help! Help!"

Then a voice bellows above the wind. "Where are you, Saralinda? Kenyon! Shout again! We've called 911! Hold on! I'll find you!"

It's not Antoine.

It's Caleb Colchester Jr.

Chapter 7. **Caleb**

You sit fully dressed in a cubicle of the emergency unit. You could walk out. Get an Uber and go right back to school. You always spend weekends there even though your parents live in the city and you could be home inside an hour. But that apartment is not your home, and why should the roof collapse make this weekend any different?

You hold Saralinda's cane. You dug it out of the rubble while Saralinda and Kenyon were being loaded onto stretchers—Saralinda protesting that she was not hurt. You like holding her cane. It is even heavier than it looks: She must be stronger than *she* looks to be carrying it all the time. You put it down and pull your phone from your pocket. You look again at the text from your father.

On my way. Don't say anything.

He thinks you did it. It angers you, but maybe he's right.

Maybe you are responsible.

Only how?

You get up. You push aside the curtain around your cubicle

and catch the eye of a passing nurse. She approaches you, smiling.

"We'll be with you shortly. You're not an emergency, I hope you understand. We'll need to check you over—"

You hold up your hands. They're filthy and covered with cuts. "No problem. Just, can you tell me how my friends are?" The word *friends* is a lie. It's what came out.

"You're the hero, aren't you?" The nurse lowers her voice. "I shouldn't say anything, medical privacy, but you deserve to know. Plus, I understand you're Dr. Colchester's son." Her eyes go starry, like most people if they have met your father, or read his articles on the human mind in *The New Yorker*. "I see the resemblance. Don't worry about your friends. That one girl has some lower spine bruising, which can be tricky, but—"

You interrupt. "Who?"

"The blonde with the neck tattoo?"

"Kenyon." You'd been scared for a moment that delicate Saralinda had a back injury.

"Yes. She'll have to wear a brace for a week or so. She's in pain, but we have some lovely meds. Don't worry. She'll be fine."

Lovely meds. Like your mother's. You do not show your distaste. "What about Saralinda? She's the one with—"

"Oh, her." The nurse's eyes roll. "The one with the mother. She just has some facial and head cuts. Her mother is with her, of course. All the parents are here." The nurse's gaze flicks behind you, as if she realizes there's a hope of seeing Dr. Caleb Colchester in the flesh. You watch her assimilate that you are alone. "Someone did call your father? That is, your parents?"

"Yes." You slip your phone back into your pocket.

A plump woman in her early fifties emerges from the curtained cubicle across the way. She grips a thick three-ring binder. Her eyes—totally different in expression from Saralinda's—fix on the nurse.

"I'd like another blood sugar reading for my daughter. My experience tells me not to trust that first one without verification." Her toe does not tap but it seems as if it might.

She's so totally not what you expected. You'd assumed Saralinda's mother—no, no, you assumed nothing, you never thought about it.

Okay. You did think about it. You thought Saralinda was Latina, like your own mother. But her mother is white.

"Just a moment," the nurse says to her. She turns very deliberately back to you and points. "The restroom is that way, sweetheart." She winks. "Then hang out near the main desk. You might hear something." She goes to attend to Saralinda's mother.

You walk slowly past Saralinda's cubicle, but all you hear is the nurse saying, "Good color. Normal blood pressure."

You linger, but Saralinda doesn't say anything.

You head to the restroom. You peel off your T-shirt and shake out dust and particles of roof debris. You brush more stuff from your jeans. You wash your face, neck, shoulders, pits, and arms with hot water and soap, ignoring the sting of the soap in the cuts that are everywhere, dabbing away blood that seeps when the cuts reopen. You fish your comb from your back pocket and repeatedly wet it and run it through your hair before fastening it into a ponytail again. Then, because you've made an unholy mess of the floor, you grab a bunch of paper towels and mop up.

Finally you straighten and check your reflection. You don't want your mother to get hysterical when she sees you, if she sees you, if she comes—which she won't, or she might need more meds. Lovely meds.

You are careful, as always, not to meet your own eyes in the mirror, in case the wrong Caleb leers back at you.

You're the hero, sweetheart.

No.

It's true you called 911 and located the other kids and dug them out. But if you had not, Evangeline would have. She had almost freed herself by the time you found her, the first one you found, and she'd snapped right into focus. She'd been very useful, which had been necessary because Antoine's left arm had been dangling from his shoulder.

Still, thank God the official help came when it did.

You feel sick, picturing what might have happened.

You push away from the sink, unlock the restroom, and head to the main desk. There's no need to eavesdrop. Evangeline is there. She's as dirty as you were ten minutes ago, with bandages on her hands and some white surgical tape across one cheek. Next to her is a redheaded woman, who has an arm around Evangeline's waist. This woman is in close, anxious conversation with a man in a white coat.

Evangeline spots you and twists deftly away from the redhead.

"Hi."

"Hi." You stuff your hands in your pockets. You nod a question toward her bandages.

She shrugs. "Whatever."

"Know anything about the others?" you ask.

"Antoine has a dislocated shoulder, which we guessed. Also cuts and bruises, but altogether, not bad. What about Saralinda?" She hesitates. "Kenyon?"

You fill her in with what you learned about Kenyon and Saralinda. It's strange to be talking with her—with anyone—so easily. You won't let it last, of course. It's not safe for it to last.

You are who you are and nothing has changed.

Then the redheaded woman is beside Evangeline again, curling a soft, tentative arm around her waist once more. Her face is oval, her eyes a deep, vivid blue, and—well.

Well. Her femininity is basically weapons-grade. It is not directed at you but is something this woman *does*, is. Still you have to work hard not to check out how her breasts push gently against her shirt as the redhead rubs her cheek gently against the tape on Evangeline's face, and a smudge transfers itself from Evangeline's face to hers.

"Introductions, Evangeline?" she says.

Evangeline stands stiffly in the woman's embrace. "Spencer, this is Caleb Colchester. Caleb, this is my stepmother, Spencer Merriman Song."

Stepmother? Really? You try to hide your surprise, but the stepmother has got to be in her twenties. Her left hand, resting tenderly on Evangeline's shoulder, bears a single plain gold wedding band. The clichéd trophy second wife, married to Evangeline's rich father before his death. You wonder how much older he was.

Evangeline's stepmother smiles at you rather too eagerly. When you reach out a reluctant hand to shake, she takes it in both hands. "Caleb," she says, lingering too long on the syllables.

Your mother is also rather younger than your father, fifteen years, though he says he thought it was ten originally, and that she lied about her age when they met. To you, looking at their wedding pictures, the age disparity is clear.

There's one picture you used to love. Your mother, Veronica, holds her head high, and her eyes glow more brightly than her rhinestone tiara. You get your father's point about the tiara; it is in spectacularly bad taste. (She hasn't dressed to go out without consulting your father ever since.) Yet you love her in the tiara.

Loved her, past tense.

Spencer Merriman Song still holds your hand. Hers are soft, with perfectly manicured nails. "So you're the one," she says intensely. "There are no words except thank you. *Thank you.*" She looks into your face as if she is trying to find something there.

You mutter something about having just been there. She laughs as if you said something witty. "Modest. Well. It's a miracle that all of you survived." Finally she lets go of your hand. She smiles tentatively at Evangeline. "Dr. Young tells me that my daughter won't need plastic surgery." She leans on the words *my daughter,* and flashes a smile at the man in the white coat, who's lingering nearby, angled toward her.

For the first time you kind of want your father to get here, so he can meet this woman. You want to hear him analyze her afterward, the way he does. Because there are times when his perceptiveness about people is astounding.

If mean.

Evangeline eels free of her stepmother. "Excuse me. I see Antoine."

The stepmother's smile falters. You nod at her awkwardly and follow Evangeline.

Antoine's shoulder and arm are supported by a sling. There's a thin woman by his side, as tall as he is, with graying hair in short dreads around a worn face that resembles his. Mrs. Dubois hugs Evangeline with one arm, and says in a low voice, "I thought he was dead! I thought I'd never see him alive on this earth again!"

Evangeline hugs the woman back. "It's good to see you, Gabrielle. Antoine's fine. We're all fine."

Mrs. Dubois nods. She clutches a small gold cross hanging from her necklace as Antoine makes significant eye contact with Evangeline.

He says, "Let's go home, Mom."

"You'll come home with me? Not back to school?" His mother's voice shakes.

"Just for tonight."

Evangeline darts a look at Antoine, and says, "Are you sure?"

He nods at her, and she frowns more darkly. You wonder what's going on. Evangeline doesn't think Antoine should go home with his own mother?

Then you hear another woman's voice, raised in demand, and look down the length of the emergency unit as the curtain twitches back on Saralinda's cubicle. Her mother emerges with her big black binder.

It's then that a tall, bulky man in wire-rimmed glasses strides through the automatic doors of the emergency unit. He's alone. He's wearing an open jacket, khakis, and a white dress shirt. He pauses for a second, looking around.

That thing happens, a small stir, a flutter, as a nurse, then a doctor, then an aide, and then another doctor recognize him.

It's as if they are iron filings and your father is a magnet. It has always been this way. Even when people don't know who he is, it is this way.

They stop. They stare. They smile.

He keeps moving.

You stand your ground.

He's in front of you.

"Caleb. What a terrible experience. I've been talking to the police. You did well." His arms twitch forward as if they might hug you.

You shove your hands more deeply in your pockets.

His arms go back to his sides.

You don't ask about your mother. You aren't disappointed that she's not here. It's better.

"Dr. Colchester?" Within seconds, your father is surrounded by his admirers.

You step away. If he notices, he doesn't stop you. It's time for you to go back to school, alone.

Wait, no, not quite yet. There's something you have to do first.

Chapter 8. **Saralinda**

My mother holds the tip of the insulin syringe against my bare thigh. "Ready?"

Since we got back from the hospital last night she's treated me like I am helpless. She doesn't wait for me to answer, but sticks me (it doesn't hurt, I am used to it, she knows that).

I finish getting dressed. She sits on my bed and watches me which I wish she wouldn't but okay yesterday scared her, me too I get it.

She hands me Georgia.

Regarding Georgia this is what happened. When my mother was not there Caleb Colchester walked into my hospital cubicle and put her down beside me and left. (Georgia is fine or will be after some wood polish plus WD-40 for her mechanisms and Simple Green window cleaner for her orb.)

Caleb did not say anything by the way. But he thought to save Georgia for me. And it was *him*. Antoine's arm was dangling from his socket and he was in shock, it was not his idea to save my cane. Also it was not Evangeline though she was very active in digging us out.

My mother says conversationally, "Maybe I'll sue Rockland Academy."

I stop thinking about Caleb.

"What?!"

She shrugs. "They're responsible for the welfare of students on their property. Ergo, they're guilty of negligence."

"But I'm fine. All of us are going to be okay."

"Saralinda, you were buried *alive*. There will be long-term effects. PTSD—that's posttraumatic stress disorder. You'll suffer for years. Possibly forever." She gestures me to follow her into the kitchen and makes me sit. "Eat this."

Food balances the insulin but it's a sad little apple not protein. "Can I have an egg? I'll make it." I start to get up but she presses me back down by the shoulders.

"Rest. I'll make eggs for you later."

"But—"

"I want you to have carbohydrate before any protein. I'll test you again in two hours."

I would prefer to test myself but instead I take a tiny bite from the defeated apple and think about suffering forever from stress. Although it was horrible in the carriage house at the same time I was under the debris with

Kenyon and we shared secrets about ourselves and we laughed.

"I'm going to research PTSD," says my mother.

"I'm going to my room," I say.

"Good. Rest."

Georgia and I retire with the wood polish etc.

It is 8:22 a.m. on Saturday.

It's going to be a long day, correction: weekend.

I used to be all right penned up at home, it felt safe and cozy. But now even when I have a delicious book (maybe I will read *Jane Eyre* again and see if Rochester is as bad an idea as I remember), I cannot disappear into it completely anymore. If only I could lock my bedroom door, have some privacy, but there is no lock on my side (renovation mistake, long story).

From my bed I can see outside my window. I am allowed to open it even though we are on the sixth floor because the window sticks firmly at eight inches. There is nothing interesting happening outside unfortunately.

Our home is a co-op on West 24th Street. It was once a one-bedroom one-bath condo that my mother bought with her divorce settlement (before my time of course). In the renovation, my mother sacrificed the living room so we would each have a bedroom and bath of our own, hers is also her office.

Having my own bathroom has never thrilled me however, because my mother thought it should be accessible in case I am in a wheelchair one day. I don't know why she would think that would happen, I am better. The shower is enormous and on every wall there are metal grab bars. All-white tiles on walls floor ceiling. Why tile the ceiling? If the tiles weren't there I would paint it blue which would help with the ambiance.

My bedroom is fine however and I also like our kitchen which is our living room as well. It has a TV and two chairs and an ottoman for my equally good foot. My mother's printer is kept there too so that I can use it to print school-work, which I do not do often to be honest. My mother prints a lot and keeps her printings in her bedroom/office (she does not trust the cloud so she must print).

My mother has a bedroom/office because she works from home. She helps scientists write grant applications. She makes a lot of money sometimes because she is very good at it, and we are very good about not spending money when we don't have it. When there is money, we splurge. It's fun. We get clothes and gourmet takeout and tech, and then last year there was enough money to send me to Rockland (and a car service every day). I asked to go to school but I did not think she would let me, and then she did and a really good one too.

I love her, I do.

I have a terrible thought which is that she wants to sue

Rockland because money is getting low again. Dilemma because I want to keep going to school but if we are poor I should not go, I should go to public school but I do not want to start all over again at a new school.

As I finish polishing Georgia, my phone beeps. I snatch it up.

—*This is Kenyon. Are you there, SL?*

It's my first-ever text from a friend! And suddenly I am SL. I like it!

I gently close my bedroom door. It might be a while before my mother notices this I hope. I text back.

—Yes! How are you?

—*Not bad. I'm on Percocet. Whee! You okay?*

—Fine. Where are you? Hospital? School?

—*No, I'm with Mr. Mayer, the teacher at my old school I told you about. He came to get me.*

—Did you talk with your grandfather?

—*They called him from the hospital. I told him I was going with Mr. Mayer. That was that.*

I am suddenly appreciative of my mother who loves me and came right away when she was called.

—Sorry.

—*It's okay. Do you know how the others are? Including what's her name.*

—Evangeline? Will you forgive her? She helped get us out.

—*It was Caleb who was in charge, not her.*

I do not answer this directly instead I type something very prissy.

—I think Evangeline could be a good person underneath. I think maybe she didn't know about your mother.

—*We'll see. Oh, Mr. Mayer is calling me. Gotta go. Bye.*

I put down my phone. I look at Georgia, who is shining with polish.

Caleb saved her for me.

Chapter 9. **Caleb**

You have felt strange and unlike yourself at school the last few days, since the carriage house collapse. People came up to you and said nice things. Awkwardly. But apparently you didn't react the way they wanted. Not that you know what they want or how to give it to them. What you know is that it didn't take long for them to take their compliments and their curious eyes and move away from you again.

You're not hungry these days. That's another change, because normally your body demands to be fed. Yet now it's as if you are sick; all you can stomach is flat ginger ale. After a while you realize something: You are filled with waiting. There is no room for anything else.

Waiting for what?

You don't know. On the one hand, it seems like waiting is all you have been doing, your entire life. Waiting for some self-inflicted disaster. On the other hand, you're trying something new now, you're trying to force something—change? That's what the confetti is about every night. It doesn't seem like much, true. You're like the fly waking up in the sticky silk of the spider's web and beginning to struggle. Or maybe just beginning to question the path you took to get here.

But still it is something.

Change is coming.

Or disaster.

Or both.

What happened in the carriage house is part of it.

What happened to *you* in the carriage house is part of it.

"Hello, Caleb," says the Head of School as you pause in the doorway to his office. To you it is a familiar place. In fact you were here yesterday. *Very possibly you saved four lives, Caleb.*

The Head of School is Dennis Y. Lee. He has a bachelor's degree in English Literature from Georgetown, a PhD in Education from New York University, and an MBA from Wharton. These degrees are tastefully matted and framed on the side wall of the office.

Dr. Lee is trying to hold your gaze but you look away.

Today you are not his only guest. Five matched chairs with the school emblem are arranged in a small arc, and in them are your—you can't say *friends*. The carriage house kids, left to right: Antoine, Evangeline, empty chair, Saralinda, and Kenyon. Kenyon is standing behind her chair with her hands on it. She wears a back brace, and her crutches lean on the wall nearby.

Evangeline directs a faintly wobbly smile your way. You have a flash of memory: her kneeling in the debris beside you, digging Kenyon out, her movements fast yet careful, with her soaked hair sticking to her cheeks and tears streaming unchecked from her eyes.

You nod at her.

You sit in the empty chair between Evangeline and Saralinda.

Dr. Lee remains standing. "I have something very serious to say to all of you. I have spent the last couple of days conducting an investigation. The five of you each received a text message inviting you to the carriage house for the first meeting of Leaders Club. It turns out that Mrs. Allyson did not send you those invitations." Dr. Lee's voice rises, incredulous and enraged. "Someone unknown wrote and sent those messages, hacking Mrs. Allyson's account."

You blink.

You don't know the first thing about hacking! It's all you can do to download an app—you fat-finger everything, and half the time something freezes or sends an error message. Plus, the text messages came during the day.

You had no blank time during that day. You were yourself.

The relief is so strong—*you really didn't do it, this is*

proof—that at first you completely fail to notice the corollary.

Somebody else *did*.

You dare to look at Saralinda. She sits leaning forward, with her wizard cane held loosely in one hand and her head tilted so that her long braid hangs over her cheek.

Her eyes are huge.

"Something else," Dr. Lee says heavily. "The carriage house was scheduled for demolition. We knew it was unsafe. There were large signs on it warning people to keep out, and the door was padlocked. Padlocked! But the lock was cut, and it and the signs have now been discovered in some bushes."

Antoine says, "They were deliberately removed?"

"Yes. They were." Dr. Lee looks searchingly from Antoine to Evangeline to you to Saralinda and finally to Kenyon. "You all see where I'm going? The bogus text messages that led the five of you to the carriage house in the storm . . . the unsafe carriage house. This is beginning to look like some kind of sabotage that was aimed specifically at one or more of you."

Saralinda makes a tiny noise of dismay.

Antoine and Evangeline look at each other.

Kenyon shakes her head.

"But the roof," says Saralinda at last. "We were only there a short time—nobody could have anticipated the roof would collapse while we were there."

Dr. Lee shrugs. "Probably this wasn't originally meant to be as dangerous as it turned out to be."

His gaze goes to you for a second.

Okay, in fairness, your evil self has the skills to remove a sign and even a padlock. But really, you don't have the skills of a hacker.

"I am postulating that this was meant as a harmless prank, which went awry because of the storm." Dr. Lee actually says *awry*. "I'm considering an announcement to the school at large to see if someone will come forward." Again his troubled gaze rests on you.

You stiffen, because you guess what he might be thinking: that you did this to set yourself up as a hero, instead of a villain.

Antoine leans forward. "Have you traced the hacker from the phone records?"

Dr. Lee shakes his head. "The police could do that, but I have not yet involved them. I would prefer to describe this incident publicly as an accident and handle any disciplinary matters privately."

Saralinda frowns. "But what would be the point of a prank like that?" Her chin lifts. "You know what? I thought it was weird that I was invited to Leaders Club. I thought it was some sort of joke. I'm not a leader."

"You're an excellent citizen of this school," says Dr. Lee, heartily but too hastily.

Saralinda rolls her eyes.

You say flatly, "I'm no school leader either. I figured I was invited as a joke too."

There is silence.

Dr. Lee says, "All right. At the risk of, er, melodrama, do any of you have enemies here? Classmates who dislike you?"

More silence before Kenyon says, "Who knows if there's somebody out there hating someone else for some reason they made up in their own head? Or no reason at all? This discussion is pointless." Her voice is high, tense. "I have to go." She grabs her crutches and lurches toward the door.

Evangeline snaps, "Oh, so there goes Martha McKenyon, rushing out again. What is this feeling I have? Déjà vu?"

Even with the crutches, Kenyon manages to slam the door behind her.

Saralinda hoists her wizard's cane and points it at Evangeline. "Why are you so mean to her? Don't you know what happened to her?"

"What, the thing with those kids at her school? Of course I know!"

"No, I mean with her mother!"

"What *about* her mother?"

Saralinda's eyes widen. "Okay. Listen to me. Before you

say another word to her *ever*, go google what happened to her mother. I'm saying this for your sake."

"Wait," says Evangeline. "What?"

The bell rings for lunch.

Antoine puts his hand on Evangeline's arm. "Later, Evan." He turns to Dr. Lee. "Can we go now?"

"I guess so," Dr. Lee says unhappily. "But if any of you think of something . . ."

You catch yourself feeling sorry for Dr. Lee, who has a few hundred kids to look after. This is a new thought, and a surprising one, but then, it's been a surprising few days. Also sometimes thoughts take shape deep inside and emerge only when fully grown.

"You can go," says Dr. Lee resignedly. "All of you."

Chapter 10. Saralinda

It's lunchtime, so after the meeting with Dr. Lee, we head to the cafeteria. I say *we* because we go as a group which feels weirdly natural. Caleb lopes along behind me and Antoine and Evangeline, I am super-aware of him maybe because he saved Georgia. I have to thank him by the way which I have not done yet. Anyway, as we walk we overtake Kenyon who is moving slowly on her crutches, and we absorb her. Even Evangeline slows her pace. I give Kenyon a smile but she is busy narrowing her eyes at Evangeline.

I sneak a quick look at Evangeline, whose face is subdued. I see her look at Kenyon and bite her lip and then Evangeline takes a deep breath.

Go on, I think at her. *Apologize. Do it do it do it.*

She says nothing.

At least I said something to Evangeline, I was not silent. Kenyon is my friend and nobody messes with the friends of Saralinda (okay, friend, singular), especially when they are being rude and unfair.

How could Evangeline not know? Then I feel a stab of pity for her because when she finds out what happened she will feel terrible, who wouldn't?

Although before I get to feeling too great about myself, I must note that I am walking next to Antoine, and I cannot think of the right thing to say to him, or indeed *any* thing.

He is frowning. He looks anxious.

So I blurt the wrong thing which is: "Antoine? Are you okay?"

He doesn't hear me because he has taken his phone out, providing direct evidence that my mother is right about humanity voluntarily embracing the zombie apocalypse in the form of our phones, hello, when life is all around you. Then Antoine shakes his head and puts his phone away, still apparently unaware that I spoke, and he reaches out and puts a hand on the cafeteria door, holding it shut so that instead of going in we all have to stop there in a clump.

He says, "Evan." He has to repeat it because she is looking down at her phone. "Evan."

Evangeline looks up which is when I see that her phone's face is blank which means she was staring at nothing. Also there is a deep furrow in her brow. "What?"

"Nobody could have expected the roof to collapse."

"Right," she says. "Although the storm made it more likely."

"But my mother," Antoine says, and then he shakes his head and makes a motion with his hands as if he's pushing something away. "Let's get lunch."

He holds the door open.

I wonder what he was about to say about his mother, and about the fact that the two of them were continuing an earlier conversation about the roof that did not include the rest of us, but then I am distracted because Evangeline slips ahead of Kenyon and takes two trays. Without looking at Kenyon, she says, "Tell me what you want."

Kenyon gives her a wary look. "Are you buying me lunch?"

"Don't push me," Evangeline snaps. "I'm just helping you get your food." There is a pause and then she adds, with her gaze on the hot entrees: "All right. I owe you an apology, Martha. I was mean." She flicks her eyes briefly at me, and then back to the entrees.

Kenyon says, "If you want me to think you're sorry, then don't call me Martha."

Evangeline nods. "Kenyon. Sorry. Do you want this soup? It's vegetable noodle. Or there's chili."

I don't hear how Kenyon responds because Antoine is next to me, and he says, "You told Evan off. Good for you. I'm impressed."

Now is the right moment to say something witty and improve the good impression I have already made on Antoine.

I say, "Where are the trays?"

I picked something up not from first-year French but from my reading, it is a phrase called *esprit d'escalier,* spirit of the staircase, which refers to the moment (*le moment*) when you think of the just-right thing to say (*le mot juste*), only it is too late to say it because you are already on the staircase leaving the party. (There must be lots of upstairs parties in France. If we were invited, Georgia and I would have to go slowly on the stairs which would give me ample time to regret the witticisms I did not think of before.)

The trays by the way are located directly in front of me, which I knew, because (1) I can see them and (2) it's the same place they have been since I started at Rockland. There is misery ahead for me on the staircase (metaphorical, but I may seek out a staircase after school and make it literal) figuring out what I ought to have said. I hate French, what was I thinking by taking it? I don't need a romance language. What I need is woodshop so I can make more friends like Georgia since I can't make them the ordinary way through interpersonal communication.

"You can share my tray," Antoine says. "So you don't have to carry one."

And he smiles at me.

A heavenly choir begins singing in my head and I discard the idea of woodshop: so dangerous anyway, power tools.

Then Caleb, about whom I had entirely and completely forgotten, says, "She's not helpless. In case you haven't noticed, she hardly uses that cane."

I would hit him with Georgia except I fear it would injure her.

But then what he said penetrates and I wonder if Antoine offered because he thinks of me as disabled, and then I wonder if Caleb thinks I'm faking it, and I have to bite my tongue not to burst into an explanation about my foot and about Georgia, who I need to lean on sometimes, I need her, and if he doesn't understand that (although why should he) then why did he rescue her for me?

I grab my own tray and catch up with Kenyon and Evangeline.

Evangeline's tray has a green smoothie on it and a veggie burger with salad.

Kenyon's tray has lasagna and a Honeycrisp apple. She is now eyeing a giant salted chocolate-almond bar, which is crafted by Vermont artisans and packaged with recycled brown paper and twine, I have noticed these myself in the past, although in favor of drug store chocolate brands such as York Peppermint Patties it must be said that they do not intimidate you into not eating them.

Then to my surprise Kenyon looks away and points instead at Evangeline's green smoothie. "What's in that?"

Evangeline's face lights up. "Kale, spinach, half a cucumber, half an avocado, green apple, and peach. Iced. It's my own recipe—they make it for me here every day."

Antoine snorts. "Even my mother makes it for her."

Evangeline holds up her glass for Kenyon. "Do you want some? It's delicious!"

Kenyon mock shudders. She points at the Vermont chocolate bar. "I want that."

Evangeline picks it up with thumb and forefinger and deposits it on Kenyon's tray as if the chocolate were poison. Then she moves to the register.

Kenyon looks at me and at my tray, which I suddenly realize is empty.

"Aren't you going to eat anything?"

I have already passed through the entire food line. Caleb is behind me, and Antoine. If I go back I will look even more like an idiot. If you care, the French word for idiot is the same: *idiot* or *idiote*. I myself do *not* care. I feel finished with French even if I do not take up woodshop.

I grab one of the Vermont chocolate bars.

Kenyon lowers her voice. "Are you supposed to eat that? As a diabetic?"

"I can eat whatever I want," I say airily. This is sort of true although my mother says it is a terrible way to be a diabetic and like playing Russian roulette with your blood sugar. I hand my student ID to the cashier while adding, "I just shoot up insulin to compensate."

At this point, though I have not had the benefit of an actual staircase for purposes of reconsideration, I understand that it was nice of Antoine to want to help me even if it was because he thinks I'm disabled. What happened was that Caleb ruined the moment. My moment. My chance. It is his fault that Antoine is not carrying my tray and that I am going to eat chocolate and call it lunch and then later play Russian roulette with a syringe.

I say grimly to Kenyon, "Where should we sit? With her?" I nod toward Evangeline, who is walking around the perimeter of the cafeteria. "Is that okay with you? She did apologize."

"Also she has my lunch."

"Please sit with us," says Antoine, who is behind us again.

At this the heavenly choir restarts in my head and this time Caleb does not interrupt it. I walk beside Kenyon to the large table where Evangeline has set down the trays. It is located at one end of the cafeteria, in a nearly private nook. I hold out a chair for Kenyon and slip into mine.

Antoine does not sit immediately however. He shouts, "Hey, Caleb!"

The name reverberates through the cafeteria.

Caleb did not follow us. He is seated at another table by himself. His back is toward us and his head is bent down and he is acting as if he can't hear Antoine, because he doesn't look up.

It reminds me of the turret.

I remember what he said in Dr. Lee's office about also thinking his invitation was a joke. Something inside me twists.

"Caleb!" Antoine bellows again, and now the entire cafeteria full of people is quiet, with everyone watching.

Caleb turns around and scowls at Antoine.

Antoine points at the empty chair beside him.

Evangeline stands up, next to Antoine.

Then without making any decision I scramble to my feet too, clumsily because it is one of those times I need support.

Quicker than thought, Caleb's eyes meet mine. Again it seems to me that there is nobody inside him, his eyes are so very blank, but now this makes me want to cry which has something to do with whatever it is inside me that is twisting. I do not cry of course. If I have to cry, I will do it privately on the staircase later (metaphorical—the staircase I mean, not the crying, I will cry if I need to, sniff, just not now please).

I am still looking at Caleb.

He gets up. He gets up and walks over to us and plunks his tray down next to Evangeline without looking at me anymore, and normal sound resumes in the cafeteria like nothing happened although of course something did. What it was I am not sure. I sit myself down very carefully.

I unwrap my Vermont chocolate bar so I will have something to concentrate on and not cry for no reason because I am absolutely okay and not sad at all and certainly not scared what is wrong with me I am shaking like my blood sugar is low but it feels different and I stuff my face with chocolate and taste nothing.

All I want is to look at him, no not Antoine, *him*. I am hormonally addled or insane or my fairy godmother hates me, whatever whichever, please let it be temporary, a crush on Antoine felt warm and good but this does not does not does not does *not*.

Chapter 11. **Caleb**

You're confused by Antoine. He has with deliberation gathered all five of you together, but all he does is hold his burger like it's a foreign object.

"Antoine?" prompts Evangeline.

He looks at her, and then, one by one, at the rest of you.

"I have a theory," he finally says.

With the part of your mind that keeps track of Saralinda no matter what else is going on, you note that she has not looked at you since you sat down at this table.

The other part of you is focused on Antoine, who is trying to smile.

He is a guy who smiles often. It is one of the reasons he is so well-liked. Nobody can resist his friendly, engaged smile. But now you see that it is a mask, one that is cracking.

"What's your theory?" you say.

Antoine puts his burger down. He speaks in a rush, his voice low so that it does not carry beyond the table. "My mother is a structural engineer. She knows how to explode a building. And it's easy to pick out a few random student phone numbers. They're all listed on the school website in the parents' section."

"Wait," says Kenyon incredulously. "You think your *mother*—"

"My mother," Antoine says, "would rather I was dead."

Saralinda freezes with a chocolate square inches short of her mouth.

Kenyon presses both hands to her cheeks.

As for you, it's like your mind is a white board that has been wiped clean.

Evangeline leans forward. "Antoine, no. Seriously. I realize your mother isn't well, but you're jumping to conclusions. Are you getting enough sleep? Are you still on that anti-anxiety pill?"

"Yes. My medication has absolutely nothing to do with this, Evan."

With the part of your mind that comes back online— *while you were worrying that it was you, Antoine was worrying it was his mother?*—you agree with him about the pills. Your own mother was alert and firmly connected to reality when an anti-anxiety pill was the only medication she took.

"This is not possible," says Evangeline. "No."

"It *is* possible. It's a hypothesis, but a possible one."

"It's a leap."

"Yes, but not without foundation. You know what I'm talking about, Evan."

Evangeline doesn't answer.

Antoine looks at you and Saralinda and Kenyon. "I want to apologize to you guys. I'm sorrier than I can say. If it was my mother, then it's my fault that you were almost killed."

"No!" Saralinda reaches forward with chocolatey fingers though Antoine is across the table out of reach. "Even if—well, you're not responsible for what somebody *else* decides—"

Evangeline cuts in sharply. "Your mother knows me, Antoine. Why would she want to kill *me*?"

"I don't know. She's gone crazy." Antoine gets up from the table. "But that's what has me more scared than anything else, Evan. She loves you—or at least, she used to. If it were only me she wanted dead, at least that would make *sense*. But you—and these kids she doesn't know! That's truly nuts."

"It's not true," Evangeline insists.

Antoine shakes his head. "We don't know."

You have never seen anything as terrible as his face. The mask has cracked entirely.

You want to leap up from this table and run away. You do not want this kinship, fellow-feeling, compassion, whatever it is. You cannot afford it, any more than you can afford to have Saralinda look at you the way maybe she did, across the cafeteria a few minutes ago.

You have no room inside you to care about anybody.

Nobody should be allowed to care about you.

It's too dangerous.

Still you try to remember Antoine's mother, from that night at the hospital. All you have is a tall woman looking at her son with an expression that you would have sworn was love.

"I'm going," Antoine says.

Evangeline grabs his arm. "Where?"

"To talk to her."

"No! Let's keep—"

He shakes his head. "I have to confront her. When I look at her, then I'll know." He pauses. "Do a favor for me, Evan? Explain to these guys about my mother and—and tell them what her reason might be. They deserve to know. Oh, and Caleb?"

You nod, surprised to be addressed directly.

"It's because of you that things weren't worse. I couldn't forgive myself if any of you had gotten seriously hurt. So, thanks."

Before you can respond, Antoine walks away, bussing his tray neatly on his way out like the well-brought-up guy he is. Only then do you realize that the lunch period has ended and the cafeteria is nearly empty.

Class starts in a few minutes, but none of you move, and Evangeline's eyes focus on you like laser beams.

"Go after him, Caleb."

"What?"

"You don't mind skipping class, right? He'll have gone to his car. You can get there if you go quickly. Stick to him like glue. He wasn't thinking clearly. See, it's true that she might be dangerous. To him. She's—there's no time to tell you everything, but he needs—just be with him, okay? He needs somebody! I'd go but he'd never take me. You can *make* him take you."

You get it. She doesn't want her friend to be alone.

"I'll go," you find yourself saying.

"I'll go too," Saralinda volunteers, and begins to stand up.

"No," you snarl, and as Saralinda opens her mouth to protest, you add frantically, "You're too slow! You can't keep up."

Her eyes flare and her face flushes, but you don't care if she's hurt. Better if she is. Then she'll stay away from you, and you'll be able to forget she exists.

You take off as Evangeline calls after you. "North parking lot!"

Chapter 12. **Saralinda**

I feel all the emotion hot on my face horrible! Kenyon understands at least somewhat because she yells *asshole* at Caleb, who I don't think hears her because he's fast and already out the door.

I grab Georgia and curl my fingers around the wood at the top below the orb and I think dark thoughts about clouting Caleb over the head, which I definitely could do (having Georgia has always given me a good feeling of being able to take care of myself if need be) but of course I would not, I am civilized.

I get up to go but Evangeline stops me although she's looking at Kenyon.

"I guess I need to tell you guys about Antoine's mother. Can we meet after last period? My dorm room? We can talk there." She looks resigned and angry and worried all at once.

"Yes, okay," I say, but Kenyon shakes her head.

"No. I've already heard enough." She levers herself to a

standing position and props her crutches under her arms. "Listen, Evangeline. I don't like being played—not by you and not by Antoine. And I don't like you playing Saralinda—or Caleb. This joke has gone far enough."

I stare at Kenyon. What's she talking about? Didn't she see Antoine's *face*? He wasn't joking! My feelings for Antoine flood back, although different now unfortunately. But no matter what, Antoine is not a liar.

"Kenyon," I start. "The carriage house—"

She stops me with a glare. "Saralinda, listen. If Antoine was seriously in danger from his mother, he'd go to the police or social services about it. Right? Somebody threatens you, even someone in your family, you ask for help. That's what you do. This is not for real. It can't be. He's making things up."

"But—"

"No!" Evangeline jumps up. "No, that's wrong! Kenyon, listen to me. I can explain why Antoine doesn't want to involve the police. It's because his family situation is sensitive. That's the thing he wants me to tell you."

Kenyon raises an eyebrow. "Okay, I'm listening."

"We have class! I have a quiz today. I'll explain later."

"Anyway, *why* would Antoine and Evangeline make this up?" I interrupt. "It's too crazy to make up."

"Thank you, Saralinda," Evangeline says. "I think."

"Omicron Kappa," Kenyon says simply.

Evangeline explodes. "You're the one who's insane!"

"Surprised I know about it, aren't you?" Kenyon says with narrowed eyes. "But I do my research when I accept a school's scholarship, and from what I can tell, this is the kind of prank they'd pull."

"Dr. Lee disbanded that fraternity," I say.

Kenyon shrugs. "Supposedly, but it wouldn't be the first fraternity to go underground at a school. I'm guessing Omicron still exists, and that's who was behind that bogus Leaders Club invitation and the whole prank. Not Antoine's mother. Dr. Lee must think so too or he would have gone to the police. That's why he said what he said about somebody here at school being responsible."

"I didn't *really* think you were dumb, Martha," says Evangeline. "But I've got to admit you're changing my mind."

One of the cafeteria workers calls out, "Kids! We have to close up."

"Sorry, we're going now," I call back.

Evangeline stalks out. Kenyon and I go more slowly, okay fine, we are slow. When we get outside the cafeteria, Evangeline is waiting.

She looks directly at me and ignores Kenyon. "Martha has made up her mind, but Saralinda, will *you* hear me out?"

I say to Kenyon, "It can't hurt to listen."

"Yes, it can. You're too innocent, Saralinda."

Oh, so I am not only slow, I am innocent. "I just think—"

Kenyon cuts me off. "Let me fill you in on my research. Omicron was supposedly disbanded for pulling a very cruel prank. On a couple of gay students, if you care." Her lips compress. "Omicron Kappa was famous for picking out certain marks at school to make fools of. I'm thinking that you and Caleb and I all fit that category." She glowers at Evangeline. "You almost had Saralinda swallowing this. I won't allow it," Kenyon finishes righteously.

She moves beside me, and she is my friend and I should feel gratified that she cares about me and also glad to be protected by her, and part of me does, I guess, but at the same time I am not a small child and I am not helpless and I have had quite enough of other people making decisions for me.

I say, "So you think that Omicron Kappa, which includes Antoine and Evangeline, invited us to their fake Leaders Club meeting. Then the roof fell by accident."

"Exactly." Kenyon points at Evangeline. "I see right through her."

"You don't see anything! You won't listen!" Evangeline turns and walks away rapidly, her boot heels clacking down the empty corridor.

I could shout after her but I don't. Without asking me,

Evangeline is assuming Kenyon has convinced me, and meanwhile Kenyon is the one shouting after Evangeline as the doors close.

"I listen to people who are worth listening to!"

Then she turns back to me. "Good riddance. Should I go straight to Dr. Lee with this?" She pauses. "I kind of hate to do that. It could be a huge deal. People could get expelled. Maybe we should wait and see?"

I sigh. "I don't know."

"Are you okay, Saralinda?"

"Yeah."

"See you later?"

"Okay."

Then Kenyon too is gone. I stand for a few minutes more and lean on Georgia. Maybe it was a fraternity prank aimed at me and Kenyon and Caleb. Maybe Antoine and Evangeline were not involved but were being pranked also. I have to admit this makes more sense than Antoine's mother hacking into Mrs. Allyson's email account and exploding the carriage house.

But here's the thing: I don't see why that means I shouldn't at least listen to Evangeline.

Chapter 13. **Caleb**

In pursuit of Antoine, you walk but don't run past open classroom doors. You try to imagine Mrs. Dubois crawling on the carriage house roof, setting explosives.

Of course, the reality of your father's controlling behavior with your mother would be hard for *his* fans to believe too.

Why would Antoine's mother want him dead?

You exit the main school building onto the square green expanse of the Rockland Quad. You are careful. If someone official sees Antoine, they will give him the benefit of the doubt. You they will screw to the nearest wall.

You head into the science building. You take a left down the stairs and emerge out the back, at the top of the hill where kids sled on cafeteria trays in winter.

Then at last you run.

There's a crisp whiff of October air on the breeze and a yellowed leaf beneath your sneakers and the sun shining warmly overhead. Just a few days ago, the ground was covered with crashed branches and green leaves torn prematurely from life.

The north parking lot is at the bottom of the hill behind a new dorm that's being constructed from smoky blue glass. You're past it in a moment and in the student lot, where Antoine's famous car lives beneath a beige canvas tarpaulin.

The tarp and car are undisturbed.

Maybe Antoine stopped to get something from his dorm room? You walk around to the far side of the car to squat out of sight and wait.

Antoine crouches there.

He straightens self-consciously. "I saw you coming. Except I didn't know it was you. I hate that building."

You glance back over your shoulder and see that the dorm's glass reflects and distorts its surroundings. You would have been a long thin shadow sprinting across its surface.

Antoine pulls the tarp off, gathering it up into neat folds, revealing an ancient Cadillac, long and sleek as a boat, bristling with tail fins and headlights, and painted a deep, gleaming, perfect orange. You have heard that Antoine calls the car Ellie Mae.

He opens the trunk and stores the tarp in it.

You clear your throat. "You probably wonder why I'm here."

"Evan sent you to talk me out of going."

You don't clarify. "So you say your mother wants you dead. If that's true, why go see her? What if she has a gun?"

"She doesn't. She hates guns."

"Guns are a good way to kill, though, if you mean it."

Antoine shrugs.

You lean one hip deliberately against Ellie Mae. Antoine stiffens.

"I'll come with you," you say. "Make Evangeline happy."

"No. My only chance of getting my mother to talk to me is if I'm alone."

You nod as if you're buying it. Then you slide your hand into your pocket.

You have a reputation for petty vandalism. Very petty. Like, one time you forced open your sticky dorm room window, breaking it in the process. You wanted air. The other time maybe wasn't petty. There was a fire on the cement floor of your dorm's main gathering room. The kindling for the fire was a philosophy essay you had handed in, which you had written in fifteen minutes after only skimming the reading on Plato, and on which you received a D. You don't remember being upset about the grade; in fact, you thought it was generous. You also don't remember setting the fire, which sputtered out by itself, leaving a single page of your essay far across the room as evidence. What you remember best is that after this, you began scattering the confetti on the floor of your dorm room. Oh, and also that your father wrote a big check to the school, and wrote a long letter of apology for you to sign, so that they'd keep you, after that.

There have been no other incidents at Rockland Academy, though there are nearly a dozen that stretch back through your childhood.

What matters here, though, is not what you do or do not remember, but your reputation, which at last is at least useful. So when Antoine unlocks the driver's-side door with a key—no automated entry for Ellie Mae—you step forward, your Swiss Army knife at the ready.

Antoine looks down at the inch-long blade and rolls his eyes. "Seriously, Caleb? That's meant to be a threat?"

"I'm not threatening you," you say. "I'm threatening Ellie Mae's beautiful orange finish."

His eyes narrow. "Don't try it." He takes a step toward you.

Which opens up enough space. You twist past him and slide into Ellie Mae's front seat. It's a bench seat, upholstered in a velvety beige fabric that is shockingly comfortable. You scoot over to the passenger side, snap your knife closed, and push it back into your pocket.

Antoine's mouth is tight.

"Look," you say pleasantly. You point at the reflective glass of the new dorm, where a figure has appeared. "Someone's coming. We can go together, or we can wait here for whoever it is. Maybe faculty."

Antoine drops into the driver's seat and starts the engine. Ellie Mae sounds like a freight train.

And you're off, Ellie Mae's wheels kicking up loose gravel in the parking lot. As the engine settles into a purr, you reach automatically for your seat belt, which isn't there.

On the main road, Antoine drives five miles under the speed limit, his hands carefully positioned on the wheel, which he grips so tightly his knuckles are pale. The second time you go past the Route 22 McDonald's, you speak.

"So your mother lives at the McDonald's? We're circling her?"

He doesn't respond.

"Why didn't you install seat belts in this thing?"

"What are you talking about? This is a classic. That would ruin it."

You're curious. "But don't they force you to do it? Isn't there some law?"

"Not for cars from before 1964. This is a 1959 Eldorado." He draws the word out lovingly.

"What if you're in an accident?"

"There are worse ways to go."

"Plus it would please your mother," you say. "I believe

you, by the way." Because you do. "I believe your mother wants you dead, even though there wasn't time for Evangeline to tell me why."

A muscle works at the side of Antoine's jaw. "Oh."

"Why don't *you* tell me why? Since I'm here." When he doesn't answer, you go on. "See, you have a mother. And I have a father."

You cannot believe you said it.

You did not plan to.

Antoine says nothing still, but he glances at you now, quickly.

Ellie Mae approaches the McDonald's again. This third time, Antoine pulls into the lot and parks at the back where there is plenty of space around the Eldorado. He turns off the car.

"You left the hospital that night alone, without speaking to your father. Everybody noticed."

"Yes," you say. "I'm sure they did."

"There was a crowd around him in the emergency room like he was a rock star."

"There often is."

"You don't get along?"

"I'm not saying he's actually tried to kill me," you say. "But I've been aware for a while that he certainly would be happier if I were dead."

Antoine's eyes are on you.

"He has an excellent motive," you add. "I can't blame him. I have to say that I understand."

"What do you mean?"

"Come on, Antoine. You know why. I'm a monster. Probably a sociopath. Everyone at Rockland thinks so. Right?"

"No," says Antoine. "Not everyone. I don't." He pauses and adds, "Not anymore."

Chapter 14. **Saralinda**

In history class I do not pay close attention because I am thinking about Antoine and his mother and also Kenyon and Evangeline.

So Kenyon won't listen to Evangeline, and Kenyon is my friend, but that doesn't mean everything she says goes with me. Those two got off on the wrong foot. It's like in *Pride and Prejudice* only without the romance, the point is that you can be prejudiced or prideful against someone who you would love if only you knew their heart. Or in this case not love, like. Or understand. Or some verb.

Speaking of love. If I were gay I would at least *like* Evangeline and Kenyon, both of them. Well, I already like them, that's not what I mean. What I mean is that if I were gay I would maybe have less heartache. Although again it is not my heart that troubles me, it is my body. Anyway Kenyon would be angry at me for thinking that being gay is easier on the heart, it has certainly not made love easy for her so I *do* know better.

Still I would (wouldn't I?) at least dare to *think* about approaching a girl I wanted, but then again maybe not if I felt about her the way I feel about—but I will not think about Caleb. Or about what is wrong with me, it feels so intense and makes me want to run away—no, be honest, what I want is to throw myself at him.

Then if I am rejected, run away.

Or maybe run away if I am accepted, I don't know!

At the same time I have not forgiven him for thinking I am slow and the harsh way he said it. Also I have not changed my mind about him, he is damage personified but that is not all he is and part of me does not care because—because!

Because *sex* I guess but I had no idea! Also no idea I could feel this way when I disapprove of how I feel!

In short I am doomed, even deceiving myself that I am thinking about Evangeline and Kenyon when really I am thinking about Caleb, yes, thinking about Caleb when I should be thinking about Antoine and his mother and also about whether Kenyon is right about the fraternity. The cherry on top of my self-absorption by the way is that I am doomed to go over the facts of the Industrial Revolution at home tonight in order to understand what I have just now entirely missed in class.

Sigh.

Beneath the desk I illegally text Evangeline and she

answers also illegally because rule: No phone use during class. I've never broken the rule before, did I mention doomed?

I also text my mother to say I will stay after school to use the library, outright lie.

But I do not feel guilty, I refuse to feel guilty as this is *my* life *my* body *my* mistakes to make if they are mistakes at all which I don't know that.

And here is the truth which she doesn't want to acknowledge so I must lie until I find courage: *I'm growing up, Mom. Things have to change between you and me.*

Also truth, I do not want to hurt her! It is so delicate.

After school I cross the quad to Evangeline's dorm and think about Antoine and how he looked in the cafeteria, and what he said about *his* mother, and if it is true it is also a reminder to be grateful for mine. When I find that courage I will also express that I value and love her which will not help because it is just not going to go well. It will be not a discussion but a confrontation and also big drama which is why I have avoided it so far (also primal *fear*).

It is not necessarily always pleasant being in my head, believe me and where is some ibuprofen when you need it?

Evangeline's room is in a corner on the first floor of Morse Hall. It has two twin beds elevated off the floor and accessed by ladders, with room beneath each for a desk and a bureau. One half of the room is scrupulously neat but the other looks like a wind has blown through, not as bad as the carriage house after the roof caved in of course, but reminiscent to me of that, although it is mostly food-stuffs on the floor, cereal boxes, Oreos, Pringles canisters, also clothing. Some dust. It is all so interesting my headache almost goes away.

"The chaos and the crap are all totally Irina's, in case you care," Evangeline says.

I shrug though actually I am quite interested because, speaking of insides and outsides, Evangeline's roommate Irina Grekova eats only salad at lunch and when she turns sideways she has the figure of a pencil with breasts.

I sneak more looks around than the ordinary person would but this is my first time in a dorm room. Could I live in one? Suppose by a miracle things go well when I talk to my mother which they won't but if they did, could I live at school? It can't cost more than the daily car service, or can it?

"Thank you for texting me." Evangeline doesn't look at me as she arranges the desk chairs near each other and we sit down. "It matters to Antoine. I felt terrible when you guys wouldn't listen, like I'd let him down."

"Maybe I can talk to Kenyon later," I offer.

Evangeline grimaces. "Because she wouldn't ever listen to me."

"Well . . ."

"I didn't know about her mother," she blurts. "I just found out."

"Oh."

"I'll apologize. But how could she believe that ridiculous story about Omicron Kappa?"

Because I have tact I do not say that we have two ridiculous stories to choose from. I say, "Well, give it time and maybe that other apology? So, about Antoine—"

"Kenyon threw herself on top of you as the roof came down. It was amazing."

"I know! She told me that she had no memory of deciding. She did it instinctively. Isn't that incredible?"

Evangeline hunches a shoulder. "Physical courage is something that can happen with someone who lives mostly in her body. I'm not like that. I have to think things through. So she and I are too different to ever understand each other."

I say, "I personally would welcome cooperation between my body and my head." It comes out sort of bitter unfortunately, and Evangeline narrows her eyes at me puzzled. Then she shrugs again and opens a small refrigerator. She takes out two sodas. I burst out, "Evangeline? Do you have any real food? Something with protein?"

"Cheese okay?"

"Yes!" I am relieved because lunch was a fiasco for diabetics everywhere or at least for me. "Also do you have some ibuprofen or aspirin or something for a headache?"

She does. She also sets up cheddar and a knife and I eat some of that.

"So about Antoine?" I prompt when Evangeline doesn't bring it up herself—weirdly, considering why we are here. "Why does he think his mother might . . . ?"

Her hands fist in her lap.

Then she tells me. Her face is rigid and her voice is tight and it is horrific.

Antoine sweet Antoine with the smile and the sports-playing knees and the way he is always so kind to everyone, his father died slowly horribly it took years from a genetic disorder that steals both your body and mind there is no cure. Evangeline says nobody at school knew it was happening except her and Dr. Lee because Antoine wanted absolute privacy and no pity or special treatment, and then finally it ended last summer with death, which had to have been a blessing although oh God.

That is what I think until Evangeline says the worst part of all.

Antoine has the same disease.

So that day in the carriage house when Antoine smiled at me and made me feel so *seen,* inside him the genetic time bomb which is called Huntington's disease was going tick-tock, tick-tock.

Evangeline talks for a while very staccato, and I take in some of it and some of it I don't but I resolve to do research later on the internet if I can bear it, I ought to bear it he has to live it.

My diabetes is nothing my foot is nothing.

When Evangeline stops, I ask her what this has to do with Antoine thinking his mother is trying to kill him. "Is it because she wants to make sure he doesn't suffer like his father?" I imagine I might feel that too: *I will do this terrible thing to the one I love, so that something even worse will not happen.* Only then I remember the carriage house and how five of us almost died and then I am less understanding of Mrs. Dubois.

Evangeline shakes her head. "Yes, sort of, and no, sort of. What happened was, Antoine was trying to reassure her, so he promised that he would kill himself once he became symptomatic."

"Wait, *what*—"

"I don't know if he *meant* it. He doesn't know either. Anyway it wouldn't be until he's in his forties or something like that. The disease has a long gestation time. He gets to have a real life for like twenty years at least. Maybe they'll find a cure between now and then. He was just trying to say something to make his mother feel better. He wanted her to know he wouldn't necessarily suffer."

I try to imagine telling my mother I will kill myself someday and having her be happy about it or at least relieved.

Evangeline says, "Only Gabrielle Dubois is Catholic, and suicide is a sin."

"Oh." I think about that and then I add, "But then isn't Antoine Catholic too? Didn't he know she'd react that way?"

"He told me he probably should have known, but he didn't. He stopped believing years ago. He stopped paying attention in church."

I nod but am still thinking. "If she commits murder, that's a sin too," I point out. "Especially your own child. Isn't that like a special sin? Not to mention, uh, killing four other kids."

"It's only been eight weeks since her husband's death," says Evangeline. "She's not exactly stable." She looks at me.

I look at her.

I say, "What can I do to help?"

She laughs but it is slightly hysterical. "Honestly, I don't know what's going on. I thought at first he had to be wrong, she wouldn't do this, but I've been thinking and now I'm not so sure. Maybe Kenyon is right, though, and Omicron Kappa did exactly what she says. I don't know. I just don't know!"

She sounds enraged at her own uncertainty.

I don't know what to do or say so I have more cheese while Evangeline fishes glumly down into the canister of Pringles for every last crumb.

If my previous fantasy about Antoine still had its roots in me, I would do everything I was allowed to do for him, now that I know about this. Only the problem is that while I still like Antoine very much, the crush part of it seems to have definitively faded. (Am I fickle by nature? I hope not.) Also Antoine should be loved and wanted, not pitied, and *also* also, I am not what he wants, I know this, I am just some girl who had a crush.

Then all at once Evangeline is crying, short sharp gasps. I hesitate, then I put Georgia down and lean over and put my arms around her. I am awkward and she doesn't accept me really, she stiffens and mumbles that she's sorry and she pulls away and dries her eyes on her sleeve and glares at me and then away.

Still I know now that she is not so tough after all.

While she is not looking at me I ask her very quietly if she loves Antoine, though it is not my business I realize that.

She shakes her head but not in the definite way that means no way, instead it is a slow movement from side to side with her head bent like she can't bear its weight.

"Sorry," I say quickly. "Never mind." I get it, she doesn't have to tell me.

She loves him, that is what I think, but it's hopeless because he is sick.

Chapter 15. **Caleb**

Antoine stares at you levelly. "I don't think there's *anything* really wrong with you, Caleb."

You have your back against Ellie Mae's door.

He says, "You found me and dug me out of the rubble. You worked to dig all the girls out, and you did way more than me because of my shoulder. You were panting. Your hands were bleeding. Then there was a bolt of lightning and I saw your face, so don't tell me you weren't scared for the girls. Don't tell me you weren't doing everything you could to get them out. Don't tell me you're a monster. I was there and I know better."

Air is available to you at last, and so is your voice, though it sounds as if it's coming from far away. "I was faking it. Doing what normal people do because in that particular situation it was obvious what normal people are supposed to do."

"Oh, so you didn't care whether, let's say, Saralinda lived or died?"

You grind your teeth. "I don't know her very well."

"I didn't say you do. I only said that I watched you dig her out."

You say, "What I am is the sociopathic son of a genius psychiatrist—"

Antoine interrupts. "Really? Your father might be a genius like they say, but Dr. Lee thinks he's also a narcissistic asshole—"

"What?!"

"Okay, so his personal notes only said *narcissist* and I added *asshole*. Fine. Your mother is present in your life, but cowed and scared of her husband. That's also from the notes. Dr. Lee's opinion, which I now agree with, is that the only thing wrong with you is a whole lot of fear. Lee doesn't know for sure what that's about, but he has his suspicions."

Your mouth opens, and Antoine cuts you off with the answer before you ask.

"I looked at your file."

"But that's—"

"Dr. Lee trusts me a little too much because I'm the senior class president. He left me in the room with his computer the other day."

"I'm a monster," you say again. Only it comes out like a question.

"Well, that isn't what Dr. Lee thinks. What kind of monster do you mean anyway?"

"Forget it. Let's go to your mother's. You haven't got time for this." You can hear it clearly in your own voice—the fear that Antoine mentioned.

Antoine half shrugs, half nods. He turns Ellie Mae back on. But as he steers back onto Route 22, he says, "I can listen while I drive."

He can listen all he wants. It doesn't mean you have to talk.

You shouldn't talk. Antoine has his own shit to deal with, such as believing his mother is a murderer.

But you're fixated on the word *narcissist* . . . a note in a file. In *your* file, where the diagnosis is not about you.

You can't take it in. You *cannot* take it in.

What does Dr. Lee know anyway? He doesn't know you or your father. He doesn't. Why should he be right?

Antoine is driving five miles below the speed limit again.

He doesn't prompt you with questions. You don't have to tell him anything.

But you say, "Have you ever heard of *Dr. Jekyll and Mr. Hyde*? It's a book by Robert Lewis Stevenson."

Antoine's gaze is on the road where it belongs. "I saw the movie. Classic horror. Hey, look in the back. There's a book on the floor there."

You fish up a copy of *Dracula*. "This isn't *Dr. Jekyll*," you point out unnecessarily.

"Yeah, but it reminds me of it. Old-fashioned horror.

Dr. Jekyll is the one about the guy with a split personality, right? One good, one evil? Ridiculous."

"Ridiculous," you echo.

"The execution of the movie, I mean. Campy. I haven't read the book." Antoine sounds conversational. "The idea itself is extremely creepy. Like *Dracula*—which is great, you should read it. You can have my copy, I'm done. So, that's what you mean when you say you're a monster? Mr. Hyde, the evil alter ego? The devil inside?"

You turn over *Dracula* and look at the back. You don't answer.

"Tell me more. I'm not saying you're a liar, okay?" He goes on. "Human chemistry is a weird thing. Did you hear about that Olympic athlete who took some antidepressant? She was a wife and mother and then started leading a double life as an escort in Vegas where she did all these high-risk things. Basically she turned into a totally different person. The medication did something to her personality."

"I'm not taking any medication."

"I didn't say you are. Look, I'm not saying you're lying about this Mr. Hyde thing."

"But you don't believe me either."

"I don't know." His voice hardens. "I'll tell you what, though, Caleb, I'm the last person on earth to think that terrible things don't happen to people and for no good reason. I don't ever expect the world to make sense or for things to be, you know, *fair*."

You watch his profile.

He doesn't look back at you.

He wants you to talk, you realize. You don't entirely understand why, but he does. Maybe he needs you to.

You tell him. You can speak clinically, because you have done a whole lot of reading, on top of the lectures from your father on abnormal human psychology and other monsters like you in human history.

Most sociopaths do not have split personalities. Most are fully aware of their desire—their drive—to manipulate, hurt, and destroy. But you are a rarer bird. Dissociative identity disorder, it is sometimes called. Your alter ego does stuff, and it steals your body to do it—usually at night. You never have any memory of it. You know your inner monster by his deeds and the trail he leaves.

Antoine says, "So your alter ego is a sociopath. But you're normal."

You frown, because how can the word *normal* apply? You say, "What if it's my alter ego who collapsed the roof, and not your mother?"

Antoine's voice is rough. "Do you think I'd accuse my mother without good reason?"

"You might be wrong. There's this other possibility, that it's me."

"Does your alter ego know how to collapse a roof? Do you believe he left your room the night before and booby-trapped the place?" Antoine's questions come out rat-a-tat.

You think of the undisturbed confetti on the floor of your room.

He goes on. "What about the email? Did you turn into Mr. Hyde one second to send the email and then pop back into being Caleb to receive it?"

You don't answer.

"Whereas my mother has motive, skills, and opportunity."

You ask, "Why would your mother do it?"

"Because. She's mentally ill. Temporarily not herself." Antoine pauses. "It's grief." Another pause. "And fear, for me."

Fear again. You are tired of it.

"What's she afraid of?"

With his fingers tight on the wheel of the car and his voice in perfect control, Antoine tells you about his own internal monster, which comes labeled with a genetic code instead of a lurid Victorian novel.

But in another way, you think, your monsters could be cousins.

Maybe what you are is also the result of some inborn genetic coding. You never chose Mr. Hyde. You don't even share a single memory with him. But saying you have a bad gene sequence is no more of an answer than believing you have an inner evil twin, or that you're possessed by a demon. None of these so-called explanations tell you *why*.

Or even: Why *you*?

And so what if one day somebody squints into an electron microscope and says, "Aha, Caleb, you have the Hyde sequence at the end of chromosome seven!"

It would explain nothing important.

Plus, this is what would follow: "Can we fix you? No. We can only see the defect."

Antoine has had this exact same experience.

"There is no cure for Huntington's disease," he says. "It's like being tied to the train tracks. I can't hear the train coming yet, but I know it's on its way." He shrugs. "I'm doomed."

And the monster's damage isn't ever confined to the monster. One way or another, the infection—the evil—spreads. Like to Antoine's mother. Like to your own mother, who is now more a shadow than a living creature.

Then there is the peripheral damage, the innocents caught in the blast—like Saralinda, and Kenyon, and Evangeline.

Probably you *are* just like Antoine. Probably you have some nonstandard gene pattern inside you. Your father too—he is no more normal than you are, the way he shows one face to the world and another to his family.

But calling it a genetic thing doesn't make the experience any less monstrous.

"I have years still," Antoine says. "Maybe twenty, or even thirty. You know what? I *want* them." He drums his fingers on the car wheel. "But my mother . . ." He shifts his attention from the road to you for one split second.

"Evangeline knows this. My mother has already tried to kill me, twice."

You sit very still while he tells you about a partially severed brake line in Ellie Mae, the week after his father died. Then there was food poisoning, the following week.

"That's really why I'm living at school this term."

You say slowly, "Maybe if you tell Dr. Lee—"

"No! He can't know. She's temporarily insane, but she *will* get over it. She's doing all the right things. She goes to a grief group. She sees a psychiatrist. She's on serious doses of some medication. She just needs time. At least that was what I thought until now. Now I'm—I'm reconsidering." He pauses.

"I don't understand why she'd risk other people," he finally adds. "Me, I get that. But you guys? And Evan? She's been my friend since freaking kindergarten. My mother loves her—or she did when she was sane."

His eyes flicker again to you, and then back to the road.

"I'm glad you came, Caleb. Let's try this with her. Let's show her you. A real person who she almost murdered.

Let's see if she can take in how far she's gone. Shock her out of it."

You're still holding his copy of *Dracula*. "If she can't?"

"If she can't—then, new plan."

"What plan?"

"I don't know."

He floors it then, all the way up to five miles above the speed limit.

It is the only indication of how angry he is.

Chapter 16. **Saralinda**

The car service gets me home two hours later than usual which is not so bad though I feel guilty about lying obviously, on top of which is shock horror sympathy about Antoine.

Also of course wretched worry about Antoine and Caleb facing Antoine's murderous mother (right this minute possibly?), and that poor woman driven mad by grief.

In short I feel choked sad apprehensive and yet at the same time I am so glad to see our building, our home. I climb out of the car utterly eager for my room and my mother, pathetic. Maybe I am not ready to leave home after all even with Georgia by my side, the world is bad and sad, I am possibly not equipped I am still little.

I enter the lobby and push the button for the elevator. I need to not seem sad when I see my mother, who has X-ray eyes, also I hate that I lied to her, maybe I could tell her about Antoine? Just the Huntington's disease part (she would be interested, she is always interested in illness), except I promised Evangeline I would not tell.

At this point however the delivery guy from the Chinese takeout place runs into the lobby and waves, so I hold the elevator door for him and he grins and lifts his brown paper bag which smells of sesame oil. He says, "Cold sesame noodles for your mother!"

"Really?" I am amazed.

The delivery guy holds out his hand for a high five which I manage (awkwardly).

More anxiety heaps on now because my mother only orders cold sesame noodles for celebrations or emergencies. Once I am in our apartment I calm down however. It is an emergency yes, but also a celebration.

My mother is happy.

"Big money, Saralinda! I have only a few days to get this grant application written!"

She scrambles on her knees by the printer where several dozen pages have landed on the floor. She runs to put them in her bedroom/office and comes out with her face absolutely split by the width of her smile. For a second I can almost (*almost*) forget everything that happened today and all I want is to go to her and hug her and be hugged. But she's not looking at me, she has already turned to get her purse for the delivery guy and she keeps talking a mile a minute. (By the way this is not usual, she is often kind of dour and fretful even when something good happens because she is "waiting for the other shoe to drop," as she calls it, which is a metaphor I truly get on account of my equally good foot.)

She rummages in her purse. "They know perfectly well they should have given me a month to do this, so guess what? There's a big bonus when I turn it in, and then there's a second bigger bonus later on, if they win the grant."

She pays the delivery guy including a twenty-dollar tip (!!!) and he salutes us with one hand as he leaves happily. Who is this smiling extravagant woman and what has she done with the real Ursula de la Flor?

"I hope I can do it," she says, and now there is the forehead wrinkle and my heart melts, it is already a puddle from everything today.

"You *can*, Mom. They hired you because they know you're the best."

"Well." My mother smooths her hair self-consciously. "Maybe. Anyway, there'll be no cooking around here for a few days. Everything happens all at once, doesn't it?"

"What else happened?" I sit down on my chair next to the printer and prop my chin on one hand.

"Oh, nothing, nothing, I just mean this job." My mother has her back to me again, occupied with the takeout. "I got you plain chicken and broccoli, okay?"

Which is my usual safe meal from this takeout place. "Sure," I say. I count the cartons as she unloads them.

"Wait, did you get *four* orders of cold sesame noodles?" Because that is unprecedented.

My mother gets all defensive which is adorable. "I need it. I'm going to live on it while I work. I don't want to have to stop and think about food."

"Good idea," I say and prepare to tell her my lie about why I had to stay at school this afternoon.

Only she doesn't do her how-was-your-day question paired with her intense-probing-look, she just says, "I have to get back to work now. No interruptions unless it's an emergency. Oh, and please don't talk to me when I take stuff off the printer. My mind will be elsewhere."

"I get it," I say.

"Thanks."

The door of her room/office clicks shut behind her and her fork and her cold sesame noodles, which is when I realize she also did not say one single word about blood sugar testing or insulin injections. So wow, it must be *really* big money. Yay!

Also, this is what I wanted, to take care of myself, so I should not feel a tiny bit bereft.

In my horrible bathroom I do a perfectly competent job of checking my blood sugar, which is high but not terrible, probably thanks to Evangeline's cheese. I consider the numbers carefully and decide how much to inject taking into account the chicken and broccoli carb count, and I write down everything in the record book very meticulous and responsible.

Then I shoot up. There is no other way to say it and along with injecting insulin, I have the not-so-good kind of thoughts where I imagine, oh, Caleb watching me do it and maybe thinking it is disgusting and so am I. The fact is I have needle scars all over me and rough places on my skin from years of injections, I am told I have sensitive skin and most diabetics do not have this problem which believe me it did not help to hear. Also there is my equally good foot which does not match the other foot and ankle, smaller yet swollen, weird bone structure beneath, so you can see there is something wrong with it.

I think about this, then remind myself not to be self-absorbed, it is truly a small problem compared to Antoine's.

On my way with Georgia to the kitchen to get my chicken and broccoli I stop in front of my mother's door. Of course she's busy I must not interrupt and I don't, of course not. I am fine after all and I am okay alone, just blue.

My fairy godmother is clearly at work again because for most people having friends is not traumatic.

Chapter 17. **Caleb**

Antoine's house is impressive, in a suburban neighborhood of large lots with plenty of trees. In the driveway, he
parks Ellie Mae next to another car, a white Subaru. "She's
home," he says, with a nod toward the house's lit window.
He doesn't look at you as he gets out and walks to the front
door. Silently, you follow.

From behind, you watch while Antoine tries to open the
front door. He tries again. And again. You realize, before
he seems to, that his mother has changed the lock on him.

Locking your kid out is a far cry from trying to kill
him . . . and yet.

You're not sure what to say. Finally you land on "Do you
still want to try to talk with her?"

He nods, his face carefully blank.

You press the doorbell. A recording of "Jingle Bells" plays.

Antoine says, "We never got around to reprogramming
the doorbell last year."

Nobody arrives to open the door.

"Stay here. I'll try the back." Antoine disappears, you wait, and after a couple of minutes, he returns. You don't need to ask about the back door's lock.

You ring the bell again. "Good King Wenceslas" this time.

"Maybe someone else took her somewhere. Or she's asleep."

Antoine shakes his head.

Your own mother does a lot of deep sleeping. Three fire trucks could race through her bedroom, alarms blaring, and she wouldn't wake. "I love to sleep," she says, but you know it's more than that. Prescription drugs are her friend. You aren't sure if your father is right or wrong to provide them to her. You cannot judge. Maybe she's better off in her haze. Anyway, it's her choice. She's the one who takes them.

You loved her once, when you were little. At least, you think you did. You'd like to think you did.

But Antoine, now. Antoine loves his mother. This woman who has locked him out. This woman who he believes tried to murder him—three times—and four other kids too.

The doorbell cycles through "Silent Night," "We Wish You a Merry Christmas," "Good King Wenceslas" (again), and "Frosty the Snowman." Antoine allows less and less time to elapse between songs. Finally he smacks the door with a flat, heavy palm.

"Mom!" he shouts. "Mom!"

He pounds with his closed fist. He adds a second fist. The door is made from good thick wood, and the house is large, but if his mother is inside (and not drugged), she must hear him. If this weren't a suburban neighborhood of enormous private lots, the neighbors would hear him too, because he's yelling loudly.

"Mom! It's me, Antoine!"

It must be hurting his hands, to pound like that. His throat, to yell like that.

"Open up! You have to talk to me! You *have* to!"

You're wondering how to stop him when a tall shadow appears beyond the decorative glass installed on one side of the door. The glass is thick and smoky and filled with a leaded mosaic of a flower, but there are bands of plain glass above and below the decoration, so you can see Mrs. Dubois standing in the entry of her house. Watching the door pulse. Listening to her son scream.

"Mom!"

Finally you say, "Antoine." He doesn't hear you.

You catch his raised upper arm. You nod toward the glass. He follows your eyes.

"Mom?" he says in a lower voice.

She doesn't move.

"Mom, let me in." Antoine has regained some calm, some patience, or at least the ability to fake it.

Still no movement.

Antoine is tall enough to look through the plain glass at the top of the decorative inset. He shields the sides of his face with his hands and presses up close.

"I came here because I know about the roof, Mom. We have to talk."

She does not respond.

"We can figure this out together."

She does not move.

"I understand the pain you're in. I understand you're trying to help me."

Still nothing.

"But it's wrong. This is not the way to handle my problem. Please. This isn't you. This is *not* what you're like. You would never do what you've done."

Silence.

"Mom. Answer me."

Finally Antoine breaks.

"*You're* the sick one! Not me! You've snapped—you need help! Don't you understand? That was Evan with me when the roof came down! *Evan!* You love Evan! No matter what you're thinking about me and what's best, why would you put Evan's life at risk? Why?"

Beyond the glass, Mrs. Dubois does not so much as twitch.

Antoine draws a ragged breath. "There were three other

kids there too. One of them is right here now. Caleb Colchester. Look at him! I dare you! Look at who you hurt! This is an innocent person!"

You, an innocent? After what you told him?

"Caleb saved all of us that day. Evan, and me, and two other kids, girls, who are good people. Saralinda and Kenyon. Those are their *names*! You owe Caleb, Mom. He might be the only reason that you're not responsible for the deaths of five people! The only reason that's not on your conscience—if you still have one. *Do you?*"

Beyond the glass, Mrs. Dubois moves at last. She takes a step away.

"You want to talk about going to hell now, Mom? Huh?" She turns away.

Then she's gone, back into the depths of her house. Gone.

But Antoine still pushes his face against the window. He still shouts.

Mom, Mom, Mom.

You don't have any idea how long he does it.

Finally he stops. He turns back to you. You simply fall into step beside him as the two of you return to Ellie Mae.

He sits in the driveway, gripping the wheel, saying nothing for a long time. You sit beside him.

"I can't believe she changed the lock," he says.

You say nothing.

"She's truly crazy. You see that, right? She needs help." His fingers drum on the steering wheel. "Do you see?" He turns to you at last. "Do you see that she must be the one who collapsed the carriage house? That it wasn't an accident?"

"It's definitely possible," you say at last.

He nods grimly.

He starts the car. He pulls out into the street, driving toward the setting sun and the darkening evening sky. It's not the direction of school.

You're thinking about the roof. If experts investigate it, they'll find evidence of whatever happened. Antoine has got to know this as well as you do. Dr. Lee will call experts in, if they don't come themselves. Insurance investigators. Police forensics.

Antoine is talking again. He has been following a similar chain of thought. "My mother is not a criminal. You have no idea what she's been through, but I do. I'll protect her, no matter what. We'll get through this. I can't figure out exactly how, but I will. I just need time to think."

He sounds certain again. Antoine the president, Antoine the leader. No longer the little boy pounding on the door, screaming for his mother.

Never that boy again, ever, you think, and you have to look away for a moment.

But he needs to go further.

You say, evenly, "Let's think this through. What if some-body had really died? Like you said before. Like Evan?"

"Nobody did, though. And now she knows I know, so it's over. You guys will be safe." He drives on for a while before adding, "I could contact her therapist. Ask him what to do."

You think of your father, the famous psychiatrist. "Do you like her therapist?"

"I don't know him. She only started seeing him in the summer. But you know, he's a professional. He'll help."

Your father is a professional too. He has helped many, many people. Who he is at home is not who he is at the office. Can't be. He doesn't mess with his clients' heads the way he messes with yours. Right? Because they pay him.

"I'd have to find his name and number, though," Antoine says.

"You don't already know his name?"

"My mother just says 'my therapist.' She probably told me; I can't remember." Suddenly Antoine catches his breath. "Caleb?" His gaze slides sideways for a second to meet yours. "The brakes aren't working," he says. "Don't panic."

Ellie Mae is going over fifty miles an hour.

Antoine's hands are tight on the wheel. "I'm off the gas now. Once we're at a low enough speed, I'll steer us onto the shoulder."

"Okay," you say as you note that there isn't much of a shoulder on this part of Route 22, approaching the McDonald's intersection with its traffic light.

Its traffic light that is currently yellow.

You will have sweating nightmares the rest of your life about the next few moments.

The traffic signal blinking from yellow to red.

Ellie Mae inexorably speeding up on the road's downhill slope toward the light.

The traffic—including a small truck belonging to Carabella's Fine Fruit and Produce—beginning to come through the intersection in the other direction.

You see what is going to happen.

You shout to Antoine: *Jump!*

In the same moment you fumble for the car door handle.

The truck brakes screech.

Your body hits the road, curled, rolling.

You hear the smash of metal on metal.

Chapter 18. **Saralinda**

Around bedtime that night I think again about Kenyon and how she refused to hear Evangeline and I decide to find information on Huntington's disease online and send it to the printer so I can show her tomorrow. Also I find a copy of the obituary of Antoine's father. She will understand that this is not the background of somebody who plays jokes. She will admit that she might be wrong about the fraternity, or that at least she should open her mind about Antoine.

Maybe it is true that when you think about someone they are often also thinking about you because at the very moment I click Print I get a text from Kenyon.

—*Where are you?*

—Home, I text back. Where does she think I would be at this hour? I consider having the conversation with her now. I could call, but I would rather talk to her about this in person.

—*Are you okay?*

—Yes, I say, puzzled. Why?

—*No reason. You'll be at school tomorrow?*

—Yes of course.

—*Text me RIGHT AWAY when you get here? I want to talk.*

—Sure. What's going on?

—*It can wait. Good night!*

Probably Kenyon also wants to talk about Antoine, which is good. Unless she has found some information about her own theory in which case I will listen because I do have an open mind.

At this point I remember the stuff I sent to the printer for Kenyon so I go out to the living area. It's dark in our apartment except for the yellow light burning in the crack under my mother's door and a pulsing red light on the printer, which has run out of paper in the middle of my print job.

I kneel to get more paper and see that a couple of my pages have fallen to the floor, so I fish them out, then load the printer and wait for the rest of my pages. I take everything back to my room.

Now it is time to check my blood sugar before bed and take more insulin if necessary, and while I do that (I do not need to give details, trust me I know what I am doing) I think about a doctor's appointment when I was maybe twelve. The doctor's eyebrows stretched high when I explained I wasn't allowed to carry my own supplies, and he turned to my mother (he was angry). "Saralinda is old enough to start taking care of herself. It's dangerous not to let her." My mother fumed all the way home and *I* felt insulted and stung too, and naturally we never went to that doctor again but now belatedly I realize that yes *of course* I should always carry supplies. So I decide to put together a kit—glucose meter, insulin, needles, glucose tabs (my mother insists I eat them instead of candy when I am low). There, my body my responsibility.

When my kit is done I start to sort the papers for Kenyon, which is when I see that some of them are my mother's and I glance at them—quite natural and not snooping, who wouldn't?

Right away I see that the pages are not about the grant; grants are all research, plans, and budgets and also the background of scientists.

This is the picture of a little girl.

She seems to me maybe three years old and she is Asian and adorable all plump fists and nervous smile and flyaway strands from awkwardly ponytailed hair.

There is also a letter.

Dear Ms. de la Flor,

We are pleased to inform you that your formal paperwork is now complete for Tori's adoption. The next steps will be easier. Congratulations! We'll start with a home visit . . .

I read the whole thing and then I read it again and again oh my God.

I am going to have a sister!

Chapter 19. **Caleb**

You are in a heap by the side of Route 22.

Not twenty feet away, Antoine is slumped over the wheel inside a smashed Ellie Mae, which has spun around to face the wrong direction on the road. Cars have pulled over to the side.

Across the street, people pour out of the McDonald's.

A small man swings out of the cab of the Carabella's Fine Fruit and Produce truck, which is not much damaged. He has taken only a few steps toward Ellie Mae and Antoine, when Ellie Mae's engine explodes.

Chapter 20. **Saralinda**

Tea parties and hair ribbons and coloring and playing My Little Pony!

Of course I shouldn't presume what my new little sister is going to like doing, maybe she will want to build LEGO star stations or run crazily in a circle until she's dizzy, wheeee—whatever she wants is fine with meeee!

As God is my witness, I am going to be the best big sister there ever was.

"This is Tori," I say to Georgia and hold up her picture.

I read the letter again. *Tori is a bright, cheery girl, who smiles often and is very loving.*

I imagine myself on my knees, hugging her close.

The letter also says that Tori is partly deaf, and possibly has some learning disabilities also. Because of this apparently the agency had trouble finding a home for her, there was a three-month trial placement that ended in disappointment—my heart twists, poor Tori, can you imagine how *horrible* for her?

But then my mother stepped up. My heart swells with love for my mother, if anybody can take loving excellent care of a child with disabilities it is she. That is an absolute fact, and I will be present to moderate things when necessary if she overdoes it. Maybe she won't. I understand that overprotective parents often calm down after the first child.

Tori and I will have looks in common too although in a weird way, simply that neither of us looks very much like our mother. In my case I have brown eyes and hair and my skin always looks tanned. My mother is paler than me and she has blue eyes. She dyes her hair reddish, which is unconvincing to be honest, but she is gray underneath, her hair was brown originally like mine. She keeps saying she wants us to do that genetic test where you get detailed information but we have not done it.

I want to rush to her waving the letter and screaming with happiness (and also demanding to know why she didn't tell me this was happening). But I soon realize I must allow her to surprise me as she obviously intends.

I am so excited. Georgia and I walk around and around and around my room I *cannot* keep still, and I am having another reaction too. Shock disappointment anger at being excluded, and also a sneaky nasty thought about being *replaced* which is totally unworthy and disrespectful of my mother, I am after all very much loved like I said.

Still her secrecy dismays me until I have a chance to think more about why and then I kind of get it. Adoption takes a long time and might not work out and my mother wanted to spare me from the uncertainty.

Then I realize something *else* which is a small but fun thing: that the cold sesame noodles truly *were* a celebration, and maybe my mother would have told me about Tori tonight except for the grant. It is just like my mother to decide to focus on the grant and celebrate with me later.

Also for Tori's sake we now need more money obviously, children are expensive, worth it but costly especially if they have issues like me and Tori. Issues are expensive.

Obviously I must learn sign language, and luckily Rockland Academy offers it. I wonder if it is too late to swap it in and drop French.

More ideas come to me such as the realization that in the future my mother will focus mostly on Tori. The lesson is this:

My mother was working the same problem as me, in her own way, about how things had changed in our family now that I am a teenager. If I had trusted her more and been open and compassionate, she might have told me about trying to adopt and then we could have hoped together and today we could have received the good news about Tori together.

Instead now I am stuck with waiting until my mother tells me herself.

Which means I need to put the papers back under the printer like I never saw them, which I do.

But I take a picture of them first so that later I can look at my phone and know it is not just a dream.

Oh my God such good news!

Chapter 21. **Caleb**

You stay in the woods where you crawled, adjacent to the McDonald's parking lot. You see no point in moving. You see no point in doing anything at all. You clutch Antoine's copy of *Dracula*. You must have grabbed it on your way out of the car. You don't remember reaching for it.

You saved a book. Not Antoine.

Time passes.

People and vehicles come.

People and vehicles go.

You stay where you are.

Hours pass as you stay shrunken down in the scrub and the dirt.

Sometimes you think: *In a minute I will get up. In a minute I will go to the police. There they are, right there. In a minute I will tell them I was with Antoine. In a minute I will tell them about his mother. I will say that the brakes stopped working. I will ask them to investigate.*

Antoine's mother must have done something.

But she was in her house. And how would somebody engineer what happened with the light changing and the produce truck?

They couldn't.

In any event you do not get up, you do not move, as the police shut down the McDonald's and shoo away the shocked crowds, and the police go too, and the ambulance with the body bag. Only one body bag. Nobody but Antoine has been killed or hurt.

Antoine would be glad about that.

At least Ellie Mae is still nearby, still with you, pulled off the road into the McDonald's lot. She is a skeletal, smoking husk. Beneath glaring lights, a tow truck and four men work over her. One of the men strokes Ellie Mae with a gentle gloved hand in a spot where a defiant orange paint patch remains. Then he attaches a hook and chain.

Antoine would want you to stay with Ellie Mae until the end.

Maybe you will stay here until you die.

Your phone buzzes with a text. Again. Again again again. When it buzzed the first time, a long time ago, it said: *This is Evangeline. Where are you guys???* You have not read her other texts. This is bad, you know. She is worried. You will respond in a minute. You will.

The tow truck pulls away with Ellie Mae.

You could get up now.

You don't.

Evangeline calls, a call not a text, but you don't answer, and then after some time passes, Kenyon texts you (you know it's her because she says so), and you don't answer her either. You want to, or at least you want to want to. But your hands won't do what your brain tells them. You are alone now, alone with Antoine's copy of *Dracula*, which is now your copy of *Dracula*. Alone in the dark. Alone, except for the traffic.

Alone is what you like. Alone is where you belong.

Antoine said, *I don't think there's anything wrong with you, Caleb.*

You wish you could believe it.

You pull out your knife that Antoine mocked. The blade is sharp and strong, though small. You test the blade against your fingertip. Your blood is warm.

Antoine should be alive, not you.

What if you had grabbed him when the brakes first failed, opened your car door, and yanked him out after you?

A beat-up Kia pulls into the now-deserted McDonald's lot and stops beneath one of the lights. Two girls get out, both medium height. One of them cups her hands around her mouth and shouts your name.

Kenyon. Distantly, you recognize her, and then Evangeline.

"Caleb!" Kenyon calls again.

"We know you're here!" Evangeline shouts. "I tracked your GPS signal!"

If anyone could and would figure out how to do that, you think, it would be Evangeline.

"Unless you're dead too, get out here!" Evangeline calls.

Well, you were going to have to talk to her eventually.

You wipe your bleeding finger on the inside of a pocket and shove the knife away. You lurch to your feet. You stumble out into the parking lot.

At least you don't have to tell them about Antoine. You read enough of Evangeline's texts to know that she already knows.

You come to a stop in front of them. In front of Evangeline.

You blurt, "I should have saved him."

She stares at you with a frozen face.

"I should have found a way. If I'd thought faster. There should have been something I could do."

"Oh, God," Kenyon murmurs. Her eyes close for a second and she puts a hand on your shoulder.

You shake it off.

You say to Evangeline, "You told me to take care of him. You *told* me."

Evangeline's face remains still. Then she shrugs, like she doesn't care.

"So when he died?" she says. "At that exact moment, or

at least near to it? I was looking at summer frocks." Her voice is filled with self-loathing. "My stepmother sent me the link. Spencer's thoughtful like that. Always trying to bond. *Frocks.*"

The three of you stand there, Evangeline leaning on the Kia, you clutching *Dracula,* and Kenyon with her arms crossed in front of her.

"I'm sorry I didn't answer your texts," you say.

"We figured you were dead too," Kenyon says.

"Just in case you care what we were thinking," says Evangeline.

You never thought anyone would worry about you. "Oh."

"Only there wasn't any mention of you on the news," Kenyon says. "Just Antoine. Didn't you talk to the police?"

You explain what happened. You add, "Then I just—I sat. I knew I should get up but . . . but I didn't. I couldn't— I couldn't."

"Like maybe if you didn't move," Kenyon says softly, "it wouldn't be real after all."

You give her a startled glance. Then you keep going.

"The brakes failed," you say. "In the car. That was what happened. Then we ran a red light and a truck hit us and—and then the explosion."

"The brakes did *not* fail." Evangeline shakes her head. "Antoine took care of his car like a baby!"

"They did," you say. "Antoine said so."

"The car was old," Kenyon says. "Accidents happen."

"Really?" Evangeline snarls. "Caleb, what about Antoine's mother? Did you see her? What happened?"

They are both looking at you.

"We saw her," you say finally. "But not to talk to. She wouldn't let us in. She didn't touch the car, though. I know what you're thinking because I was thinking it too, but she didn't leave her house. She'd changed the locks. We stood outside, and Antoine shouted at her." You pause. "Sometimes brakes fail, right?"

Evangeline shakes her head. "Not on Ellie Mae." Her eyes burn. "It *was* his mother. It *was* Gabrielle. Somehow she did it, just like she did the carriage house, and we have to figure out how, and we have to do something about it! She can't be allowed to get away with it. She can't!"

Her hands fist. "Promise me. Promise me you guys will help me. Help me get her. She almost killed you two, after all. Even if you won't do it for Antoine, do it for yourselves!"

Do it for yourselves.

"I'll do it for Antoine," you say.

Chapter 22. **Saralinda**

In the morning my alarm jolts me awake, I am stunned that I slept because what I remember is my eyes wide in the dark and my brain total chaos. I stagger into the shower and grip the handicapped rail. My brain is all Tori Tori Tori and also what I learned yesterday about Antoine having Huntington's which my mind wants to wince away from (too painful), but I breathe it in with the steam of the water because it's real. Also real: Evangeline who is not simply shellacked perfection and knifelike brain the way I thought, her veneer thick but intended to protect vulnerable insides, it turns out. I get that.

After all, life is hard sometimes, also surprising shocking unfair sweet—all beauty and terror. Our hearts need to be brave however, and what we have to do is put ourselves out there even if it means we could be crushed.

I hope I can be brave like that I don't know.

Anyway, for now I have other concerns too, I am going to have a sister and help Antoine all I can and tentatively I can now say that I have two friends, Kenyon and Evangeline. Which wow.

Also. Also last night in bed I thought more about Caleb, my feelings such a surprise—what to do I don't know probably nothing, because although in theory my heart is brave, in reality it twists backward like my foot.

I get dressed and leave for school without seeing my mother. Her door is closed, which is good because as much as I want Tori to be my sister I am still just the *tiniest* bit angry at my mother.

For basically *lying* to me, not that I am guilt-free in that department.

In the hallway at school there is a low buzz of kids talking and eyes are wide and shoulders are hunched. I am halfway aware and halfway not because I am thinking about Tori—about learning sign language (will she already know it?) and about sharing my bedroom as there is no third bedroom obviously. I am willing to redecorate in any style even pink canopy twin beds, although maybe Tori will be okay if only *her* bed is a pink canopy, not mine. If Tori is into it we could have a Disney wallpaper border such as Elsa and Anna (sisters!). Also if in the winter we build a snowman, Georgia can be part of it too because a snowman (or maybe better a snowwoman) would look good holding a stick. Temporarily of course. I would not leave Georgia out in the cold.

Or maybe I'll move to school and live in the dorm with a roommate and visit my mother and sister on weekends . . .

But as I get to my classroom it penetrates my stupid skull that there are these small groups everywhere huddling and whispering, and some people are actually crying and Olivia Fourier is having hysterics. She's leaning against her locker and her sobs are operatic. (Not that I have ever been to the opera.) Her best friend Anindita is patting her back and sees me and makes a face full of woe.

I say, "Is Olivia all right?"

"Oh, just really, really upset. They went out freshman year."

"For six weeks!" Olivia looks up, her eyes glistening. "I never forgave him for dumping me! Why didn't I forgive him? We were fourteen! Now it will be on my conscience *forever!*"

Anindita gives her an extra pat.

"I wasn't here then," I say. "Who didn't you forgive?" Then belatedly the clues come together. "Wait. Did someone *die?*" As I say it I know it must be true and horror fills me: Who was it?

Olivia is incredulous. "You don't *know?*"

"Antoine Dubois," Anindita says. "A car accident yesterday evening. That old car!"

"I was in it once!" Olivia bursts into renewed tears. "Ellie Mae!"

Anindita says, "They say it was quick at least."

Antoine.

No. It can't be. No.

I mutter something to Anindita and Olivia and then Georgia and I hobble away very carefully and find the door to my classroom and go inside and sit. People are talking about him in here too so I learn everything that happened.

For all of last night, Antoine was dead.

This morning therefore he is not at school and never will be again.

Because he is dead.

I think of his knees poking out of his jeans when I went to the carriage house and he welcomed me. The knees were alive and now they are not.

Evangeline said his mother wanted him dead and now he is dead.

In a car accident.

Yesterday Caleb and Antoine went away in Antoine's car.

My heart has a tiny seizure.

Nobody has said Caleb is dead however.

To calm myself I try to meditate which involves consciously staying in the present moment, you do not think of the past or the future. I have never shown much talent for meditation and now I get why, it is because whenever it occurs to me to try meditating I am desperate which means that the present moment sucks and therefore I don't *want* to be in it. An announcement comes on about an all-school assembly which is happening now, proving again that *now* is a dreadful thing. Everybody files out but I don't, I stay in my homeroom, and the teacher doesn't notice because she goes out with everybody else. I am not so sure I can walk, to be honest. Even with Georgia. Anyway I stay behind with Georgia, and five minutes later Kenyon and Evangeline and Caleb find me and when I see Caleb I breathe sharply in because he is okay (except his expression says he is not okay). Then I remember that Kenyon called me last night and wanted me to text her this morning only I forgot because of Tori. She must have wanted to tell me.

Then I focus on Evangeline.

She loved him she loved him, her friend, her friend is dead.

I say her name but I say nothing after that because everything I might say dries up and sticks to my tongue.

Evangeline is the one who talks.

She says, all in a rush, "Saralinda, the three of us are sort of running away together for the night so that we can talk, we need to figure out what to do about Antoine and his mother, was this an accident or wasn't it. Can you come?"

I look at Caleb. He was with Antoine, he nearly died too and now his face. His face.

"Please come," says Kenyon.

"You were in the carriage house," Evangeline says. "You belong with us. We need you."

Caleb nods.

What I think is this: Evangeline is my friend and Kenyon is my friend and Caleb is Caleb, so come what may, if they want me with them, then I am with them.

Antoine is dead.

I just want to be with my friends.

I think about asking where we are going and what we are doing but I don't because to be honest? I don't care so long as I can be with them.

"Of course I'm coming," I say.

Chapter 23. **Caleb**

You sit in the passenger seat of Kenyon's Kia while Kenyon drives and you navigate using your phone. Saralinda and Evangeline are in the backseat. The four of you are going to Fire Island, where there is a beach house belonging to friends of Kenyon's.

You keep returning to what Evangeline thinks. That Ellie Mae's brakes should not have failed, not the way Antoine took care of her. That Ellie Mae shouldn't have exploded either; she was hit broadside.

Evangeline has moved into take-charge mode, explaining things to Saralinda.

"So what we're doing is, we're giving ourselves some private time to discuss Antoine's mother. Here's what we know: Antoine believed she wanted him dead, right? She tried to stage an accident that would kill him along with—incidentally—the four of us. It didn't work, so what I think—what *we* think—is that she sabotaged his car, the brakes, hoping for an accident that would do the job for her. And it worked."

145

"It almost killed Caleb too," Saralinda says.

You angle yourself in the passenger seat so that you can see Saralinda's face.

Evangeline nods vehemently. "Yes. She didn't care who else she hurt or killed, obviously. So long as she got Antoine. He gave other people rides in his car all the time! She could have killed more people!"

"If she did it, we'll find a way to prove it," Kenyon says calmly. "We'll sit down together and talk it out in peace and quiet, and then we'll do research and put our case together for the police."

You wonder if that will work or not.

"We *have* to get Antoine's mother," Evangeline says.

"If there's evidence. If she did it," Kenyon adds.

Evangeline directs a glare at Kenyon's neck. "She *did* do it." Then she leans in toward Saralinda. "Are you in?"

"Of course I am," says Saralinda, simply. "But um . . . can I ask a question?"

"Okay," says Evangeline.

"Should we talk to Dr. Lee too? He's already suspicious about the carriage house, right? I mean, he seems like a good guy to me . . ."

You remember what Antoine said about Dr. Lee's file— the one about *you*.

"That's not crazy," says Evangeline slowly. "But . . ."

"I'm not saying we shouldn't all go away to be together

and think and stuff," Saralinda adds. "I mean, I want to. But what if, you know, Dr. Lee has already found evidence about the carriage house?"

"Caleb? Kenyon? What do you think?" Evangeline asks the two of you.

Kenyon says, "I like the idea of having an adult on our side. If he's trustworthy. Caleb?"

"Let's keep talking about it," you say. The fact is, you don't know. You have never known what to think about Dr. Lee. You're even more confused by his supposed opinion on your "narcissistic asshole" father. You say, "We don't have to loop him in tonight. It could be later, after we've all talked. Tomorrow."

"Oh, I *definitely* don't want to loop him in tonight," Evangeline says fiercely. "I want this just to be us tonight. We're the only ones who—who—" She stops. Swallows.

"So that's settled," you say. You're relieved. The thought of making yourself vulnerable to an adult terrifies you. Talking to Dr. Lee, asking him to listen, to believe you . . . about Antoine's mother . . . about *anything* . . . it makes your stomach clench. Why should anybody believe you? *You* don't believe you.

You look at Saralinda. "Just us tonight. Okay?"
She nods.
After that, there is silence until you see the sign for the

Fire Island ferry. "Wait, we have to take a boat?" you say. "There's no bridge?"

"It's because cars aren't allowed on the island," Kenyon explains as she drives the car into the line for the parking garage. "It's a short walk to the cottage after the ferry dock. We won't need the car."

"I'm not afraid of walking," you snap. "Although maybe *you* should be, Kenyon. You just dumped your crutches and you're still in a back brace."

"I'm doing fine. Also I have plenty of Tylenol."

You stare at the ferry. "We could find a hotel or something."

"Yeah, but we'd need a credit card for that," says Evangeline. "My stepmother is totally over-controlling. She might check and find out where we are before we're ready. We *agreed* on Fire Island."

"My friends' place is free," says Kenyon. "And nice. There are three bedrooms!"

The car behind you honks.

"All right," you say at last. It's not like you have a reason for your sudden objection. It's more a feeling. You just . . . would rather have the car.

Kenyon pulls into the garage. None of you say anything else as she finds a space to park. You grab Antoine's copy of *Dracula,* which has not left your side, and stuff it into your pocket.

Evangeline buys four round-trip tickets with cash; her paranoia about any of you being tracked by your parents has caused her to make everyone promise to keep away from debit and credit cards. You don't have a lot of cash, the four of you, even when pooled, but it should be enough.

You board the ferry as a group. Saralinda has her far-away expression on; the same one you saw on her face during the drive, when you sneaked looks at her. You wonder what she's thinking.

You're glad she agreed to come.

You admit it to yourself now: You have a thing for Saralinda de la Flor. It's not a big deal. It's only physical or chemical or whatever. It's a *thing*. It isn't mutual; of course it isn't. Even if it were, you're dangerous and she should stay far away from you. She belongs in some super-safe place with some nice—no, you won't imagine her with some imaginary nice guy. There are limits to self-torture.

You wonder who will look for which of the four of you tonight, and if the various excuses all of you left will hold up.

You're pretty sure your father won't be checking up on you. You can go weeks without a text between you.

On the ferry deck, you pull the ocean air into your lungs. There are some other passengers boarding, but it's far from crowded. You move away from the girls and stand on the deck alone to read the first couple pages of Antoine's book.

By the time the ferry pulls up at the dock, *Dracula's* Jonathan Harker has been warned that *when the clock strikes midnight, all the evil things in the world will have full sway.*

You stuff the book back into your pocket and disembark with the girls.

Fire Island has nothing in common with Castle Dracula. Well, maybe signs of wealth. There's a fenced marina next to the ferry dock. Its slips are filled with sailboats, motorboats, and sleek large yachts. You stare at the ten-foot chain-link fence around the marina, which you doubt is about boat theft. The fence says: *If you don't have a key, you don't belong here.*

In the same way that Jonathan Harker doesn't belong in Transylvania. He's an innocent heading into trouble. Like Antoine was, you think.

"Caleb?" says Evangeline. "Coming?"

"Coming," you say.

As we walk on Fire Island, with me and Kenyon and Evangeline abreast and Caleb trailing by himself a few yards behind us, I think of questions. These are the questions it did not occur to me to ask back at school before I got into the car, and mostly they are about what my mother will think. Running away is a rash thing to do. But then again how can it be bad for the four of us to be together? We have to figure out what to do about Antoine's mother, who *must* be brought to justice.

Also, we need to grieve. Evangeline needs it especially. I wonder about making a ceremony tonight, such as lighting a candle and standing in a circle and maybe there could be a poem?

We are not *running away* running away because we are not children and it is only for one night. I rehearse telling this to my mother later. The thing is, I have never been away from her for an entire night before. I was never allowed.

Now I'm allowing myself.

We have to do this. It is not fair and not right about Antoine. He was already destined to have his life cut short and now the rest has been stolen from him. Also I hope he didn't know what was happening and didn't have time to feel oh God the smash, the fire, please let Anindita have been right about it being quick at least.

Please.

It is obvious why the island has the no-car rule. There are no streets, just narrow sandy pathways and boardwalks for people to walk on. It's quaint and appealing, and though it is the off-season there are a few people around, such as a woman riding an old-style bicycle and a male couple walking toward the beach.

"Kenyon, what did you tell your friends about us?" Evangeline asks as we walk.

Kenyon smiles at her and at me. "Nothing! See, my friends gave me a general invitation to come anytime, and they showed me where they hide the spare key."

When Evangeline doesn't reply, Kenyon's smile fades. "Does that meet with your approval?"

"I guess. It seems, I don't know, over-generous. Who are they? How did you meet them?"

"They're friends of a teacher—who is also my friend— from my last school."

"What are their names?"

"What is this, the Spanish Inquisition? They're Erin and

Cordelia. They're adults, in their thirties. Does that meet with your approval?"

"Yes. I guess so. Sorry, okay? I want to know. What's wrong with that?"

"Look, Evangeline. My friends figured there might be times when I'd want to get away. They understand me. Also, they understand what happened in my life."

Kenyon's voice is tight and angry. The tension between her and Evangeline is too much for me. I slow my steps and let them go on ahead.

Caleb comes up beside me.

"I thought they got past their first reaction of hating each other," I mutter to him. "And now Evangeline knows about Kenyon's mother . . ."

He shrugs.

I sigh.

He says, "Maybe she doesn't want to treat her differently than she would otherwise."

I recall my first reaction to Caleb. That was not a positive one either. I sneak a glance at his profile.

I now know for sure that he is not the thuggish boy I once thought. If he were, there would never ever be the kind of look on his face that is on his face at this moment.

Suddenly he looks at me too.

I look away.

Oh, God, why am I here, why? At least I should have

already called my mother, so what if she is working on her grant. My mother has so much love that she needs two daughters to express it. She has taken care of me all my life and she does not deserve to have me run away, she will worry (if she knows I am gone). And then I realize that my mother will also worry about my insulin level, but I have insulin and the glucose tabs in my emergency kit that I packed just last night in my backpack, and of course my glucose meter to test with, isn't that odd and lucky?

It makes me feel better to think of that—like fate intervened, like I am meant to be here. I am meant to be here with the others, and maybe my fairy godmother is not useless and obstructive after all.

Ahead of Caleb and me, Kenyon and Evangeline are now silent.

I look at Kenyon's vulnerable bare neck. I say, "Kenyon? Are you all right? I mean, your back and—and things?"

There is a very long pause and I think she will not answer in which case I will not press her. Then she says, "You know what's funny? Antoine's mother—it makes me think about my grandfather. I keep remembering how he was when I was little. When he loved me. Before everything happened. Now I don't call him Grandpa anymore, you know? I don't call him anything."

Evangeline says, "I don't call my stepmother anything

either. She's 'hey, you' to me. She only married my father for his money."

I don't think her stepmother has anything to do with anything, and also Evangeline has interrupted Kenyon. Yet I am curious and cannot stop myself from asking.

"How much money do you have, Evangeline?"

She hesitates, then shrugs. "Forty million, give or take."

My eyes bug out, seriously I feel them bulge and in front of me Kenyon twitches.

"It's not so much." Evangeline's voice is defensive. "Also I don't have it *yet*. Not until I'm eighteen."

I am overwhelmed. I think of the money my mother will get from completing the grant work and maybe it will be fifteen or twenty thousand dollars which is a lot of money but still it will not go far for us especially because of Tori and also because of me, as Rockland Academy is not cheap.

"It's good to be rich," I blurt, as I realize fully that having two daughters is going to put serious financial stress on my mother and she will need to write a lot of grants assuming she can even get the work which does not always come regularly. Maybe I can get a part-time job?

"Or at least," says Kenyon, "it's good to have enough money for a beach cottage like this one." She points. "We're here!"

Chapter 25. **Caleb**

The cottage has weathered shingles and turquoise shutters and is crowded onto a tiny lot. You are dismayed. You'd imagined an isolated house tucked into the dunes. This place has—you count—eight equally cute neighboring cottages in its cluster. They look closed up, at least, but in the summer when they're fully occupied, people can probably hear each other dream.

Saralinda has brightened, however. "It looks so cozy!"

"Wait until you see the inside!" Kenyon runs her fingers under a windowsill and holds up a small box. "Key."

The girls crowd behind her into the house, and Saralinda makes a noise: part intake of breath, part hum of pleasure. The sound whispers seductively over your skin. But you're desperate to run, alone, back to the ferry, back to the mainland. Find some way to handle what happened to Antoine all by yourself. You've been alone all your life . . . how can you step into that small house with those girls?

You linger on the cottage doorstep, where you can see the ocean.

You have never been to a real beach before. Your family is not the kind to take vacations. True, you went to camp the summer you were eleven, upstate at Lake George, where there was something they called a beach. You left camp after a few days. It was one of those few times when you remember exactly what happened, and why; you were not then and are not now sorry about that kid's smashed nose, which he deserved.

Your father had come to get you and take you home. He bought you an ice-cream cone. He'd been cheerful and talkative and said, "Don't worry about it, son."

You always felt uncomfortable when he called you son. That day, it made you realize something new: that you could not give in anymore, not *ever*, to an impulse to be violent. You had to control it when you could, because of all the times when Mr. Hyde, inside you, could not.

You don't belong here with the girls. What if . . . what if . . .

But you have no choice now. You already made your choice.

You go inside.

It's nice, you guess. There's a combination kitchen and living room, with cream-colored walls and a wooden floor and turquoise trim around the windows. A motley collection of mason jars, bowls, coffee mugs, and spices crowd a long open shelf above the kitchen counter. Over the sink, a sign says FRESH VEGETABLES. In the living room, there's a white-brick fireplace with six comfy, mismatched chairs grouped in a circle before it, and a big, low wooden coffee table.

You hear Saralinda in the hallway beyond, where she is checking out bedrooms. Evangeline stands in the living room, hands on her hips. Kenyon has a kitchen cabinet open and says something about wanting to eat and a nearby convenience store and who can cook what.

"We are not here to play house!" The words explode from you.

Saralinda sticks her head back into the main room and stares at you.

"We're here to talk," you add, more moderately. "About Antoine."

Three sets of eyes narrow, but it's Saralinda who responds. "We know that. But I also need to eat. I'm diabetic, for your information. But actually, we all need to eat."

Diabetic?

Saralinda turns to Kenyon. "I'll go to the store. What do we need?"

Kenyon says, "We won't have a lot of choice. It's a convenience store. They have lightbulbs and toilet paper, and some basics like bread and milk and, you know, cookies and chips. Will that be all right for you, Saralinda?"

"Sure. I'll find something."

"I'll go," you say. "You guys don't have to."

"I need to come," says Saralinda, without looking at you. "And pick out my stuff."

"I'm coming too," adds Evangeline.

You look at Kenyon, but she shakes her head and points to an oversized armchair. "I'm staying right here."

The three of you retrace your steps to the village near the ferry dock and into the store. You're the only customers, and there's a bored-looking cashier.

You check out the aisles. The contents of the store are less limited than Kenyon led you to believe. There is a small counter with produce and a refrigerator case with milk and cheese and yogurt. Saralinda gets lettuce, cheddar cheese, and a package of Slim Jims. Hands stuffed in your pockets, you trail behind her into the next aisle, where Evangeline holds a shopping basket with M&M's and cookies in it. She's holding a family-sized bag of Cheetos.

She looks up. "So this is what *I* want. Orange chemical goodness. Saralinda, I know you can't, but is it okay if—"

"Actually," Saralinda interrupts, "I can, a little. How about these too?"

She picks up York Peppermint Patties and tosses them into her basket.

You pick up microwave popcorn.

"That's practically real food," says Evangeline disapprovingly.

"I beg to differ." You peer at the label. "It's got something called Flavacol."

Your reward is a halfhearted smile and the extension of the basket.

The girls pick out more junk food. At the register, before you realize what she's doing, Evangeline pulls out a debit card and gives it to the cashier.

Then she blinks. "Wait! Not that card!"

For the first time, the cashier really looks at Evangeline. "Overdrawn?" He smiles and gives it back.

Evangeline turns to you. "Your turn to pay," she says airily. "I paid last time."

The thing is, you only have thirty dollars. You hand it all over, and it's not quite enough. Luckily, Saralinda can cover the rest. She counts out quarters.

All of this catches the cashier's interest. Then he's checking you out. Slowly.

Well. It's good to know you attract somebody.

"Do you need bags, darling?" he says.

"Yeah," you say.

"I always forget to bring mine too," he says chattily. "Where are y'all staying?"

"At a friend's place," you evade. You pick up the groceries and turn to follow the girls out.

The cashier calls after you. "There's a movie tonight. Eight o'clock at the firehouse. It's *Alien*. Sigourney Weaver! Gotta love her! Y'all come!"

You sort of nod, without meeting his eyes, but Saralinda smiles and waves good-bye.

Outside, Evangeline is several paces ahead, walking fast. The three of you return in silence to the cottage, but then as you approach the door, Evangeline says tightly, "Sorry about the debit card."

"It doesn't matter," Saralinda says.

"It *does* matter. My stepmother is really nosy and if I'd used that card, she'd know exactly where we are. Plus, I don't *make* mistakes, and I was the one who told you guys it was better for us to use cash for anything we had to buy." Evangeline grabs the bag of Cheetos. She rips it open, crams a handful into her mouth, and orange powder explodes down her chin and onto her chest. She stomps inside with the smell of her Cheetos trailing behind.

You hold the door open for Saralinda. "After you."

Saralinda says, "Evangeline's hard on herself."

"Yeah."

She tilts her head back to look up at you and smiles, a quirk at the edge of her mouth. "Caleb, that guy liked you, you know."

Shock poleaxes you.

Saralinda knows you're straight, right? You fumble for something, anything to say.

When you finally look up, she has gone inside.

Chapter 26. **Saralinda**

I slip into the cottage bathroom, my face hot and no wonder. I sit on the closed toilet seat with Georgia gripped
in one hand for comfort. I attempted to flirt with Caleb,
stupid impulse also shameful because inappropriate, Antoine died exactly one day ago. Anyway Caleb looked away
probably embarrassed on my behalf, also not interested,
hello humiliation.

I set Georgia aside and test my blood sugar. I am 112
which is excellent, that helps me feel better emotionally,
also relieved—it is scary being a diabetic all on my own,
this is not exactly the way I thought it would happen. I
know what to do however, careful calculation of how much
insulin to take because eating can bring you up or down
depending on what you consume and also depending on
your own particular body and how it reacts to various
foods and exercise. In short figuring insulin dosage is an
art and frankly I am not as good at it (yet) as my mother,
about whom I also do not want to think.

Only I should, I am doing her wrong.

I notice orange Cheetos dust on my shirt from Evangeline (is this why Caleb was put off?) and I pick it up with a fingertip that I then put to my lips (civilization crumbles fast when teenagers are alone), but I can't get a real taste. Speaking of civilization crumbling it was an education to watch Evangeline shop the chips and cookies aisle.

I wonder what kind of treats Antoine liked and if anything Evangeline bought reminds her of him, and if so we should all eat it to honor him. Okay no matter what I am going to eat something junky. Because. Because I need a treat. My options from the things we bought are:

Oreos.

Pepperidge Farm Pirouettes.

Pringles. (There is something fascinating about the physical perfection of the Pringle.)

Lindt chocolate truffles. (Evangeline bought two packages: caramel and dark chocolate.)

York Peppermint Patties. (*Love.*)

Gummy worms. (Not a contender.)

M&M's.

Ritz Crackers. (This was nice of Evangeline to get because she said they were to go with my cheese. It is best to eat cheese straight no crackers if you are a diabetic because of the extra carbs, but it felt rejecting to say so to her.)

Microwave popcorn. (My mother makes unbuttered

popcorn sometimes from actual kernels popped on the stove in canola oil, I am allowed three level cups which do nothing for me.)

I know why my mother does not butter our popcorn, it is because she always wants to lose weight—which she does succeed in doing periodically and then she struts around in skinny jeans so happy, though I like how she looks ordinarily, more soft and round. I say nothing and she never stays skinny long anyway because of the stress of life which is to say the stress of me, and yes I would rather think about Cheetos, which is my final option for my treat. I have never been near them before. Orange chemical goodness! I like the sound of that plus Evangeline likes them and she is no fool.

Next I text my mother and tell her I am fine, I am with friends can't give details but don't worry, and I send her a picture of the test and the insulin too. It shows that I am okay on my own, not that I am on my own, I am with my friends.

Last night's not-much-sleep is catching up with me. I sit on the closed toilet for another minute with my head down, then I go out and join the others.

"There you are, good," says Evangeline. She empties the grocery bag in the middle of the living room's wooden coffee table and everything we bought tumbles out to make an altar to the gods of Salt and Sugar. Soon the Pringles canisters are on their sides with stacks of potato chips fanning out, and the cookies and crackers and chocolate and candy packages are ripped open.

I move the York Peppermint Patties aside to make room for the popcorn that Caleb has popped. I sink into an empty chair and pour Cheetos out onto a paper towel which will serve as my plate.

To these—slowly—I add caramel chocolate squares, my York Peppermint Patties, Pringles, M&M's, and Oreos. (My lettuce, cheese, and Slim Jims are off to the side.)

Then Caleb says to me, "I thought you said you were diabetic?"

He is sitting next to me.

I blink up at him and he looks back questioningly and shame fills me—again—and the Cheetos turn to chalk in my mouth whereas a second ago they were the most delicious thing I ever ate.

Then I am enraged! I was enjoying myself for a second. Also I had to have a treat because my absence might be worrying my mother plus Antoine's death twists my heart chokes my throat. I deserve Cheetos and also anything else I might want to eat, I deserve it so just try to stop me. Not that he did just try, there was a look *just a look,* only there is nothing "just" about a look, believe me.

"I can eat whatever I want!" I say sharply. He is visibly taken aback at my tone and the next second I have tumbled completely into the pit of self-torture remorse regret hate.

I reach for Georgia and hold her. Okay so the truth is that I have not yet made peace with my body and its problems, I have tried I will keep trying, I hate myself I wish I loved myself. Well, sometimes I love myself, okay today I am a wreck. Today is not a good day period although falling apart is not allowed, deep breath, Saralinda, good girl.

To repeat, I didn't sleep much last night.

Now Caleb is not looking at me but at Evangeline. Fine I don't care. I am letting him have power over me by valuing his opinion over mine so I will simply stop doing that. Simply.

We are all in a circle eating, soon we will talk, for now I will breathe and maybe eat some cheese.

Evangeline has picked up a photo from a side table. She asks Kenyon, "Are these your friends?"

I crane my neck to see, glad of the distraction. In the photo there are two women and they are wearing white with their arms around each other's waists and their cheeks pressed together and big smiles.

"Yes," says Kenyon. "That's Cordelia in the suit and Erin with the flowers in her hair."

"It's their wedding?"

"I guess so," says Kenyon. "I only met them last summer so I wasn't there."

"How did you meet them?" Evangeline asks.

I am listening. Also I want to eat cheese. It has nothing to do with Caleb. I cut off a slice and then I eat a Pringle, balance.

Everything I eat decomposes into sugar in my stomach pushing into my blood but I know what I'm doing and I have insulin and I planned for this, he doesn't understand. I feel okay, I think I do. Still maybe I've had enough of the bad food for now. Although I will have more if I want, it's my choice.

Kenyon says, "They're friends of my teacher Mr. Mayer. He had Erin contact me. We had a lot in common, though Erin is older. Then she invited me here for a weekend in the summer to meet Cordelia and hang out and meet some of their other friends."

"Just like that, she invited you?" Evangeline puts the photo down. It now has her orange thumbprint on its frame. "You came here to spend the weekend with people you didn't know? Weren't you scared?"

"I was socially scared." Kenyon picks up the photograph to polish it clean. "But Erin and Cordelia and their friends are awesome, and they were nice to me." Kenyon looks directly at me. She adds, "And that weekend, I got, like, this transformative vision for my future. For the first time, I believed that I would, you know, survive. That it would get better."

I smile back, we are both remembering our talk in the

carriage house under the debris, isn't it strange what a good memory it has become? Kenyon puts down the photograph but keeps a hand on it as if it's a good luck charm.

She says, "That was when I began to understand that I could do things to help myself, and start to solve my problems." She laughs. "My many problems."

"Gay teens are not the only ones with problems," says Evangeline.

"I'm not saying they are! Give me some credit." Kenyon pauses. "I was being honest about myself. Is that not okay? Listen, Evangeline, you were the one who asked in the first place about Erin and Cordelia. You with your fairy-tale problem."

"Fairy-tale problem?" Evangeline's forehead wrinkles.

"Oh, beautiful you, beautiful stepmother. I figure any minute we'll find out she has a magic mirror telling her you're the one who's more fair so she's jealous."

Evangeline's jaw drops. "What are you imagining? That's not my story."

"Okay. Then what is?"

Evangeline hunches a shoulder and doesn't answer.

I clear my throat. "I'm glad you met Erin and Cordelia, Kenyon."

She seems relieved to look at me instead of Evangeline. "Yeah. Now, when things are bad, I think how someday I will meet someone, like Erin met Cordelia. It will happen, if I don't give up."

"Everybody wants that," I say. "To meet someone." I do not look at Caleb.

Caleb says, "But not everybody can have it."

We are all silent then.

"Gummy worms?" Evangeline says brightly. "Everyone? Antoine liked them." She puts three in her mouth and then spits them back into her fist and coughs.

"Maybe you've had enough?" says Caleb.

"Don't tell her what to eat!" I snap. "She can eat whatever she wants. Whatever. She. Wants!"

Three heads turn to me.

"Sorry," I say. "Sorry, sorry, *sorry*. Oh, God."

"No, I'm sorry," Caleb says.

I look at him for a second, ashamed. "Sorry," I mutter again and he says it too, at the same time.

"Yeah, you're both sorry," says Evangeline. "Anyway." She raps on the table with one hand. "Time to discuss Antoine's mother. Time to discuss Gabrielle Dubois."

Chapter 27. **Caleb**

You listen as Evangeline talks about Antoine's mother, and a picture forms in your head, not only of Mrs. Dubois, but of a small girl with no memory of her own mother, and a father who did too little, and a grandmother who did too much.

Evangeline.

"So it's like a week into kindergarten," Evangeline says. "Beginning of the day, I'm standing all alone with my grandmother lingering in the doorway like she always did, and Antoine comes up to me and holds out his hand and after a few seconds I take it. Which is when my grandmother springs into action." She grimaces. "So the thing is, some Koreans and Korean Americans are kind of, uh, prejudiced, especially when they're from the older generation . . ." Her voice trails off.

"Your grandmother's racist," you say. "Is that what you mean?"

"Well, she's dead now, but yeah." Evangeline grips the

back of her neck with one hand. "That's it. She was. She had good qualities too—but anyway. African Americans . . . any dark-skinned person, really. She didn't want anything to do with them. So anyway, the next thing I know, my grandmother is right there, grabbing my other hand, trying to pull me away from Antoine. Only I won't let go!"

"You just hung on?" asks Kenyon.

"I did. For dear life. It was like a tug-of-war, my grandmother pulling me away from Antoine, and me screaming for her to let go. Which was when Gabrielle Dubois intervened. She said something to my grandmother about how she told Antoine to play with me, because she noticed I was all alone. It was, uh, kind of humiliating." Evangeline shrugs like this doesn't matter, but you can see that the memory stings her a little.

Only then she smiles, if briefly. "But somehow I just kept on holding Antoine's hand anyway, and he kept on holding mine. And even though my grandmother was awful about Antoine until the day she died, he was my friend from that moment. And Gabrielle was my friend, too. She noticed me and she took action to help me, because that's who Gabrielle Dubois is." She pauses. "Used to be."

"Until her husband got sick?" Saralinda asks.

"Yes. Although she was still herself then. It's since his death that she got so strange." Her chin points out. "Listen, before the carriage house, she tried to kill Antoine a couple of other times too. Including messing with Ellie Mae's brakes. I wanted to tell you guys that."

Saralinda sucks in her breath sharply.

"He told me," you say. You've been turning this over in your head for hours, since you remembered. It is unbelievable to you that it was only yesterday.

"So he never got in his car without checking thoroughly," Evangeline continues.

"He didn't check yesterday," you say, interrupting again. "I guess because of me. I distracted him. So maybe she cut the brake line again? Is that what you're thinking?"

Evangeline chews the inside of her cheek. "Maybe. All right, Caleb, now go ahead and tell us every single thing you remember about yesterday."

You open your mouth, but Kenyon cuts in.

"Look, you guys. I mean this kindly, okay? We can talk all night, and I'm happy to do that. It's why we came. But I think we all know where this has to end, right? We have to go to the police. We tell them everything we know, including that the two of you heard Antoine accuse his mother of poisoning him and cutting his brake line, and that Saralinda and I also heard him accuse her of sabotaging the carriage house. Then the police investigate and they find the evidence, if it's there. After which Mrs. Dubois goes to jail, or gets psychiatric help, or both. The end. Right?"

"Yes, police, of course," Evangeline says. "But I want to go to them with something solid. Evidence, not hearsay. Maybe we can find some if we try. What's wrong with that?" She glares at Kenyon. "On the news they said it was an accident, after all. Why should we trust the police to investigate this and do a good job? I *don't* trust them."

"Well, you should," Kenyon says. "They'll investigate when we tell them to."

"How can you be so sure?"

"Because I grew up around cops. My *grandfather* is a cop, okay? I know how the police work. They have procedures. They follow them. So they'll take care of this. They'll figure it out. That's their job."

You are surprised to learn that Kenyon's grandfather is a cop. Although there was no reason for her to mention it before.

Evangeline's lip has curled. She says to Kenyon, "So would you suggest we go to your grandfather with what we think?"

Kenyon winces. "No. He'd never listen to me."

"But you think other cops would. Even though we have no evidence."

"They'll find evidence for us. That's their job. Why wouldn't they?"

"Oh, maybe because Antoine wasn't white?"

Kenyon makes a face. "That's paranoid."

Evangeline looks at you. Of course she does; you're not lily-white either: She waits.

Diplomatically, you say to Kenyon, "They might investigate. But it would be naïve not to understand that Evangeline could be right. If we can possibly find some evidence, it can only help." You pause. "For when we do go to the police. And to Dr. Lee. Because yeah, we have to do that in the end." You nod at Kenyon. "You're right."

Kenyon bites her lip.

Saralinda pushes a York Peppermint Patty off the napkin in front of her, as if it were a chess piece. She says, "But it is hard to believe the police wouldn't care that Antoine is dead and maybe was murdered."

"Happens every day," Evangeline says bitterly.

You nod.

Kenyon says, "Okay, so let's see what we've got to work with. Caleb? You were going to tell us what happened yesterday?"

But before you can start speaking, Evangeline's phone beeps.

"Irina," she says, making a face. She jabs at her phone with one finger, and then her expression changes as she keeps looking at it. Her shoulders tense.

She holds out her phone.

"Look at this. It's our evidence! It's our *evidence!*"

Saralinda and Kenyon crowd on either side of you as you watch.

It's a video: a grainy image of a parking lot. The student parking lot at school. There's a time stamp. Evening. Day before yesterday.

A man—short, heavyset, with gray hair—crosses the parking lot, passing car after car, until he stands beside Antoine's car, which is covered by the tarp. He glances quickly around. He kneels, and his arm moves under the car. A few seconds later, he gets up and walks away.

"This is it, right?" says Evangeline. "Won't it force them to investigate?"

When you look up, Evangeline babbles at you. "My roommate Irina has been meeting this new boy by the parking lot. Because it's private there. She says they thought they were being followed, so they recorded the guy. Do any of you know Irina much?"

You all shake your heads.

"Okay, well, let's say she's always looking for privacy and she always thinks she's being followed. Irina lives in a very dramatic world. This isn't the first time she's done a recording or taken pictures. Anyway, she forgot about it until now, which is typical of her too. But then she remembered and of course she knows Antoine is my friend and that's his car, so she sent this—"

"But that's not Antoine's mother," Saralinda says. "That's

some guy. What are you thinking, that she got someone to help her, like a mechanic?"

"Yes," says Evangeline. "And—"

"No," says Kenyon, in a strangled voice.

"What—"

"I mean no, that's not some guy. That's my grandfather." Kenyon pauses. "My grandfather, the cop."

Chapter 28. **Saralinda**

I sink into my chair by the coffee table and push all my delicious junk food aside. I don't want any of it anymore not even a York Peppermint Patty, and I stare at Kenyon. All of us stare at her.

"Are you sure?" Caleb asks at last. "It's not like the video shows a close-up of his face."

"Yes, I'm sure." Kenyon is pale in the artificial light of the cottage and her neck tattoo stands out as if it's raised. WHY BE HAPPY.

Evangeline sinks down onto the floor and draws her legs up against her body and puts her cheek on her knees. "Really *really* sure?"

"I know how he walks, how he turns his head. Also, that's his coat with the ripped back seam." Kenyon's voice dips. "It pissed my mom off, that he wouldn't get it fixed or wear the new one she bought him. They had a whole thing about it, her saying it looked terrible, and he'd just keep saying it was comfortable."

Kenyon laughs but it is a short unamused bark. "So. My grandfather killed Antoine? My grandfather killed Antoine! Only why? Why would he *do* that? I mean, he didn't *know* him."

"As far as we are aware," Caleb comments. Abruptly he pulls the rubber band out of his hair and twists it over his fingers. "Probably there's other stuff we don't know . . ."

"At least we now have actual evidence of Antoine's car being sabotaged," Evangeline says. "So the police . . ." She falters as she remembers what I am remembering, which is that Kenyon's grandfather *is* the police.

Then my mind tilts with an outer-space idea. I say it anyway, these are my friends.

"Kenyon, your grandfather blames you for your mom's death. You told me that he wished you were the one who died." They all look at me and I go for it. "So this thought I'm having, not saying it's true, just, um, what if Kenyon's grandfather met Antoine's mother at some school thing and they got talking and, uh . . ."

"Swapped murders?" Kenyon says sarcastically. "Are you suggesting I should watch out in case Antoine's mother pushes me under a bus? Now it would be her turn, right?"

I hunch my shoulders. "It's just an idea."

"There was a movie about something like that," Evangeline says doubtfully. She looks at Kenyon and raises an eyebrow.

Caleb shakes his head. "How would the subject come up? 'Here, have some pita and dip, and by the way, do you want your kid dead like I do mine?'"

"I meant it as a thought experiment," I say defensively. "I mean, we have to explain why Kenyon's grandfather would even do this."

"For money?" asks Evangeline.

Kenyon holds her elbows.

There is silence again and into it I keep babbling. "Anyway. Back to Antoine's mother. Is there a word for when you plan to kill your own child? Opposite of patricide and matricide. Fratricide? No, that's when you kill your brother."

"Infanticide," Caleb says. Without the rubber band his hair hangs down around his face and I long to push it back, I ache to do that. I look away quickly to Kenyon, who is the important one here, what is wrong with me.

"Antoine was not an infant," Kenyon says. "And I'm not one either."

"I'll find it," Evangeline says, and taps on her phone and we all watch her intently as if finding the right word is so important. Kenyon is now upright and standing very still in the middle of the room. Finally Evangeline looks up. "Well, there's something called *filicide*. Not an everyday word. Latin root, *fils* meaning son—"

"I get it," Kenyon says.

Carefully she sits down.

"It was just a thought," I say. "I don't believe—"

Kenyon swivels toward me. "But *I* believe it, Saralinda. Suddenly I do. I tried to fight it, but my heart did this thing when you said it—like it popped inside my chest. It's like—it's like I heard the bell of truth."

I bite my lip, I can think of nothing to say.

Words pour from Kenyon. "He *hates* me. And Antoine is dead, and he *did* it." Kenyon waves a hand toward Evangeline's phone. "Oh my God. We have *evidence*. And—and Antoine's mother already tried to kill me once, in the carriage house. Right? Along with Antoine. Why else would I have been invited to that meeting? I was new to the school!" She sinks her head into her hands. "*I* was a target too. They were freaking conspiring to kill Antoine and me."

"Saralinda and Evangeline and I were also invited to the carriage house," Caleb points out.

Kenyon waves a hand. "We've talked about that. It was random coverage. Collateral damage—there had to be a few other kids there."

I say, "But I don't know if *I* believe this." I feel afraid of what I have unleashed and of the expression on Kenyon's face.

"My heart believes it," Kenyon says.

Evangeline for once says nothing, but she watches Kenyon.

"But really, how would they have even met?" I ask. "Because Caleb's right. It's hard to imagine them talking about this at some school event. Also, Kenyon just started at Rockland a few weeks ago."

Caleb pulls at the green rubber band. After some silence, he says, "Antoine told me his mother was going to a grief group. Was your grandfather doing grief therapy too, Kenyon?"

She shrugs. "I wouldn't have thought it was his kind of thing."

"My father leads group therapy sessions." Caleb snaps the rubber band around two fingers. "It seems to be a pretty common thing."

A furrow appears between Evangeline's arched brows. She tilts her head to the side. "Nah," she says softly.

Caleb looks up from his rubber band at her. "What?"

"Nothing."

"*What?*" This time it's Kenyon.

"Oh, my stepmother was doing that too." Evangeline's mouth compresses. "It's been two years since my dad's death, and she suddenly tells me she's getting help to work through it and is that all right with me. What a hypocrite! So just now, when we were talking about swapping murders . . ." She shrugs. "I had this thought. It's craziness, though. It's that if I die before I turn eighteen, Spencer gets all my money."

My jaw hinges open like an oven.

"Holy—" Kenyon says.

"No." Evangeline cuts her off. "Absolutely *not*. I just had this what-if moment. Because of the carriage house, and it's not like Spencer and I get *along*. But I can't see her having the guts to kill anybody." She shrugs.

A chill has literally zipped up my spine.

"Does she have her own money?" I ask.

"Some," says Evangeline.

"Forty million dollars like you?"

"No."

It's Caleb who asks: "So how much does she have?"

"I don't know exactly. Two, three million?" She looks at the rest of us and we look back at her.

It sounds like a lot to me, but then again . . .

"When do you turn eighteen?" I ask.

"A month," says Evangeline. "After that, the lawyer has the papers for me to sign, to leave my money to the Upper East Side Cat Society." None of us laugh though amazingly she seems to have been trying to make a joke. "Okay, no, not really. I picked some extremely responsible foundations and charities. Spencer doesn't need my money, you guys. She doesn't care. She didn't say a word when the lawyer said we needed to get my affairs in order for my birthday."

Kenyon and I exchange a glance, not Caleb though, who is looking at Evangeline with no expression at all.

"Stop it," says Evangeline. "Spencer has her faults, and I don't like her. But I mean, if she finds a spider, she has someone set it free outside." She rolls her eyes. "She can't even kill a bug."

"How do you know what she really thinks, though?" Caleb asks. "How would you know for sure?" He is again watching his hands as he winds the rubber band across all four fingers and pulls so that his fingers turn white.

Evangeline shrugs. "I'm pretty certain Spencer's an airhead and could never manage the logistical aspects of a murder. Let alone a murder swap. If that's still what we're talking about here."

As for me holy cow my head is exploding because Evangeline has forty million dollars and she already called her stepmother a gold-digger and honestly it is hard for me to think of a better motive than money for killing someone except maybe love/jealousy/revenge/hate.

I look at Kenyon and I can tell she agrees with me.

"Your stepmother could pay off my grandfather or Antoine's mother," says Kenyon tentatively. "To do things for her. So she wouldn't have to dirty her hands."

I nod.

Evangeline snorts. "Oh, please. Seriously? Exactly how would this conversation take place? This conversation where three people agree to swap murders? Who raises the idea first? Okay, so maybe I can imagine two people doing it. I mean, we *have* to imagine it because of the video." She taps her phone. "But three? It wouldn't happen—and stop giving me that look, Kenyon—it seriously would not happen. Even if Caleb's right about them meeting at a grief group, or if they met at a school function, what do you think—that they came up with the idea during a coffee break? Somebody has to bring it up first, and who would? Seriously, who would? Who would be able to get away with saying that kind of thing out loud?"

The rubber band snaps in Caleb's hands flinging itself across the coffee table to land in my Cheetos.

Chapter 29

Caleb

Saralinda picks up your rubber band and tosses it back toward you. You duck your head as you catch it. You're afraid of what she might see in your face.

You're afraid you look insane.

Your flash of insight is fading now, like lightning overtaken by darkness.

It can't be. Can it? Your father can't be involved in this, right?

Evangeline is talking, which thankfully shifts Saralinda's attention away from you.

"Okay, so assume Saralinda is right and Gabrielle and Kenyon's grandfather swapped murders. That would mean that Kenyon is in immediate danger."

"You figured that out, did you?" Kenyon snipes. "Thank you for caring."

Evangeline smiles grimly. "In fact, I do. Listen, it's a good thing we got you out of there today. I mean, think about it. Your dorm room might have turned into a fire-trap or something. Gabrielle has skills."

Kenyon exhales. "Great."

"So, to work. What kind of policeman is your grand-father? Where does he report? What's his rank? We'll have to go around him when we show our evidence. The police won't want to believe in the involvement of one of their own."

Saralinda puts in, "Most importantly, we have to protect Kenyon. That means we have to throw suspicion on Mrs. Dubois immediately. Get her arrested if at all possible, which—oh, God. Back to square one. We have evidence on Kenyon's grandfather, but not on Antoine's mother. Huh. What to do, what to do."

You say, "There might be something in the carriage house. Something pointing to her." You are astonished that you can pay attention, because your mind is still spin-ning on its own track. Your father. Your father. Your father.

"We need Dr. Lee," Saralinda says.

"Yeah, if we can trust him to believe us," Evangeline comments. "Anyway, these are problems, but not impos-sible ones. Hopefully."

"I don't get why you're so positive all of a sudden," Kenyon mutters.

"Because we have a thesis and a potential pattern," says

Evangeline defensively. "When there's data, there's hope, okay? I want to make a list—"

You listen but say nothing else as you turn the impossible idea over in your mind.

There's no *reason* your father would manipulate grieving parents into swapping murders. *Multiple* parents? Why would he do that? It would put him at huge risk, and what would he get out of it?

Although you've never understood him.

No. It's truly nuts. Totally implausible.

Does your father want you to die? Yeah, maybe.

But if he wanted to kill you, he'd find an easier way. He could slip you an overdose of some opioid and blame it on you, for example.

You rub your eyes.

Kenyon is describing her grandfather's job. He's a lieutenant for the New York State Police, Criminal Investigation Division.

Evangeline leans her chin on her hands. "That's pretty high up?"

"Yes," says Kenyon. "People report to him."

Evangeline moans. "That's not good."

Saralinda says, "I have an idea."

Without consulting your brain, your mouth opens. "Uh-oh."

Saralinda glares. "What's that supposed to mean?"

"Nothing," you say. "Sorry. It's just—your previous idea was, uh, disturbing."

"But it's the best working theory we have so far," Kenyon says.

"It's kind of mad genius," Evangeline says.

"Yeah," you say frankly. "And it scares the hell out of me."

"Say it, brother," says Kenyon. "Anyway. Saralinda?"

"Okay." Saralinda laces her hands together and presses them under her chin. "What if we *don't* try to make a case for the police? What if we go *public*? I'm talking YouTube, Tumblr, Twitter, Facebook. We put it all out there, our suspicions, our accusations. We accuse Kenyon's grandfather and Antoine's mother so that there'd be no chance they could get away with it if anything did happen to Kenyon. Maybe this would push an official investigation into Antoine's death that Kenyon's grandfather won't be able to finesse. See?"

"Oh," says Evangeline. "Oh. Huh."

Kenyon frowns. She holds up a hand. "Let me think."

"No," you say flatly. "I don't see."

Saralinda gets to her feet. She makes a gesture with her cane like she's the grand marshal of a parade. "If we do this, we don't have to figure out how to persuade the police to do anything up front. They're free to ignore us even, if they think we look like your garden-variety internet crazies. Which we might be. But that doesn't matter! What matters is that Antoine's mother and Kenyon's grandfather would know that our accusations are out there. If anything happens to Kenyon, then wham: The police are forced to take notice. It's like taking out *insurance*."

"It might buy us time," Kenyon says thoughtfully. "To talk to Dr. Lee. Persuade him to do an investigation of the carriage house—"

"Which he might be doing already," Saralinda puts in.

You see it now too. It would also put a spotlight on Mrs. Dubois and Kenyon's grandfather, whose name is Lieutenant Stewart Kelly.

You say, "But what if Mrs. Dubois doesn't care? She's got what she wanted—Antoine's death. She doesn't have anything to live for." You remember how that tall, straight-backed woman stood on the other side of the glass wall from her son, expressionless. "This is a plan that would work for someone who doesn't want to get caught. We don't know if she is that woman. We don't know what's in her head." For you, everything always seems to come back to a final question. "We don't know if she's sane."

"Oh, she's not," says Evangeline softly. "You should have known her—before." She ducks her head down, so that her expression is completely hidden.

There is silence.

Evangeline says, "Antoine wouldn't want her to go to prison."

You say, "Antoine would want Kenyon alive."

Evangeline nods. "I know. I know. That's our focus now."

You push all thoughts of your father aside. You ask, "How would it work? We'd show the video of Kenyon's grandfather? Make a statement of some kind?"

"We'll have to figure it out," Saralinda says. "How to make a campaign. How to make it go viral." She looks at Kenyon expectantly. "Kenyon has experience."

"Not pleasant experience," Kenyon mutters. "But yeah. Yeah, I have experience." She is paler now than she was before.

Evangeline hesitates. "Back to Gabrielle for a moment. I'm thinking that maybe we—I guess it would have to be me—I could talk on a video about Antoine's dad and how his mother suffered. That would be sympathetic, not accusatory." She picks at the skin on the back of one of her hands. "Establish that she is crazy with grief and not herself."

More silence. You think about how Evangeline goes back and forth between rage and compassion. Maybe you aren't the only one who is not entirely okay.

Kenyon's voice is gentler when she speaks. "Nobody would lock Antoine's mother up in a jail cell. She'll get help, therapy, whatever she needs. She wasn't ultimately the one who murdered her son—even if she did blow up the carriage house." Her voice hardens. "That was my grandfather. It's hard to imagine her blowing up the carriage house all by herself, isn't it? How much do you want to bet they did that together?"

"This will be huge," you say at last. "We'll definitely go viral."

Evangeline shakes her head. "It'll probably be one more stupid thing on the internet. We'll look like crazy kids, and the only people who will notice are people we know. But maybe it will work anyway. Maybe it will do what we need. At least we're not sitting around doing nothing, or waiting on other people to act." She looks up. "Saralinda, you are brilliant."

Saralinda blushes.

"It's decided, then?" you ask. "We'll do this?"

You look from face to face and each one nods.

Kenyon grabs paper and begins to scribble a list, taking charge. "We have to have scripts. Keep in mind too, this is theater. Advertising. We should be outrageous. We don't want credibility as much as we want readers and we want shares. If we can pound this out tonight, that would be great. Then we go back to school tomorrow, talk to Dr. Lee."

"Let's do it," Saralinda says.

Chapter 30. **Saralinda**

Using Evangeline's phone which has the best video recorder, we record some footage in which Kenyon explains who her grandfather is and narrates what's happening in the video of him with Antoine's car. Caleb finds some pictures online of the car crash and also a local news story about it. Evangeline and I start working on another part of the script about Antoine and his mother and father, but when Evangeline says that she is going to be completely melodramatic in it, Kenyon speaks up.

"You guys? I have to mention something." She clears her throat. "What about college?"

Evangeline and Caleb and I look at each other and then back to Kenyon.

Evangeline says, "What *about* college?"

"So, colleges do internet searches of their candidates. They look on Facebook. Right? I already have a reputation. After we do this, I'm afraid I'll look like—you know, the kind of person who wants attention." Kenyon scowls at Evangeline and adds, "Like *you* said, that first day in the carriage house."

Evangeline blinks. "What are you talking about?"

"You said that."

"I did not."

"You did."

"Well, you were annoying me. And I didn't know you yet."

Kenyon scrunches her eyes shut for a second. "Fine. Whatever. But you got that idea from what you knew about me online, right?"

"I guess. So what?"

"Well, I was thinking—I want a regular life on the other side of this. Assuming I survive. College and, you know— a life."

Evangeline says, "Um. Nobody gets into college when they're dead."

"I know that! But can we at least, in putting all this stuff online, can we *not* act crazy or melodramatic? Can we achieve the exact same ends by being calm and clear?" Kenyon lifts her chin. "Can we *try* for credibility?"

We look at her.

Finally Caleb says, "Doesn't matter what you do. People are always going to think what they think."

Kenyon sighs. "All right. So I should accept it? No matter what, I'm going to look bad. My grandfather's a cop.

You guys don't know—cops are revered in a way. Who am I kidding? I'm going to be a pariah. At least I'll be a living pariah. If I'm lucky. Never mind. Forget I said anything."

"There's community college," I say tentatively. "Don't they let *everybody* in?"

Kenyon gives me a look that makes me shrivel. But stubbornly I add, "I know it's not, you know, Harvard."

"Wellesley," says Kenyon. "My dream is Wellesley. Hillary Clinton's college. Just in case anyone happens to care."

"College can't be your priority," Caleb says quietly. "Or ours."

"I know I know I know," says Kenyon. "One more thing, though, while I'm talking. Just to get it off my chest. None of you have a *clue* what it's like to be a so-called internet celebrity. The hate mail. The—the rape threats." Her fists clench. "And—and worse."

We are silent and I don't know about Caleb and Evangeline but I am thinking about Kenyon's mother, killed by a stranger who had decided he hated Kenyon because of what he saw and read about her online.

"It's not *fun* to be hated by strangers. It affects you. It does damage." Kenyon shrugs then, like it doesn't matter. "Okay, I've said my piece. I only want all of you to know in advance what we're doing if the viral thing happens. Just—you know. In case."

"I never thought of any of that," I say.

"Well, who would? Not until it happens to you. Maybe I shouldn't have said anything. It's not like you can really be prepared anyway." Kenyon's shoulders slope down. "I don't know what to hope for," she adds. "If we get some traction and go viral, that'll be good. Except for all the ways in which it won't be. Okay, stop with the big eyes, Saralinda. I'm fine. I'm just fine."

I don't think she is, but it can't matter because this is when music rings out from somebody's phone. Somebody's phone is ringing and then it turns out that it's mine.

"My mom," I say.

"Don't answer," Caleb says.

But I have to answer she is my mother who loves me.

My hand is shaking for some reason however and then my mother's voice is on speaker and she is furious, yelling:

"How dare you run away? How *dare* you, Saralinda! Well, you're to come home right away. I'm sending the police for you! Yes, I know exactly where you are! Go outside right now and wait for the helicopter and you come home!"

My mind swoops and swirls—police, helicopter?

"Mom," I say. "Mom, calm down—"

"There is nothing to be calm about!"

"Mom," I say, and then Kenyon grabs my arm and snatches the phone away and hangs up on my mother.

I stare at her. "Kenyon, what—?"

She is breathing so hard her chest is going up and down.

"You're not getting on any police helicopter, Saralinda. I don't know what the hell is going on, but—but the police wouldn't be sending a fricking helicopter after a girl who's been gone from school for a few hours! Which means my grandfather is involved somehow, and *that* means . . . I don't know what it means, but—"

"It means we need to get out of here immediately," Evangeline says. She hesitates. "And our phones . . ."

All four of us have been using our phones. For research, for starting to record the video, for making all the plans to save Kenyon.

"We have to leave our phones," Evangeline finishes. "So they think we're still here while we run, and so they can't track us."

"You don't have to come too," Kenyon tells her. She's on her feet, facing Evangeline with her hands on her hips. "I can take Saralinda with me, while you and Caleb finish up." She swivels toward me. "Saralinda, you do have to leave—I have this bad feeling about you, about your mother. About what you told me when we were in the carriage house."

"Uh," I say, because I don't remember exactly what I told her.

"We're all going," Caleb says. "Together. Now."

"But all our work on the phones," I wail.

"We'll get new phones," Caleb says. "We'll do it all over again, with phones they don't know belong to us."

Chapter 31. **Caleb**

You push everyone out the door. Outside, while returning the key to the hiding spot—a nicety that Saralinda insists on—Kenyon stumbles. Her back is hurt, you remember. You offer your arm. "Lean on me."

"No. It's time for more Tylenol, that's all."

She shakes out four and swallows them dry.

You set a fast (given the situation) walking pace toward the ferry. The ferry! There's no other option. You knew the island was a bad idea, you knew it.

The girls talk, because the time will never come when girls don't talk.

"Main thing, we need money," Kenyon says grimly. "We definitely can't use credit cards if they're following us."

"And at least one phone," Saralinda says. "To record video on."

"Also, a safe place to do the recording," adds Evangeline. "Maybe a hotel room?"

"Money," says Kenyon. "Money buys everything else."

Evangeline says, "I'm not sure cash is the answer to everything. We'll need a credit card for a hotel. You can't check into a hotel room with cash."

"If it's a skanky hotel you can," says Kenyon.

"Really?" Evangeline raises an eyebrow.

"That's my impression. From, you know, TV."

"Fount of all knowledge."

"You questioning it?"

"Actually, no. I don't know."

The four of you now have about fifteen dollars. Mr. Hyde has never performed a robbery that you know of. But how hard can it be? You run it through in your mind: a small store, a mousy clerk, dead of night— which is on its way now, as the sun sinks fast toward the horizon . . .

Abruptly you turn and walk backward, facing the girls. "Kenyon, you're right. When this is over, none of us will be Wellesley material. I just caught myself planning a robbery. I was, like, seven detailed fantasy steps into it, with some kid at the cash register handing over money."

In the next instant you can't believe you told them that. It felt . . . intimate. And you've probably shocked Saralinda with your inner criminal.

"Caleb?" says Evangeline. "Just so you know? Wellesley is a women's college."

"I knew that," you mutter, although you didn't.

You turn back around and say over your shoulder, "Maybe prison will be sort of like college."

"We haven't committed any crime," Kenyon says.

"Yet," you respond.

Your imagination zips off again. You could be on the same chain gang with Saralinda, picking up trash by the side of the New York State Thruway. She would lean on her trash pick-up stick. You could superglue a plastic snow globe to the top for her. If snow globes are allowed in prison.

Kenyon says, "With luck, we'll be gone long before the helicopter has time to get here. If Saralinda's mother called soon enough. But when we get to the other side, should we keep using my car? Probably not, right? Also, where should we go?"

"The city," says Evangeline. "Best place to get lost."

"Do we take the train?"

"Not enough money. Listen, let's cross that bridge when we come to it."

Kenyon says, "I thought you liked to plan ahead."

"I am. I'm thinking!" Evangeline says.

The ferry dock comes into sight.

That's when you hear a whirring from above, growing louder by the second.

Saralinda cranes her neck and points.

Kenyon says, "We're screwed."

Evangeline shakes her head. "The ferry's coming in now. We can make it."

But the helicopter is huge overhead, silhouetted against the dusky sky. It's white and black. It says NEW YORK STATE POLICE.

Kenyon waves a desperate hand toward the marina, which is crammed with countless docked boats. "Come on! Let's go hide in there." The helicopter engine is so loud that she has to shout.

It's tempting to run and hide, like children. But you'll be caught, because the marina is a dead end, with the water beyond it.

Anyway, it's already too late. The helicopter moves into a hovering position directly above. A door on its side opens. A ladder drops, and a man moves onto the ladder. He's wearing a uniform, with a gun on his belt. Police.

A second man begins to climb down the ladder.

"That's my father," you say evenly.

"What?" says Saralinda, and at the same moment Evangeline exclaims, "Why is he here?"

Kenyon squints upward. "That second guy is not my grandfather. That's some ordinary police guy."

Saralinda says, "Kenyon, before, you said that the police wouldn't pursue runaway teenagers who've skipped out on school and been gone a few hours."

"My grandfather has friends. But he isn't here. I'm confused . . ."

You're confused too. Confused, but also tense. Very tense, as your father and the policeman maneuver down the ladder rungs and reach the ground. They unhook their safety harnesses. The cop waves upward. The helicopter swoops off, its engine noise fading.

The four of you face your father and the policeman. He is white and young and big, with wide shoulders that strain his uniform. His badge is shiny. He places his hand on his weapon and draws it, though he keeps it pointing down.

"Come on," Evangeline mutters. "He can hardly shoot us down in cold blood."

Saralinda nods. "I'm not scared."

"I am," you snap, and bite your tongue on what you could say. The girls can't conceive that a cop would shoot them? You know different.

You put your hands up as your father speaks.

"Martha. Evangeline. Saralinda. I can't say I'm happy to see you under these circumstances, but I *am* glad you're all well. You're feeling okay, Saralinda?" Behind his glasses, your father's gaze is humane, kind, troubled. "Your mother is beside herself with worry."

Saralinda doesn't answer.

Your father indicates the cop. "This is Officer Perotta.

He came with me to make sure that all of you would be safe. We'll all go back to the mainland together. The helicopter will meet us at the helipad."

The police officer's teeth have had the benefit of a superb orthodontist. "That's correct." He raises the gun slightly. "Come along."

What will happen, you wonder, once all four of you are in the helicopter?

The gun is pointed at you. You lift your foot to do as they say.

Only then Saralinda says, "Let's see if he really does shoot."

The cop begins to talk, but Evangeline speaks at the same moment.

"The marina, like Kenyon said. Now."

And Saralinda simply runs, holding her cane. Kenyon swears and swivels to follow, and—now that you have no choice—you go too.

But first you scoop Kenyon up in a fireman's carry. Then you race just behind Saralinda, with Evangeline keeping pace beside you. Kenyon bounces on your shoulder, but it must be true about panic giving strength. You hardly feel her weight.

"What are you doing?" Kenyon yells.

"You hurt your back. You can't run."

"You're insane."

"Maybe." You can't believe you're all doing this. You might die any second—

Only there is no gunfire, and the marina is a hundred yards away.

"The cop is running after us," Kenyon says. "He's put away his gun. But your father is just *walking*."

He knows we're trapped, you think. There is nowhere to go from the marina. The water lies beyond. You run anyway, watching Saralinda's backpack jounce as she moves.

Saralinda gets to the marina gate, which is as tall as the fence. The gate and fence are both made of chain link, with barbed wire eighteen feet up. She rushes through, and one second later, you and Kenyon and Evangeline follow. Evangeline says something you don't catch as the cop pounds up, but the girls are ready and they slam the gate shut in his face.

The cop throws himself against the other side, pushing, but there are four of you pushing back. Then Saralinda snakes a thick chain into place and snaps its padlock shut with quick, competent fingers.

The cop stops pushing. Evangeline slips an arm around Kenyon's waist. "Come on! Everyone, let's go hide!" Those two stumble off into the maze of the marina.

Hide? You sigh.

There is nobody else here. It's an autumn weekday evening, and the boaters of Fire Island are in the city. They're thinking about dinner.

You look beyond the cop, at your father, at how the setting sun glints off his glasses as he approaches.

You wouldn't have said he was walking. You'd have said he was *strolling*.

You realize again that you don't understand this man who is your father, and you never have. And maybe— though you still don't know why he would have done it—maybe, just maybe, he is behind what has happened to Antoine . . .

You slip your hand in your pocket.

"Go with them," you tell Saralinda as the cop eyes the chain-link fence and, matter-of-factly, starts to climb.

"But—"

The sun is halfway down the horizon. Your knife is out and ready. "I'm going to buy us some time. I'll be five minutes behind you."

You have no idea what you're doing.

"Promise?" she says.

You don't look at her. "Promise." You hear her footsteps recede.

The toe of the cop's shoe is in a fence link at your shoulder level. You feel inside yourself for some remnant of Mr. Hyde, or failing that, a brave version of yourself. You reach through the link below and grab the cop's pants, pulling the fabric and wrapping it around your fist. This slams his leg against the fence. Your blade slices through the fabric and along his calf. He screams. You dig deeper. He drops backward to the ground, clamping a hand to his calf.

There is blood on your knife, dripping onto your hand.

Staring at you, the cop reaches for his gun.

Your father stops beside him. He lays a hand on the cop's hand. "Now, now," he says. "Remember what we agreed."

The cop snarls something. He drops the gun. Then: "Help me, dammit! I thought you were a doctor. I need, like, a tourniquet."

"In a minute," says your father, serenely, and turns to you. "Hello, son."

You don't move.

Your father puts his hands in his pockets. "A professional tip," he says. "Your computer search history should be cleared daily. It's simply good technical hygiene. If you'd done that, I might not have found out how often you visit little Saralinda's page in the Rockland student directory."

Truly, you do not know this man. But you still know better than to let your face show anything.

Including bewilderment.

"Maybe you'll do better at protecting her over the next day or two." He winks. "We'll see, won't we?"

The marina lights come on, soft white bulbs strung from wires overhead.

"But what about Antoine?" you blurt. "Antoine and the other girls—what's going on—what are you *doing*—"

You clamp your mouth shut.

"It's a multifaceted game," your father says, in the warm explanatory voice his patients probably love. "We'll see if you can figure it out. I'm curious. For now, run along."

He turns his back. He bends to help the wounded man at his feet.

What is going on?

If only you had the gun. If you had had some way to take it from the cop.

You would kill him.

And then—yourself? No. Or not yet. The girls need you.

You back away, one step, two, three. Then you run—you can't help it—your sneakers pounding down on the metal of the piers. And all at once you realize you're not looking for the girls. You let yourself be swallowed by a forest of tall powerboats with elaborate fishing gear, and wide catamarans, and sleek cabin cruisers, and elegant sailboats with towering masts. As you run, automatically, you squeeze your knife closed with one wet sticky hand, and push it into your pocket.

The dock comes to a dead end. The water lies before you. You face it.

You suddenly realize that your father has been playing some game or other with you your entire life. And now he has involved other people.

Maybe you should dive into the ocean now and swim as far out as you can. But would that satisfy your father and end his mysterious game?

What if it doesn't?

So you can't die. The girls need you. And Antoine needed you, but you didn't realize it. You didn't understand. And what you didn't understand is this: If this is your father's game, then *you* are the one responsible for Antoine's death.

You.

You you you.

You stare at the cold water. If you can't stop him, then you should end it, here and now. It would mean you don't risk witnessing any more death. Being responsible for any more death.

Cowardly, but maybe you are a coward. Maybe it would be better to be a coward—

A voice pulls you back. "Caleb."

It's Saralinda.

Chapter 32. **Saralinda**

I move as unobtrusively as I can between Caleb and the end of the dock, except I am probably quite obtrusive because I sort of lurch and I need to lean heavily on Georgia after having run earlier which I am not exactly accustomed to doing, I would never have believed how fast I could go and pain totally did not matter. But what is important now is to get in Caleb's way because before he knew I was here he was leaning toward the ocean in a very scary way.

Caleb is lethal it turns out just like I always thought, but it is not in the *way* I used to think. I am upset about what might be going on with my mother but right now more upset about Caleb because not only is he dangerous to himself, he is dangerous to me.

Because when I look at him with his hair hanging down around his face I could drown in his pain and go down almost willingly.

I ask, "What happened just now with your father?"

"Oh." He pauses for a second, as if he forgot and has to

remember. "The cop was trying to climb the fence, and I have this folding knife, and I stopped him." He looks at his hands. "I, uh. So I stabbed him in the leg and he fell."

On one of his hands I see dark stains in the folds of his knuckles and around his fingernails. I blink. He used a knife to do physical harm to another human being on our behalf, me and Kenyon and Evangeline.

"Are you hurt?" I ask feebly.

"He's the one who got hurt." Suddenly Caleb grins which makes my stomach lurch in a melty way.

I manage to say, "Let's go. Kenyon and Evangeline are waiting."

Caleb doesn't move though. "Saralinda, listen. My father is letting us get away. He wants us to run, that's what's going on. He's giving us rope. This is fun for him. A game. It's not only about Kenyon and Antoine."

I look up at him again. "He *said* that?"

He holds my eyes. "He said it. He said he was playing a game."

"What does it mean, a game?"

"For now, it means that we have to stay alive. All of us."

"I guess that's not brand-new," I say slowly, as I try to take this in. "But what kind of game? Was Antoine a game, or—wait, what does your father have to do with, well, me? Or Kenyon, or her grandfather, or—" I stop. I am totally confused.

He shrugs. "I don't know those things either. We'll have to all talk, I guess, except right now—we have to get out of here." He looks beyond me. "Where are Kenyon and Evangeline?"

Silently Georgia and I lead the way to a large sailboat and I motion to Caleb to get on board, then Georgia and I clamber after him. We duck beneath a loose tarpaulin and call out that we're coming (although they probably heard us already, as Georgia and I are more clumsy than usual).

In the boat's cabin, Kenyon leans against the wall and aims a flashlight toward us. Evangeline is talking before we get all the way in. "There you are. Caleb, you'll tell us what happened, but first, do either of you know how to sail?"

Caleb says, "No."

I shake my head and sit down on a bench along one side of the cabin.

"It'll have to be a motorboat, then. Kenyon will pilot it. We'll take the boat along the coast and then up the East River to the city. It'll still be dark when we land. In the city somehow we'll get money. And a phone. We'll redo our videos and stuff and go ahead with our internet plan." Evangeline nods toward me. "Then we'll contact Dr. Lee."

"Uh, what's this about me piloting the boat?" asks Kenyon.

"You're the one who knows how to drive a car. A motor-boat is similar."

"What? How do you know?"

"I've been out on motorboats. I trust you to figure it out." Evangeline waves her hand vaguely.

Kenyon's jaw drops. I guess it's from hearing Evangeline say that she trusts her, on top of the blithe statement about how driving a car is the same as driving a boat. Then Kenyon recovers and says in almost (but not quite) her usual sarcastic voice, "You also trust we'll find a key in order to start this hypothetical boat?"

"Yes. Boating people often hide keys onboard." Evangeline lifts her chin challengingly. "We're improvising. We find a key, or we'll hot-wire the engine. Or something."

"Really. You think it's that easy?"

"I think that if one thing doesn't work, we'll try another."

They lock eyes. Kenyon is the one who looks away. "Caleb?" she says. "I want you to know something. You might have saved my life before by carrying me. I think I could have run, but honestly, I'm not sure how fast. So. Thank you."

Caleb looks shy. "You're welcome. I didn't think about it, though. I just—I did it."

Which is basically what Kenyon said about shielding me in the carriage house.

Caleb tells the other girls what he did at the gate. "My father's playing a game with us," he finishes. "He wants us to escape for now, so that he can torture us longer. Torture *me,* in particular." He hesitates. "I think—he's a strange guy—he said something about seeing if I could—could protect Saralinda . . ."

"*What?*" I exclaim.

Caleb doesn't look at me. "He said, and I quote, 'It's a multifaceted game. We'll see if you can figure it out. I'm curious.'"

We are all silent as we think about that.

Finally, Evangeline says, "What's *with* him? You said he was strange. But this—I don't even know what this is."

Caleb shrugs. "Me neither." After a second, he adds, "I—you guys, I'm sorry."

"A game?" Evangeline's voice rises. "A game with Antoine's life?"

Caleb shrugs again. "I know," he says.

I have never heard anyone sound so miserable.

Kenyon's face hardens. "Well, listen. My grandfather doesn't play games. He plays for keeps, and he's in this too. Obviously."

We are quiet again.

"Okay," Kenyon says. "Caleb. Before we do what Evangeline is suggesting, are you sure that at this point we're not being, well, *herded* by your father into something? Like drowning at sea?" She glances at Evangeline. "Or stealing a boat?"

"No, I guess those are possibilities," Caleb says.

"We have another choice. We could sneak back out of here and onto the ferry later." Kenyon pauses, thinking it through.

"They'll be waiting," Evangeline says. "The ferry only lands in one spot. My way, they don't know where we land."

I say, "Let's take a motorboat. We're trying to get someplace safe—or safe enough—so we can make our videos. Caleb's father is giving us space for his reasons, but we're taking it for *our* reasons. He doesn't know what we're planning. And once we get a phone, we won't need much time! It's dark, so they won't know what boat we're in or where we're going. That is, if you can drive it, Kenyon." I pause. "And we can put this stuff about the game online too. We can say that this is what's going on and that we don't understand it. Why not?"

Caleb nods. "Agreed."

He still looks horrible.

Kenyon pushes herself away from the cabin wall. "I guess we're borrowing a boat."

We troop down one pier and onto another, looking.

Kenyon gestures to a catamaran called *Ship Happens*. Evangeline hops up to see if its owners left a key in any obvious spot but no. We check other boats, searching under cushions and seats and in storage compartments. After what seems like forever and in the total dark night we get lucky with a not-too-small open boat called *Après Ski*. Its key is actually in the ignition.

"I knew it!" Evangeline says as if she willed the boat and its key into existence.

Après Ski feels like a car. At the front, there are two cushioned chairs behind a windshield and control panel. One chair has a steering wheel. There are two more chairs at the rear and also a bench. I find an operator's manual which I examine immediately.

Then I crow, "Guys, this is an *unsinkable* nineteen-foot Boston Whaler!"

Kenyon smiles. "I like the sound of the word *unsinkable*."

"Also, it has GPS," I say.

"Now we're talking!" says Evangeline. "We can do this."

Kenyon moves to the instrument panel. "Let's hope for a full tank of gas."

Chapter 33. **Caleb**

You investigate the boat. *Après Ski* comes with supplies: flashlights, life jackets, a blanket, a couple of oars, an ancient first-aid kit, flares, and several college sweatshirts.

"Colgate! That's where Cordelia went," Kenyon exclaims when you hold one up.

"You're obsessed with college," you say.

Kenyon shakes her head. "I can't believe none of *you* are. I mean, what do you guys *want*? For your future?"

Your mind fuzzes.

Saralinda shrugs. "I'm still figuring it out."

"Antoine had a clear plan," Evangeline says. "He wanted to go to Boston College. He visited it last fall."

"And you?" Kenyon challenges Evangeline over her shoulder as she slides into the pilot's seat with the manual and a flashlight. She scans diagrams as she touches the wheel, the throttle, and the dashboard instrumentation.

"Oh, I just want my money," Evangeline says airily. "Counting the hours."

You turn away, glad the girls are not pushing you for your answer. Because though a few seconds ago you bit your tongue on the old reflexive want—death—it's not actually true anymore. When Evangeline said Antoine's name just now another want welled up in you, an impossible one. You want Antoine to still be alive.

You touch the copy of *Dracula,* which has miraculously stayed in your back pocket.

"Let's get out of here," Kenyon says, and starts the engine. "Life jackets, people," she adds as she leans over the dashboard and mutters, "The GPS seems like the one on my phone. What's this?"

"Radar," says Evangeline, sliding into the seat next to Kenyon.

"Great! Uh, what does radar do, exactly?"

"It locates objects in the water so we won't hit them."

"I like it."

You sit down in a rear seat beside Saralinda and put on your life jacket. For no reason at all you think of your mother. Before you abandoned your phone at the cottage, you received today's text from her. *I love you.* You didn't reply. You never do.

With one hand on the throttle, slowly and carefully, Kenyon maneuvers the boat out of its slip. The navigation lights try to light the way, but the water ahead is black. As Evangeline gives advice ("Cut left, now right, okay . . ."),

Kenyon guides the boat through the maze of the docks and out onto the open water, where the boat rocks alarmingly on the choppy waves. The wind is strong and cold and wet.

You fold your arms around yourself. Saralinda does the same.

Evangeline and Kenyon talk.

"Wait, what? Evangeline, the GPS says those small islands are Fire Island! I thought we left Fire Island!"

"We're going west. We're exactly where we're supposed to be."

"What if we hit something?"

"We won't. The radar shows us obstructions, remember? You can steer around them just like you'd steer around something on the highway. We're totally safe out here."

"Really."

"Every obstruction is mapped," Evangeline says in a gentler voice. "Listen, you're tense. Why don't you take a nice deep breath, hold it in your lungs, exhale, and say Namaste. Okay? Na—"

"Namaste, motherfucker," Kenyon growls.

You snicker. Saralinda giggles.

"Fine," says Evangeline. "Be like that."

The Boston Whaler jounces on the waves, with the lights of Long Island glowing alongside. The only sounds now are occasional soft instructions from Evangeline and muttered replies from Kenyon, along with the vicious chop of the ocean, the cut of the wind, and the reassuring low rumble of the boat's engine in the back. Saralinda is a vague shadow beside you.

It would be good to get some sleep, if possible. You say so to Saralinda.

"I can't shut off my mind." Her voice is wry in the darkness.

"Yeah. Me too."

Kenyon calls back, sounding a tiny bit more relaxed. "So you guys, guess what? I'm not so sure about going to Wellesley anymore."

"College again," you say.

"I'm thinking positively about the future, Caleb. You should try it."

"Why change your mind about Wellesley?" Evangeline asks.

"Before all this happened, I thought I wanted to go to a women's college and focus my world entirely on women. But now I'm thinking, they say you make lifelong friends at college. I already know I'll marry a woman, so why miss the opportunity for male friendship?"

You clear your throat. "So how about this Colgate place? Do they take men?"

Kenyon says, "Yes."

Saralinda adds shyly, "Maybe we could all go there. Or—or somewhere, together. Is that—is that crazy?"

"No," says Evangeline. "Not crazy."

For a few minutes you let yourself dwell in a fantasy future in which you go to college and have friends. These friends. Only you can't afford fantasy, and neither can the girls, not now. "Saralinda?" you say, more harshly than you intended.

"What?"

"Let's talk about your mother. Is she in this—this game thing too?"

"No! I don't think so! You're thinking about the murder swap idea, right? No! I mean—I—" She stutters to a stop and then adds in a low voice, "She loves me."

Kenyon says, "Saralinda, you have to consider the possibility. You guys, the story is that Saralinda's mother is single, and Saralinda is sick a lot. It wasn't the parental experience that her mother signed up for . . ."

"Seems like an unlikely reason to kill your kid," Evangeline observes. "But she did call you when we were at the cottage, Saralinda. And she'd been talking to Caleb's father."

As slowly as if the words are being dragged out of her by force, Saralinda says, "Yesterday I found out my mother is adopting another daughter. A little girl named Tori. She kept it secret from me." She tells all of you about accidentally discovering the adoption papers. "I was so excited. I had a whole Disney movie going in my head about having a sister."

Evangeline nods thoughtfully. "How old is she?"

"Three."

"Easily controlled," says Kenyon. "Why's she adopting? Is she too old to have another baby herself?"

"Probably, my mother is fifty-three. And—"

The boat rocks violently sideways. You and Saralinda are thrown to the deck. You grab for her at the same moment that you hear a very loud, very unnatural noise.

It's fiberglass smashing. All three of the girls scream. You too, although you would prefer to say that you yell.

The Boston Whaler has hit a rock.

Chapter 34. **Saralinda**

I land on the deck of the boat and scramble with one hand for Georgia, who is there under my fingers not lost overboard thank God. Caleb has grabbed me by the life jacket and I grab back at him with the hand that isn't making sure of Georgia. He and I tangle together helped by another terrible heave of the boat, it bobs up and down and Caleb holds me tight and my foremost thought is that I did *not* like the sound of whatever happened when we hit whatever it was we hit.

Caleb loosens his grip on me and we both crawl up on our knees and there is no mistaking what has happened because the bottom of the boat is filling up with water.

"Don't panic!" I yell, as much to myself as to everyone else. "The manual said this boat is unsinkable!"

"Do you believe everything you read?" Evangeline yells back.

Yet the boat is not listing to one side, it is sort of floating partly submerged like a wounded rubber ducky in a giant horrible tub, so I dare to hope.

Only then Evangeline shouts:

"Kenyon? Kenyon!"

Now I remember hearing a big splash and a scream (well, we were all screaming), and I am on my feet sloshing toward the front of the boat with Caleb. Evangeline has the flashlight aimed down into the ocean where—we see her—Kenyon thrashes in the black water. She is yards from the boat, she is in her life vest at least, only she is not screaming for help which scares me.

I call her name as Evangeline kicks off her shoes and jumps into the ocean at a distance from Kenyon. She surfaces.

I pray.

Caleb grabs the flashlight and directs its beam out toward the bobbing heads.

Kenyon windmills her arms wildly. Evangeline swims a short distance away and treads water. Her lips move but I can't hear what she's saying.

"I can't swim," I say to Caleb.

"I can. I'll go." Caleb toes off his shoes.

I grab his arm and it's not that I am afraid of his leaving me (though I am), but that I have an idea. "No, instead, can you turn off the motor?" Because crazily the motor is still running. "It's taking us away from them."

Caleb nods and seconds later the thrum of the motor stops, and now I hear Evangeline shouting.

"Get onto your back, Kenyon! Remember, you're in a

life vest. You're going to float. Do you hear me?" She keeps her distance while Kenyon makes very bad swimming motions with frantic arms.

"I need you to float on your back, Kenyon," Evangeline calls again.

"Why won't she just go get her?" I mutter to Caleb, who is beside me again.

"People who think they're drowning sometimes drown their rescuer, because they're panicking," he whispers in my ear, and then adds, "Tell me if I should go help." Instinctively I grab his hand and he grips mine back.

Evangeline's hoarse voice turns rhythmic. "You're going to float, Kenyon. The vest holds you up. Be still!"

Kenyon stops thrashing for a few seconds but then she starts again. My heart is in my throat.

"Are you a *good* swimmer?" I ask Caleb, and the way his fingers tighten tells me the answer. "Then no," I say in a definite voice as if I knew what I was talking about which I do not. "Evan is handling this."

Evangeline says, "Just let the vest hold you up. It will keep you safe, and then I'll come and get you. Once you are still, I will come and get you. But not before. Only after you are still."

Kenyon's frantic splashing slows.

"Good. As you slow down, remember to breathe. Breathe deeply, in and out, as you shift to lie on your back." Then Evangeline adds, "Namaste, Kenyon!"

I gasp, but somehow this is the right thing to say because Kenyon shifts until she's floating on her back, bobbing on the waves.

"Let the life vest hold you up. Do you feel how it does that?"

Kenyon says, clearly, "Yes."

"Say: The life vest will hold me."

"The life vest will hold me."

"Say Namaste."

"I'll say Namaste when I'm dead."

"That proves it. You're fine," says Evangeline and swims toward her, a powerful breaststroke with her head above the water.

"It's going to be okay," Caleb says in my ear.

I continue praying as hard as I can.

Evangeline is now behind Kenyon. "I'm here. Feel that? That's my hand."

Kenyon tries to turn toward Evangeline.

"No, stay still! Stay entirely still or I'll go away. Don't grab me!"

"Don't go!" It is a piteous wail.

"I won't go. I want to make sure you understand. You are not to do anything. You are not to help me. Stay still and let me do the work. I'll tow you. All right? Say my name so I know you understand."

Kenyon's voice is strong again. "First you say mine."

"Fine. Kenyon."

"Evangeline."

"Good. Now—I've got you. You're safe. I'm going to swim you over to the boat. It's not far." Evangeline raises her voice. "Where are you guys?"

Caleb directs the flashlight. "Head toward the light!"

"We're not quite ready for that, buddy."

I choke back a laugh.

Caleb says, "We'll hold an oar for you to grab."

It seems like a long time before they are beside the boat, reaching. Caleb and I haul them up. They are on the deck at last dripping and shivering. Caleb helps Kenyon into a seat. Evangeline stands, leaning over with her hands on her knees and her eyes closed.

Caleb says, "Hypothermia danger. Saralinda, get the blanket and sweatshirts."

I grab them, glad to have something to do. "Evangeline, that was amazing. Were you a lifeguard or something?"

Without opening her eyes, Evangeline says, "At camp."

Kenyon says, "I went to Bible camp once, but all we did was learn about hoarding supplies in case of the apocalypse."

"Nonsense," says Evangeline, panting. "I'm sure they taught you to make s'mores."

Chapter 35. **Caleb**

You turn away politely as the trembling Kenyon and Evangeline work on stripping off their wet clothes, sopping away water—yeah, good luck with that, considering all the water sloshing in the bottom of the boat—and getting into the sweatshirts and the dryer life jackets previously worn by you and Saralinda.

It's all the clothing you have for them.

Saralinda leans in next to you. She is a warm spot in an ocean of cold. "We have flares," she says.

You nod. Yes. You could summon rescue.

"That will bring in the Coast Guard," you point out.

"Or some other boater. Somebody we can spin a story to. We could give them false names, maybe?" Saralinda chews her lip. "Let's think."

You doubt if it makes a difference who comes, Coast Guard or otherwise. Communication is too swift, too good. *Après Ski* will be identified. It'll be known that you are not its owners. All roads lead to parental custody.

On the bright side—

"Maybe we should embrace getting arrested," you say. "Immediately confess to stealing the boat." You look at Evangeline and Kenyon, who are now more or less dressed. "Let's get ourselves into a nice safe jail cell. Hey, won't they have to get us lawyers?"

Saralinda makes a noise of approval. "Lawyers! Now there's a thought."

"We'd get handed over to the custody of our parents or guardians," says Kenyon firmly. In the oversized sweatshirt, with her wet hair and bare legs, and her arms wrapped around herself, Kenyon looks as small as Saralinda. "You think random lawyers might believe us and decide to be our allies? Hardly. Also, it's an entirely different thing to go to the police voluntarily, up front. This way, we're dragged in, having stolen and wrecked somebody's boat."

"We don't have a lot of options," Saralinda says worriedly.

Evangeline slicks her hair back with both hands. "I see another choice," she announces. "We continue as originally planned."

You and Saralinda exchange glances. Maybe Evangeline cracked her head.

Saralinda begins, "Evan—"

Evangeline raises a hand. "Hear me out. This boat floats. Sort of. It'll be slower, with all the water, but we have a working motor and a rudder. Also, the tide is going in. I bet we can still get ashore on our own steam."

"I like it," says Kenyon after a moment.

"I think you've both lost it," Saralinda says with uncharacteristic harshness. "We can't possibly get to Manhattan by boat now!"

"Not Manhattan. The nearest dry land." Evangeline throws up her arms. "*Any* dry land."

Chapter 36. **Saralinda**

Grimly I hold the boat wheel steady with two hands and keep Georgia safely trapped under my equally good foot. I am happy that I did not lose Georgia in the collision which I cannot say for my insulin kit, it was in my backpack which went over the side, my mother is right I am not sufficiently responsible.

At least the boat's motor thrums reassuringly which makes me love it, a kind of Stockholm Syndrome love which is a psychological response in which you get attached to someone (usually a kidnapper) because your subconscious decides that identifying with that person lowers the odds that they will kill you. Stockholm Syndrome is interesting to read about but not to experience, however if while drained and exhausted I imagine that the motor will not break or run out of gas because I praise it under my breath, where is the harm?

All of which is to indicate that (insulin loss aside, I will worry about that later, as it is not an immediate emergency) my current job is not proving easy physically or mentally. Kenyon and Evangeline have been forbidden to help (by me) because their job is to huddle and get warm, and there are only two active jobs available anyway: navigating like Caleb is doing and driving like I am. Much as I hate what I am doing it is not as difficult as I thought and I would much rather drive than navigate because what if I were to steer us into another rock? (I wonder if the accident was Evangeline's fault or Kenyon's or maybe a malfunction of the radar, oops don't want to go there.)

Caleb squints at the dashboard display leaning close to me to do it, he is no longer wearing his shirt by the way because he gave it to Evangeline and also by the way he has very nice shoulders and arms. Even though a girl is tired she notices how a dim flashlight beam throws interesting shadows over muscles and how shadows linger on those muscles—focus, I must focus.

I am saved by a witty thought. "Hey! We're all in the same boat here," I say. Humor should be shared it is a gift to the world. Nobody laughs so I helpfully explain. "Being in the same boat is a metaphor about being in a bad situation which for us is ironically literal." I snicker.

Kenyon says, "We got it, SL. It's not that funny."

"It's not entirely bad," Caleb says but since he didn't laugh I conclude he is being polite. Nobody gets me which truly is their loss, fine. I snicker again and have trouble stopping but then I manage (focus, must focus).

"Want me to take a turn with the wheel, Saralinda?" asks Kenyon.

"No, I'm good," I say because I hear Evangeline's teeth chattering. "You stay where you are." Caleb looks at me, and I stretch my eyes wide open which helps me stay awake. "I'm good," I say again.

We are quiet then. After a while, behind me, Kenyon mutters to Evangeline, "This is not me making a pass at you."

Evangeline says softly, "I didn't think you were."

"It's just that some straight people have strange ideas."

"Isn't saying that sort of an insult to me?"

"Well—I didn't mean—"

"Good."

Bickering again. I reflect that the universe certainly does like to throw Kenyon into intimate situations with straight girls. She might be correct about her bad luck although then again we're all in the same boat when it comes to luck. Ha! I try to keep my laughter to myself.

"Saralinda?" Caleb says.

"Same boat!" I snicker again.

"Don't start, Saralinda," warns Kenyon. "At least not until we're on land."

This is a hopeful thing to say and not entirely crazy either, as we are definitely nearer to land now. There is something unusual about the lights on the nearest shore although maybe it is simply that they are plentiful like party decorations. I continue to steer while Caleb watches the radar and GPS and tells me what to do and the lights keep getting closer and I slip into a kind of trance.

Fingertips graze my shoulder. I startle awake although I could not really have been sleeping could I? I find our boat rocking more gently like a cradle which is quite different from the choppiness of the ocean.

Caleb is standing above me.

"I've dropped the anchor," Evangeline calls. "We did it!"

I guess we have done it. I look up and around. Thick pillars hem our boat in on one side and light filters down on us from cracks above. We are partly under a ginormous pier and I must have been the one who drove us here. Go, me.

"Only where are we?" I ask. "Long Island? Brooklyn? New Jersey? Does anyone know?" Caleb gives me a look and I add defensively, "So geography's not a strong point."

"I assumed you'd guessed from the lights. It's Coney Island."

I stare with new eyes. Beyond the pier, bright strings of lights outline the swoops of a roller coaster, the giant circle of a Ferris wheel, and the length of the boardwalk.

"Ah," I say. "Of course. Coney Island."

I grab Georgia and we stand up cautiously in the

sloshy water as I try to remember how long it has been since I had insulin, but since I don't know what time it is I can't be sure. I decide I feel okay however and it's not as if I normally take insulin in the middle of the night. I step—stagger—Caleb grabs my arms with both hands. "What's the story with you needing a cane?" he asks bluntly.

"Oh. It's just—I was born with this thing, a clubfoot. It's fixed."

"Does it hurt?"

"No. I told you, it's fixed. Mostly." I push him away. He lets go immediately and I stand on my own in my soaked sneakers.

I move to stand by the other girls, who are looking out at the lights.

"A deserted amusement park by dark of night," Evangeline says. "What could be more fun?"

"This isn't a bad place to land," Kenyon says thoughtfully. "I'm pretty sure there's a subway stop here."

Caleb says, "There is."

"Perfect," Evangeline says.

I clear my throat. "We'll need to get clothes first. And food. And money. And phones. Some sleep if possible."

The boat rocks and none of us move and for my part this is because suddenly our ruined Boston Whaler feels safer than whatever's next.

"How are we going to get up onto the pier? Climb?" I crane my neck looking for a ladder.

"We have to swim to the beach," Caleb says.

Kenyon sucks in her breath.

I peer dubiously over the side. It looks deep. Also dark. Also cold.

"I am not going in again," Kenyon says.

To that nobody says a word not even me.

"All right, fine," says Kenyon. "I'll go in again."

"Good girl," says Caleb.

"Don't give me that male condescension."

"Good woman," says Evangeline.

"No strong woman crap either."

"Good mammal," I say wittily but no appreciation this time either, my friends just do not get me. Then I have a question. "If we're going to abandon the boat, shouldn't we at least leave an explanation? An apology? Some kind of note? We stole it, then we crashed it."

"When this is over, I will find the owners and pay them," says Evangeline tiredly.

"But they won't know that when they find the boat," I insist.

"What do you want to do, Saralinda?" Caleb asks. "Leave our names?"

I consider. "At least an anonymous note with an apology."

Evangeline sighs. "Fine. Write it. Quick."

I find a pen in a compartment. On the back of the operator's manual, I write:

Sorry we took your boat. No choice, emergency. We'll find you and pay you back later, I swear. Bless you.

All this time Kenyon stares down at the water.

"I'm ready," I say.

Without another word Caleb lowers himself over the side of the boat. The water comes only midway up his chest and Kenyon heaves a sigh of relief. She slides down into his arms. Evangeline goes nimbly over next and I hand Georgia down to her. I climb over the edge and slip down into the murky water which is shockingly cold, my head goes under and my sneakered feet flail, then they find the slippery bottom and I stand. I sputter, salt water nearly to my shoulders and in my mouth.

Evangeline puts an arm around my waist.

I say, "I'm okay. I'll hold my cane now."

But I let her help me and, staying beneath the shelter of the pier, the four of us lurch our way to the beach, where we stand together on the sand and shiver. We are wet and our clothing is scanty and before us the amusement park is all lit up and empty and looming.

It is a big victory to be here and alive but I do not feel victorious.

Kenyon says in a low voice, "You know what, we're

idiots. We should have waded in naked. Carried our clothes on our heads."

Evangeline makes an impatient noise. "I should have thought of that."

Caleb says, "Uh . . . you would have done that?"

"*You* thought of it?" I swing to face him.

"Yeah, but I figured . . . you know."

"That we would rather preserve our maidenly modesty?" I am indignant and glad of it because better to be angry than scared. "You might have *mentioned* it."

"Sorry."

"Seriously!"

Chapter 37. **Caleb**

You trudge up the beach behind the girls and smash your nose on a metal pole that's planted in the sand. You squint upward. The pole has five identical fronds spiraling out from the top.

"Because nothing says beach like a fake palm tree." Evangeline comes up beside you.

You wrap your fingers around your nose. As you wait for the pain to ebb, you think of the soaked and ruined copy of *Dracula*. It wasn't that you didn't think of dragging it along anyway.

It just seemed pointless.

"Look, there's more of them." Kenyon points to a whole line of the fake palm trees.

Saralinda says, "They add a certain something. Caribbean flair?"

"Florida surrealism," says Kenyon.

"They're not surreal, they're macabre," Evangeline corrects, which is all that's needed for her and Kenyon to start in.

"They wouldn't be macabre in daylight."

"Yes, they still would."

"No—"

Where are they finding the energy for this? You interrupt. "This place is surreal *and* macabre, okay? Can't you imagine, like, a toddler impaled on one of these?"

They stare at you. You clutch your nose. "Kiss and make up," you say sourly, and turn away. "We don't have time for one of your pretend arguments."

You plod onward. The girls follow.

When you reach the boardwalk, Saralinda boosts herself up, inelegantly but with determination. Once on her feet, she leans on her cane. You've heard of a clubfoot before, but you're not sure what it is. She said it was fixed, mostly. What does that mean? She still needs her cane.

Meanwhile Evangeline heads with determination toward a small industrial building. The rest of you trail her, arriving as she wrestles fruitlessly with the knob of the locked ladies' restroom door.

"There's always that metal palm tree," says Kenyon. "Or you could dig a hole in the sand."

"I'll wait," says Evangeline.

"Can you?" asks Saralinda practically. "How long?"

Evangeline sighs. "Be right back."

She slips down off the pier and underneath it. The rest of you step away politely and look at the storefronts along the boardwalk. Beach Shop. Sunglass Hut. Nathan's Famous hot dogs. Saltwater taffy. Tight metal shutters telegraph rejection from the front of each shop, and behind the row of stores, the giant skeleton of the lit-up roller coaster dominates. There's also a barred gate at the entry to the amusement park, and above it, a cartoon man's wide, disembodied face leers down.

"That's one happy vampire," says Evangeline, returning.

"Is he a vampire? He doesn't have fangs," Kenyon says.

"Only because he's waiting for us to get within snapping distance. Then they descend."

You're annoyed again at their pointless chatter but they stop and the four of you shuffle wearily along the boardwalk. Everyone has their arms wrapped around themselves for whatever small heat it gives. You try to imagine what this place would be like on a hot summer's day, with the taste of salt in the air and tinny calliope music teasing people toward the rides. But the wet cold is seeping from your clothing through your skin and reaching for your bones, and you keep thinking of that imaginary toddler impaled bloodily on the fronds of the metal palm tree, because his mother—yes, you blame his mother—didn't protect him.

"We'll have to break in somewhere," Saralinda says quietly. "You guys realize that?"

Of course you realized. But shopfront after shopfront is shuttered and impenetrable. You pause before a place that sells Life is Good T-shirts and other clothing. It has a small, unprotected glass display window.

"We could throw a rock through it. But I bet it's alarmed," Kenyon says.

"Plus," says Evangeline, "I won't wear their clothes. Because life sucks."

The back of your neck prickles a microsecond before you hear hoarse laughter. You spin to face two bulky men who emerge from the shadows, wrapped in heavy coats. Alcohol wafts from them. Your shoulders tighten.

"You got that right, girly," the first one says. "Look at you! Look at all of you! Half-naked! And wet." He's white, tall, heavily bearded, wears a Mets cap, and waves a bottle expansively with one hand as he speaks.

"What's with the life preservers?" asks the second man.

You have your pathetic knife in hand.

The second man is broadly built, darker skinned, and wears a knitted cap pulled low over his brow. He hangs behind the first man.

"They seem to have violent tendencies," says the first man mockingly. "They're planning to break into a store." He takes a pull from his bottle.

They block the way forward.

You don't want a fight, for countless excellent reasons, the first of which is the man's bottle. If he cracks it against metal shutters, it's a weapon. All you have is your knife.

But maybe the girls will run if you tell them to—a big maybe—and then you can at least try to delay the men so the girls can get away . . . but to where? Your thoughts chase themselves in a grim circle, and meanwhile the man in the knit cap says, "There was a story on TV tonight about four teenagers."

Your breath stops.

He continues. "Three girls. One boy."

Saralinda can't control herself. "On TV? What did they—"

"Saralinda!" Kenyon warns, too late.

"—say about us," finishes Saralinda defiantly. She puts her hands on her hips.

Silence.

The two men look at Saralinda, who seems tinier than ever in her sopping clothing and life preserver, and then at Kenyon, and then Evangeline, and then finally at you.

You stand as still as criminals in the dock.

"Runaways," says Knit Cap. "That was what they said you were." He leans slightly on the word *you*. He drinks and hands the bottle back to his friend in the Mets hat.

"Is there a reward?" Mets Hat asks. "For information?"

"The TV said nothing about a reward."

"Well, then," says Mets Hat. "These teenagers are not our business."

"Correct." Knit Cap nods.

Are you about to have some luck? Will they let you walk away?

"We'll forget we ever saw these strange and violent runaways," Mets Hat says.

Yes. You are about to have some luck.

"For a consideration." He lifts his hat. "If you would be so gracious."

Evangeline says, "Okay, fine. That's reasonable."

"Kind and generous teenagers," Knit Cap says with a bow.

Then Evangeline gasps. She holds out her hands, palms up, fingers wrinkled like prunes. They're trembling. "So, it turns out that I'm wrong. We don't have any money at all. What we had was in—uh, my pants. Sorry."

Kenyon says bitterly, "Life sucks."

"Your friend mentioned that already," says Knit Cap. "Try to keep up."

A grin splits the face of Mets Hat.

Then Saralinda laughs out loud.

You and Evangeline and Kenyon stare at her, and inside you are freaking out, but she steps forward, holding out a hand to the man in the knit cap. "Hello. My name is Saralinda. Who are you?"

Knit Cap smiles at her. "I am Marcial."

Mets Hat says, "I'm Troy."

Marcial and Saralinda shake hands. Then Troy and

Saralinda shake hands. Then Saralinda says, "Marcial and Troy, these are my friends, Evangeline, Kenyon, and Caleb."

Everyone shakes hands.

Then Marcial turns a serious face to Saralinda.

"Saralinda?"

"Yes?"

"I don't want to know how and why you are here, Saralinda." Marcial waves to indicate Coney Island by night. "All of you. Running away, without clothing and without money and without the sense God gave even to small scurrying mice, and with the police asking after you on TV."

Saralinda presses her hands together. "Well, there's a long story. We—"

Marcial holds up his broad hand to stop her. "Troy and me, we do not care why. We *all* have a long story. Every human one of us."

Troy nods. Saralinda blinks, looking rebuffed.

But you get it.

You watch as Troy hands Marcial his bottle and Marcial takes another drink. You wonder what Marcial's story is. How did he end up on the street, one of society's throwaways? How did Troy?

Because it has hit you like the rock that the boat slammed into. You are *all* here in this place, on this night. Them, and you. Thrown away. Trying to survive.

Long story.

Same boat.

Troy says, "Yes, but Marcial, what if they just told us the part about being half-naked?"

Marcial smiles. "No, better not."

Saralinda says earnestly, "If we did have money, we'd give it to you. We absolutely would."

Troy and Marcial look from Saralinda, to Evangeline, to Kenyon, to you, and finally back to Saralinda. At last they look at each other and nod.

Marcial bows slightly. "But we would not take it," he says.

"Not now that we know you," says Troy gallantly.

There are a few seconds of silence.

Marcial raises an eyebrow at Troy. "Johanna's?"

"Yeah. Let's get them out of the cold." Troy holds up his bottle. "But first. Vodka, anyone?"

"I thought you'd never ask," Kenyon blurts.

The men laugh.

"Small sips," cautions Troy.

The vodka goes to Kenyon, then to Evangeline, and next to you. It burns down your throat and warms your grateful body. Saralinda drinks last, after a slight hesitation.

"Johanna's is a secondhand store," Troy says as they walk with you away from the beachfront.

Marcial adds, "We will let you in. You will be safe for a few hours. Yes?"

"Yes," says Saralinda. "Wow. Thanks. Thank you!"

The six of you keep sharing tiny sips of the vodka. Saralinda walks next to Troy and Marcial into the back streets, with the rest of you a few steps behind.

You've given Kenyon one arm and Evangeline the other, and as you turn a corner, Kenyon's grip tightens on it. She nods upward at a set of boarded-up windows and the big yellow sign beside them. It says TERMINAL HOTEL.

The three of you trot closer to Marcial and Troy and Saralinda.

A few blocks in from the beach, you are even more grateful for the men. In the doorways and entryways, shadows move within shadows. Sometimes Marcial and Troy look in at the shadows and greet them by name.

Saralinda says, "On TV, what else did they say?"

"They are looking for you," Marcial says. "That is all."

Ten cold minutes later, you stop before a small, weather-beaten store that looks to have been converted from a previous existence as a house. The window of Johanna's Miscellany & Consignment Shoppe is small. Though barred, it showcases a mannequin in sunglasses, a yellow dress with a poofy skirt, and a dark-blond wig of luxurious locks. There's a homemade pink sign, with words inside a heart: WELCOME, MY FRIEND!

Troy produces a key and opens the door. Inside, it is

shockingly warm. A small lamp next to the cash register offers enough light to see.

"There's a restroom in the back," says Troy. "With a shower."

"You can stay here until dawn," Marcial says.

"Leave everything in good shape for Johanna," says Troy. "That is our deal with her."

"We'll take good care of it," Saralinda promises.

The two men start to turn away, but then abruptly, Marcial turns back. He pulls out his wallet. He empties it and hands the money to Saralinda.

"No, no, we can't possibly—"

"Yes. You can."

"Pay it forward someday," says Troy.

Saralinda stares down into her hands. "I will." She sounds choked. She puts the money down and reaches up. She kisses Marcial's cheek. The next moment she's hugging him tightly, and then Troy.

"Maybe let us know how you are later on," says Troy. "Johanna can get us a message."

"I will."

Troy and Marcial look at the rest of you, one by one. "God bless," Marcial says. Then they are gone.

You are conscious of the others talking—about the money, about showers, about finding clothes to wear, about what time it is (11:53 p.m., which is earlier than you guessed since it felt like you were on that boat for a hundred years). Everything they say is important. You'll pay attention.

Just not yet.

You need to absorb something more important.

No matter what material things you do or do not have, if you have a friend who walks by your side, you will never ever have nothing.

Also.

No matter what is wrong with you and your life, if you can help someone who needs your help, then you will never *be* nothing.

You used to want to be nothing.

You have just been taught better.

Chapter 38. **Saralinda**

Three steps inside her shoppe (I pronounce it shop-PEA) I am ready to write sonnets to Johanna, who (I imagine) has fuzzy gray hair and laugh lines around her eyes and an enormous bosom like a pillow and glasses on top of her head. Mentally I try her in a twin-set but it's not right on her. On the front counter of the shoppe is a spinning rack of costume jewelry which makes me realize Johanna would wear her glasses dangling from a sparkly beaded necklace. Purple.

Around the shoppe Johanna has put up heart-shaped directional signs. I would never hurt Johanna's feelings by saying that the hearts are too much and maybe actually they are not.

The signs say:

BEACHWEAR

WOMEN'S

JEANS & SWEATS

MEN'S

SHOES

HALLOWEEN

HOUSEWARES

KITCHEN

BOOKS & MUSIC

MISCELLANEOUS

OFFICE

I interrupt Evangeline and Kenyon, who are counting money, to say, "We're in heaven, you guys!"

Caleb's mouth twists. "I guess that would explain the two angels."

"I know!" I say. "Did that actually happen?"

His gaze and mine tangle. His face is intense I can't look away.

He says, "You were brave, Saralinda. When you introduced yourself. That was when things turned around."

I hear Kenyon and Evangeline agreeing, only that wasn't what happened so I shake my head. "No, they were laughing and joking with us before that so I already knew they were okay."

Caleb says, "Or maybe you held out your hand and said your name and *then* they knew *you* were okay."

He is still all intense his eyes fixed on mine we are standing rather close together and my mouth goes dry, then Caleb pivots and says over his shoulder, "I see towels." He steps away and tosses a towel each to me and Evangeline and Kenyon, who are right here and it is therefore not the time for anything quite extremely personal between Caleb and me which is what for a moment I crazily thought was going to happen.

I dry off Georgia and then myself as best I can. My towel has a jolly mermaid on it wearing a bra made of two daisies, unfortunate choice as daisies are a land flower, nobody thinks these things through. And by the way speaking of towels (and fashion) when Caleb was looking at me before, my clothes were sopping wet. Which is to say they *clung*. As for Caleb, he is shirtless but has his towel (featuring a picture of Nessie) slung over his shoulders.

God I am tired. Tired but I still notice things. Tired.

I can't move even for a shower at the moment and so I thank Evangeline for offering it to me which she just did. "You go first," I say.

Why won't he look at me again he wants to I feel it.

Evangeline closes the bathroom door and Kenyon turns to me and says, "I wonder if there's a computer here somewhere."

"Let's try the office," I say, pointing to the heart sign and I make for the back of the shoppe with Kenyon and Caleb following.

Is he looking at me from behind?

The office computer is a big metal box paired with a heavy old-fashioned monitor. With difficulty I locate the power button and we crowd around while it spins and wheezes to life.

"Windows 2000?" says Kenyon incredulously. "Does that seriously mean the year 2000?"

"Yeah." Evangeline is in the doorway with a towel wrapped around her head and another around her torso.

"You were quick," I say. She smells of soap.

"Yeah," she says again. "Let me drive, and please pray for internet." She sits down and clicks on the browser. The rest of us lean in and nobody mentions going for a shower next.

There is internet. There is Google.

Kenyon breathes down Evangeline's bare neck. "Check the New York news stations."

I say, "No, no, don't bother with that, google our names."

The internet connection is not exactly fast. Eventually however the results of Evangeline's search appear. She taps on a link and from behind me I hear Caleb suck in his breath.

Son of Dr. Caleb Colchester Sought as Witness to Accident

Rockland, NY – Emerging testimony in the death of Antoine Dubois, the 17-year-old Rockland Academy student killed yesterday afternoon in a traffic incident, points to the presence of another student in the car with Dubois. Caleb Colchester Jr., 17, had accompanied Dubois on an unauthorized trip off-campus. He did not remain on the scene after the alleged accident.

Police seek to question Colchester as a person of interest, but he has disappeared. He apparently departed Rockland Academy this morning, while the student body was reeling from the news of Dubois' death.

Colchester is the son of psychiatrist Dr. Caleb Colchester, writer for *The New Yorker* and author of the bestselling book *The Woman Who Chased Love, and Other Strange Twists of the Human Mind*, and his wife, Veronica Silva Colchester, of New York City.

Antoine Dubois was the son of Gabrielle Dubois, an engineer and architect, and the late Laurent Dubois, of Scarsdale, New York. His paternal grandmother was the poet Julietta Bandoni. Dubois was president of the senior class and a starter on the soccer team, according to sources at Rockland Academy. "He was a young man of remarkable character, who was admired by everyone," said Dr. Dennis Lee, Head of School at Rockland Academy.

Rockland Academy has released a letter, which

reads in part: "This is a tragedy for the entire Rockland Academy community. Our thoughts are with everyone whose life Antoine touched, and especially with his mother, family, and his many friends."

Also missing are three female Rockland Academy students: Saralinda de la Flor, 16, Evangeline Song, 17, and Martha McKenyon, 17. They are believed to be with Colchester. Song, McKenyon, and de la Flor are known to have been on campus at the time of Dubois' death yesterday, however.

McKenyon was in the news last spring for providing controversial evidence leading to a confession in the Perrytown High School alleged gang rape case, which is expected to come to trial next year.

Asked about his son, Dr. Colchester said, "We are hoping that Caleb comes home soon and tells us what he knows about the death of his classmate." He added that he had no idea why Caleb or the other students had run away.

The families of the other runaway students either had no comment or could not be reached for this story.

An AMBER Alert has been issued for the underage runaway students. Anyone with information regarding their whereabouts is asked to immediately contact the police hotline.

I wonder: What is this story insinuating about Caleb?

Caleb says to Evangeline, "I didn't know Antoine's grandmother was Julietta Bandoni."

"Yeah, well," says Evangeline. "She was."

"Do you know her work?" I ask him. I have never heard of this poet myself.

He says, "My mother likes her."

"Antoine never knew her really," says Evangeline. "He kept meaning to read her poems but I don't think he ever did."

This is so sad I have to look away.

Kenyon leaves to have her shower and the rest of us browse through the pictures with the article. However they are just our school ID photos and height, weight, and last-known-clothing information, yay the clothing has nothing to do with us anymore. Caleb's picture is a horrible unsmiling head-and-shoulders shot that makes him look like he is holding a prison number below the photo's bottom edge. The slideshow ends with a shot of Antoine in mid-leap on the soccer field. As he kicks out you can almost hear his living yell of triumph so the photo goes blurry before my eyes and I have to blink and lean on the edge of the desk.

Evangeline says, "It sounds like they're sort of hinting that Caleb had something to do with Antoine's death."

"That won't stand up," I say.

Caleb doesn't say anything.

"Is this part of the game thing your father is playing?" Evangeline asks.

Caleb shrugs. "Maybe, I guess."

Evangeline clicks on another link. However instead of loading, the computer makes a grinding sound like a dentist's drill and shows a blue screen with white lettering.

From the doorway, Kenyon says, "That's not a good noise."

Error occurred

Operating system stopped to protect file from damage.
Press any key twice to reboot.

Executed code dump:

0x4A757374 0x20696E20 0x7465726D 0x73206F66
0x20616C67C 0x6F636174 0x696F6E20 0x6F662074
0x696D6520 0x72655736F 0x75726365 0x732C2072
0x656C6967 0x696F6E20 0x69732061E

Evangeline puts her head down on the desk.

"To hell with the computer," says Kenyon, who is wearing khaki pants and a plain black long-sleeved T-shirt. "We don't need it."

Evangeline raises her head. "We do too." She presses the Escape key twice. The computer whirs and grinds and as we stare at it hopefully it chooses once more to come to life and say:

Windows shut down unexpectedly.

"Evangeline?" I say. "If we get out of this, can you please buy Johanna a Mac?"

"Freaking yes." She tries to restart the computer.

Caleb says, "Saralinda, do you want the next shower?"

"You go," I say.

The computer runs a diagnostic.

Evangeline says, "I'll get this piece of crap working. Meanwhile, we need to think about how to use our hundred and twenty-nine dollars—"

"Not too bad," I say. "Thanks, Marcial and Troy."

"Not great, but not bad," says Evangeline. "Way better than nothing. Also, we need to figure out what we're going to wear."

"Who cares?" says Kenyon. "We're going to wear clothing, Evangeline. Clothing that we borrow from Johanna. Unlike you in that tiny damp towel."

Evangeline doesn't look up from the computer. "No, we're not. We're going to wear *disguises*."

Chapter 39. **Caleb**

You clean up rapidly, because Saralinda needs to shower too—
no, no, *no,* you can't think about her in the shower. This same
shower. She is not for you, nothing has changed, all you've
done is endanger her. When you step out of the shower, you
notice the old mirror over the sink. Because of how the mirror's
silver has worn off the back, your face is reflected in disconnected, smoky pieces.

That's who you are.

Outside, you hear the murmur of the girls' voices and
a geyser of laughter—all three of their voices, pealing out.
It is enchanting to hear their laughter and then abruptly it
is terrifying. You try to get back the feeling you had from
meeting Marcial and Troy; the idea that no matter what
your father does, who *you* are is in your control. But what
good does that do if you can't protect them, her?

For a moment in your head you are back in Ellie Mae
with Antoine, and now you can feel your father's puppe-
teering hand, the hand that somehow killed Antoine.

"Why?" you whisper aloud, even though you know better than to ask that question.

You *almost* think about your mother then. She was younger than you are now when she met him; she was alone and she had no one, and really that's still her life—but you can't, you won't, go there.

You emerge from the bathroom wearing pants and a chamois shirt that you took from the men's department. The clock now says 1:17 a.m. You follow the girls' voices to the two racks of the women's department—and your mouth literally drops open.

Kenyon is wearing the wig from the mannequin in the shop window, along with too-snug lilac yoga pants and an enormous matching sweatshirt. The sweatshirt features a Siamese cat and the words *I'm Purr-fect.*

Somehow too she has acquired a pregnant stomach.

Saralinda has a huge grin on her face.

"Well?" Evangeline asks. "Would you recognize Kenyon?"

Speechless, you shake your head.

"I look about thirty, right?" Kenyon's expression is half-pleased, half-appalled.

"Here's the pièce de résistance." Evangeline gestures at a stately, old-fashioned baby carriage. "It was in the storage room."

You *are* impressed. The carriage is not just a disguise; it's also walking support if Kenyon needs it. Which makes you think of—

Kenyon looks at you and nods, as if she reads your mind about Saralinda and her cane. "Saralinda's going to be an eleven-year-old boy. Hey, SL, go shower."

Saralinda departs—you will *not* think about her standing naked under the water exactly where you just were. You pretend interest in the Yankees shirt that Kenyon holds up, and on second thought, Saralinda dressed as a boy couldn't be more perfect and you completely approve.

Fifteen minutes later, Saralinda sits on the stool behind the cash register in a white pin-striped Derek Jeter #2 baseball shirt and baggy boy's jeans, with her freshly washed and braided hair tucked up under a Yankees cap. Her face is grave, her eyes are alert, and she doesn't look at all like a boy.

It was easy at school when you only saw her occasionally in the hallways. She wasn't entirely real to you then—you know that now—and thinking about her was recreational fantasy.

But the reality of her is nearly unbearable. You want—so much—

Kenyon says, "SL? I'm sorry, but we need to cut your hair. Maybe then you'll look more like a boy."

Saralinda's hand inches up and cups her bare nape.

"Hold on, I'm not sure we can even do that," Evangeline says. "I haven't been able to find scissors."

You hold up your knife, which you cleaned thoroughly earlier. "I volunteer as tribute."

Saralinda takes a deep breath. Then she pulls off the cap. Her braids drop. She undoes them, combs her fingers through the loosened wet hair, and it tumbles down her back.

"Okay," she says.

You're going to get to touch her.

You don't ask if Kenyon or Evangeline should do this instead. You stand behind her. "Are you ready?"

She looks up at you and nods.

Her hair is soft, yet each individual strand is wiry and strong. You hold the first lock gently. Its wave curls around your fingers. You try to saw through the hairs a few inches away from her scalp. Inadvertently, you pull. "Sorry."

"It's okay."

Neither of the other girls offers suggestions as you cut, for which you are grateful, and after a while you figure out how to do it. You take your time, strand by strand. But the knife is small and not suited for the job, and you have no clue, so by the end you've made a mess. The lengths are anything but even. Some of Saralinda's hair sticks up, and there's a strange curl over her left ear.

"Hmm," says Kenyon.

Also, Saralinda still doesn't look like a boy. She looks like a girl with a bad haircut.

You ram the Yankees cap down over her head. "Don't look."

"How awful can it be?" Saralinda puts a hand to her head, and looks at you, and then at the other girls.

Evangeline's hand makes an "a little up, a little down" motion.

Kenyon makes a face.

Saralinda laughs. She swivels back to look at you—

You know better than to let her know what you feel about her; it would make things worse in so many ways. But you're looking down into her laughing eyes, and everything you feel for her is plain on your face, whether you want it there or not.

You see her see it.

In fact all three girls look at you with their all-seeing, all-knowing girl-eyes.

But you don't die on the spot from their knowing, and then you realize: You can't bother with secrets anymore. No more secrets, *none*—they have to know it all. They *need* to know. Even if they don't believe you. Even if they think you're insane. Even if they cringe away. To have any chance of defending themselves, they need to know what you know.

You blurt, "My father isn't the brilliant, wonderful man

the world thinks he is. He's someone else too." You pause, shocked at yourself. Words rise up in you from seemingly nowhere—thoughts you never even realized you had. And then they come out.

"He's this sick, sick fuck. But he hides that side of himself. I know you won't believe it but—"

"He did chase us," Kenyon points out. "On Fire Island. That was weird."

"And my mother," you burst out. "My mother . . ."

"Does he mistreat her?" That's Saralinda.

Slowly, you nod. "I think so. I didn't always see it, or understand what I was seeing, but yes . . . it's not physical, you understand . . ." Now that you see it, you can't understand how you missed it. "Yeah, he does."

"And you?"

"Same. It's psychological . . . warfare, I guess."

Then you're talking rapidly, to get it all out, all these new thoughts tumbling in your brain. Back at the cottage, Kenyon mentioned hearing an internal bell of truth. You've got a whole carillon concert: *true, true, true.*

"With my father, the brilliant, wonderful man is a cover for a bad guy. An intelligent cover. He knows what he's doing. It's deliberate. But I'm not an innocent party. I told Antoine—I told him in the car, before—you have to know this too. See, I'm like my father. I have a bad guy inside, just like him."

You tell them about Mr. Hyde. About the first time, when you killed the squirrel. You tell them everything. Then—not looking at them, not looking at Saralinda—you say, "But I repress my bad guy. He's in there but I can't talk to him or control him. He's . . . he's in there. The difference between me and my father is that I wish he wasn't. We're alike. We're both monsters. We manifest it differently, that's all."

You stuff your hands into your pockets.

"Caleb?" says Saralinda.

You can't tell anything from her face, because she always looks kind.

She says, "About the squirrel? I don't believe it."

The squirrel. Its blood spattered the white and black squares of the chess board.

"Okay, fine," you say tensely. "Don't believe me."

"Oh, I'm not saying I don't believe *you*. I'm saying that I don't believe the *story*."

You did this wrong. You said it wrong. Why would the girls believe you? It's useless to try. Your story about Mr. Hyde is ridiculous. You can't even be sure Antoine believed either. Maybe he just said he did. Maybe he was being nice.

You repeat, "I killed the squirrel. I did it. I've done many horrible things. Many."

You look at the other girls. You have no idea what they're thinking. Saralinda shakes her head.

"I don't think so. Now, ask me why."

You shake *your* head. You *need* her to believe you and—

"Saralinda," Evangeline says, "why don't you believe Caleb?"

"Thank you," says Saralinda. "Well, Caleb saved all our lives in the roof collapse. Then we spent the last thirty-six hours with him. So we know him. We've seen him in operation. I believe him about his father. Just not—let me ask you a question, Caleb."

You clench your teeth. "What?"

"That fire at school. Did you set it?"

"I don't know," you say. "I don't *remember* doing it, but then I wouldn't, if it was Mr. Hyde. I don't know."

She nods. "Do you actually remember torturing and killing that squirrel?"

"My father showed it to me."

"Do you remember *doing* it?"

"I already told you. I don't ever remember what Mr. Hyde does. He's another personality."

"You don't ever remember anything bad that you did."

"Not the serious stuff. No," you say impatiently. "That's the whole point."

"Okay, what if your father showed the squirrel to you and he said you did it but he was lying. You were a little kid. How hard would it have been to mess with you?"

Kenyon draws in a breath.

Evangeline nods in agreement.

They are naïve idiots all three, but you can be patient with them. They don't want to believe you . . . but they must. For their own safety, they have to understand what you are.

You say, "Mr. Hyde is real."

All three girls shake their heads.

"Look. It's not about the squirrel. The squirrel was the tip of the iceberg. I explained this all wrong. Mr. Hyde has done more than I can ever tell you."

"Maybe," says Evangeline. "Maybe not. You don't remember the fire either. Could your father have done that?"

"That's beside the point. Listen. You guys don't understand abnormal psychology." You look at Kenyon. "Split personalities aren't frequent, but they happen. I'm one."

Kenyon says, "Yeah, there's room for doubt."

"I tortured and killed the squirrel."

Saralinda says, "You were small. You were vulnerable. You were easy to deceive."

You wish she were right. Oh, how much you wish it. You think of the confetti on your dorm room floor: evidence that you haven't done anything lately. That you know of.

But you don't dare believe you *never* have. It's not safe.

You are your father's son.

"I won't lie to myself," you say. "Or to you guys. I know what I am. You need to know too."

"Fine," says Evangeline. "We have other stuff to do. You have a disguise waiting, Caleb. But consider this while you get dressed: Your inner six-year-old is still thinking for you. He needs to grow up so he can review the situation as an adult. We'd love to give you a couple years to figure it out, but we don't have that kind of time."

"Right," says Kenyon. "We have to fix Saralinda's hair."

Chapter 40. **Saralinda**

I stand in Johanna's bathroom in front of its tiny old mirror as Kenyon and Evangeline work on my hair until I say, "Enough. I'm going to put on a baseball cap. Evan still needs a costume—I mean, a disguise. You guys go do that."

I can mourn my hair later on, if I am in mourning because I might be glad to be rid of it, I can't decide. Also if they leave me alone I can think about the expression on Caleb's face when he insisted he was a monster which I refuse to believe although a small part of me is afraid I'm wrong. Another part of me doesn't want him to know that there is that small scared doubting part, and then yet another part inside me believes precisely what I said to him about his absolute bastard of a father—who (in case it is not clear) I hate with a black hatred that bubbles away in my soul like lava in the hottest pit of hell. Also before he told us about his father, Caleb *looked* at me in the exact way that I've been hoping for and in short I want to be alone (which is a phrase my mother says with a fake accent that she claims is Swedish, baffling, but about which I have never asked because I don't care and also I don't want to think about my mother, not now).

I do *vant* to be alone though.

Kenyon glances at Evangeline. "I have an idea for your disguise. I saw a baby stroller in the storeroom. I was thinking you could be, uh, my friend. Like, another mother."

Evangeline frowns. "A folding stroller? That won't work. Pushing a stroller with no kid in it is a bad idea."

"Oh, really? Then why do you think people will be fooled by *my* stroller?"

"It's a ginormous baby carriage, not a stroller. We'll cover it. People won't see inside."

"Why don't you at least look at it?"

"If you insist. Even though I'm right."

They leave at last and I breathe in and out a few times. Finally I put my cap back on (I wish it were a Mets cap like Troy's) and wonder if I do pass as a little boy. I can't tell and this is the kind of thing I have never bothered to think about before—while I could use some improvements such as a working pancreas I feel right about the gender I was born with.

Speaking of my pancreas it is entirely possible that my blood sugar needs attention and while I can do nothing right now I *can* think ahead. The facts are these: I can get a test kit at any pharmacy. But I cannot get insulin for which I need a prescription. I do have a prescription and it is on file at Duane Reade. Any Duane Reade can fill it. Except there is an AMBER Alert out with my name on it. So I cannot get insulin without risk, possibly grave risk (pun unintentional if witty although I am not laughing so maybe not witty).

I probably don't need insulin though, it's the middle of the night and I never get up and take it in the middle of the night. If I don't eat I will be okay a while, maybe a day or longer and also maybe I can get insulin somehow. I need a creative idea for how. Think, Saralinda.

Think.

I leave the bathroom and look at Caleb, who doesn't see me because he is standing up near the front of the store with his back toward me and he doesn't know I am watching him. I want to believe in Caleb. Just because his father is psychotic evil personified (why do I have no trouble believing that? Instantly I know, it has to do with his expression when he came down out of the helicopter and looked at the four of us) doesn't mean that Caleb is or could be. He is not.

But the part of me that doubts him directs my feet away and I go instead to the storeroom to find Evangeline and Kenyon. The door is half-closed and inside Kenyon and Evangeline stand across from each other with a small umbrella stroller and a beat-up kid's scooter and a rattan basket near their feet.

My mouth opens to say something to them but I change my mind and shut it, I can't say why exactly.

They are paying no attention to the stroller they're supposedly in there to look at and they are unaware of me, Evangeline looks only at Kenyon and Kenyon looks only at Evangeline. Evangeline has her hands on her hips. Kenyon's arms hang at her sides.

I hear their breathing which is louder than normal and quick.

I should turn away but instead my hand covers my mouth so that I won't make a single noise and I step to the side so I am hidden by the door and I watch.

I watch as Kenyon takes a step closer to Evangeline.

As she pulls off her wig and drops it to the floor.

As Evangeline tilts her head back and her eyes lock with Kenyon's.

As the pale pink of a flush appears and spreads on Kenyon's neck, filling in the skin around her tattoo.

As they sway closer together and their noses touch.

As Kenyon loses her nerve and takes a step back, nearly tripping over her own feet.

As Evangeline's arm catches Kenyon around her waist and pulls her in again.

As they talk in the same way they always talk, like conversation is a battle, but now they whisper and Evangeline's fingers lightly touch Kenyon's tattoo. "What does this say?" She pulls the fabric away and silently reads what's there.

"It's from a book."

"What does it mean?"

"It means—oh—to be yourself. Only it's ironic."

"You're all red. Why?"

"How dare you tease me? Don't you know how much I don't like you?"

"Oh, yes. I know. It's a problem. Because I like you."

"What?"

"You heard me. I like you. *I like you.*"

"No. It's not true. It can't be true. You hate me. You hated me at first sight."

"I felt *something* at first sight."

"I—you—but I was being such an incredible asshole that day—"

"Yes, you were. It got me all hot and bothered and angry, and for the longest time, I didn't know why. Then I did, because I'm smart."

"What? I got you hot?"

"Yeah. Take your time to assimilate it. I can wait." Evangeline smooths her hand gently around the curve of Kenyon's neck. Her every move is confident, but there is a vulnerable undertone in her voice and then she blurts, "What do you feel for me?"

"Oh, God. *God.* Evangeline—why do you think I turn into such an idiot whenever you're around? But I thought— I thought you were straight."

"I like who I please. I want who I please."

"You want . . . ?"

"I want."

Evangeline doesn't move, she waits and waits (and behind the door, Peeping Thomasina waits with hammering pulse) until Kenyon tilts Evangeline's chin up with one hand, until Evangeline's hands twine together behind Kenyon's head, until finally their mouths mesh like puzzle pieces.

My body is in flames.

I make myself back away so that they can be alone the way they deserve and also so I won't be caught, I am desperately ashamed of myself for watching but I couldn't *not*.

Back in Johanna's bathroom I sit on the edge of the tub and press my palms together.

I want to kiss like that and I want to be kissed like that and I want to hold and be held like that and if not, if I can't have that, then I will die I will dissolve in wanting I will drown in a lake of longing I will disappear in need.

Chapter 41. **Caleb**

You sense movement and swivel in time to see a rat scurry
from one trash bin to another. It is between six and seven
o'clock as sunrise lightens the horizon on Coney Island.
Mermaid Avenue, which is supposedly a main commercial
street, has completely failed you. You curl your lip at the
posted hours on the third closed drug-and-convenience
store.

How can you and Saralinda buy an insulin test kit if
all the drug stores are closed until nine a.m.? Let alone a
phone.

"Isn't this still New York?" you demand of Saralinda in dis-
gust. "The city that never sleeps?" But it is clear that Coney
Island not only sleeps, it snores. At least, going by the bum
huddled in the next doorway.

"Maybe there'll be something open nearer the subway."
Saralinda hesitates by the sleeping guy's doorway. He isn't
Marcial or Troy. The size is wrong, the coat is wrong. But it
could be one of them. Or someone like them. Or someone

like you or Saralinda. The point is, that guy is definitely someone. Everybody is.

He snores again, louder, and Saralinda sighs, her fingers tightening on the handles of her scooter. She pushes off with one foot—her good foot.

She's fast with the scooter. You lengthen your stride to catch up, which makes your Kate Spade handbag ("Fake," Evangeline pronounced authoritatively) swing awkwardly from the crook of your elbow.

Silently, you continue to fret. Evangeline and Kenyon won't be able to linger much longer at Johanna's, waiting for you and Saralinda to reestablish contact with a new phone, the one you haven't been able to buy yet. The plan calls for them to then head to the city on a different train, an hour behind you, with a phone of their own.

You hope they won't get distracted. Love is grand, but they still need to stay focused.

You need a phone to call them on. Maybe the phone is more urgent than the insulin test kit, though you feel more desperate about the kit.

You pass a bodega, which taunts you with a sign advertising prepaid T-Mobile. It is closed. Of course it is.

One good thing: As the sun rises, Mermaid Avenue is marginally less terrifying.

You try wearing your bag over your shoulder and also

try to remember that you are a woman who is taking her child to school by subway.

Evangeline said that a woman like you would carry her money in her purse. "You can't go into a store and fumble in your pocket," she insisted, and then Kenyon chimed in. "Yeah, it lacks authenticity." A Wellesley word, that, you assume.

Those two. You saw it coming. Did Saralinda? Did she notice what just happened with them?

You're not jealous. You're glad for them. You wish—but no.

You glance at Saralinda. You feel self-conscious in your red long coat, floral polyester headscarf, enormous black tie-up shoes, and handbag, and it would have been worse if you hadn't been able to shave at Johanna's. At least Evangeline let you wear a regular T-shirt and pants on underneath the woman's coat. Still, you know you are a freak show.

On the other hand, Saralinda's little boy disguise mysteriously became perfect with the scooter.

Plus, look at her go. You wish she could have a scooter in the hallways of Rockland Academy. You wonder if she misses her cane, which is now hidden inside Kenyon's baby carriage. It's strange to see her without it.

Saralinda pauses to consult the tourist map from Johanna's.

"The subway isn't far now."

"Yeah." In the new light, you can also see the roller coaster rearing up over the amusement park. You add, "Once we get out of here, I am never ever coming back."

Saralinda makes an attempt to fold the map. "You're not curious to see it in the daytime?"

"No."

"Ride the Ferris wheel?" She hands you the map.

"No."

"Eat saltwater taffy?" She pushes off again.

"Dental disaster," you say to her back, which is you getting way too much into the mom role. You refold the map properly and put it in your bag. You catch up to Saralinda, who points.

"There's the train station."

It's a massive beamed structure, aloft against the sky, open to the air. Most importantly, it's active. Proof is the elevated train coming to life on one of the platforms. It moves slowly, tracks rattling beneath it, and speeds up as it heads toward the city.

"Also, there's the bodega of my dreams," you say. It's across the street; a narrow store with a neon pink OPEN sign.

Within five minutes, you and Saralinda buy a phone from a sleepy-eyed clerk who doesn't give either of you a glance. Another minute and you're back across the street, ducking inside the train station. You find a corner, rip open the phone packaging, and activate it.

A signal.

Hallelujah!

Kenyon answers the phone at Johanna's. You tell her your phone number and where the open bodega is so they can buy their own new phone. You're about to hang up when she says, "Evangeline got an email from Antoine's mother."

"What?" you say. You listen to Kenyon, bite your lip, and finally say, "Don't do it until we get a chance to talk. Okay?" You hang up. You turn to find Saralinda staring at you, her hands on her hips.

"What?" you say.

"Don't do *what* until we talk?"

"I'll tell you when we're on the train," you say. "We don't have a lot of time."

She doesn't look happy, but nods. You follow her to the MetroCard machine.

This station is the end of the line, and the Q train waits with open doors. It's the express train to the city, which will still take over an hour. You enter a car that's nearly empty and choose seats positioned so that most people in the car will only have a view of your back. Saralinda sits beside you and parks her scooter at her feet.

"Do you see a camera?" she whispers.

"I don't know. I don't want to look around for it. Let's assume there is one."

"I'm not sure I'd recognize it." She pauses. "Could you

hold your purse in your lap? Also, you're sitting like a guy. Pull your legs closer together."

You adjust your handbag and cross your ankles and rearrange your headscarf to hang over your forehead. Ten minutes later, the train doors close, with five people in your car—the other three clustered at the far end.

You're off, clattering your way north.

Saralinda exhales. "I hope the other two make it."

"They'll be fine. They're leaving to catch the train soon." You keep your voice low.

"So, what did they just tell you?"

"Antoine's mother emailed Evangeline. She says she was tricked and she wants to talk to Evangeline and tell her something important. She wants Evangeline to meet her."

"No."

"Yes." You rub your forehead. "And Evangeline wants to go. She knows it might be a trap. I made Kenyon promise they wouldn't decide until after we all meet up in the city and talk."

"I don't know what to think," Saralinda says.

You are silent, and so is she.

You watch out the train window, which is spattered by drizzle. Beyond the window, Brooklyn spreads out, its lights misty gray.

Saralinda's eyes drift closed.

It would be good to pull her head down on your shoulder, to hold her. If there's a camera on this car, cuddling would look entirely right. Mother and child. It would help you hide your faces too. But you can't think how you'd suggest this to her.

You don't dare close your eyes, or sleep.

Her head drifts down on your shoulder.

You hold her after all, very gently, and she doesn't pull away.

At Johanna's, there was an attempt at getting some sleep. Evangeline made the suggestion. But as soon as everyone agreed to try, she and Kenyon went into the storeroom together and closed the door. Which left you alone with Saralinda. So you got out of there. You went to use the ancient computer.

Clubfoot is a birth defect in which an infant's foot is turned inward and the bottom of the foot faces in the wrong direction. Without treatment, normal walking is not possible. Most cases of clubfoot are treatable in childhood, however, using nonsurgical and/or surgical techniques.

Now you look down at Saralinda as she stirs in her sleep on the train. A frown deepens across her brow. She mumbles something you can't make out, and then she calms and settles down into your arms like she belongs there.

You check your phone for Duane Reade locations and

find one near Times Square. If there's anywhere on earth that a pharmacy would fill a prescription without cross-referencing the name to some AMBER Alert, it would be in Times Square. Right?

Once you get her insulin, then you will worry about Evangeline wanting to meet Antoine's mother. One thing at a time.

Chapter 42. **Saralinda**

I come awake and the subway car is rocking and there are warm strong arms around me. I know Caleb instantly by the vibration of my hummingbird heart. Everything is not cake and rose petals however because he holds me stiffly as if he doesn't want to be too close, which what? This is not what I was expecting from the way he looked at me earlier at Johanna's. Although then again I can present the following additional evidence of WTF also from Johanna's:

In the wee hours we all agreed we should (try to) sleep for a few hours before heading out at daybreak. Caleb and I were alone since Evangeline and Kenyon closed themselves up together in the storage room "because it's quieter." This left me and Caleb alone (opportunity!), only then what happened between us was this:

NOTHING.

Not even a kiss.

Okay I am not the center of the universe and so my wanting something doesn't mean I get it and let us also remember my obstructionist fairy godmother who I thought I'd invented as a private joke. She is not funny anymore and if I did manifest her in my life by imagining her, then all I can say is that if I find her alive I will stomp her fairy face in with my heaviest orthopedic shoe. Although when I clear a tiny space in my brain I am aware that wanting to stomp the fairy is not just frustration but also other feelings such as fear and other thoughts such as ones I'm having about my mother which I can't help.

I have lost my point. I am tired, also my blood sugar may be wonky which affects rational thinking.

Oh. Caleb. NOTHING.

So Caleb and I were together alone side by side in the dark on some piles of clothing between women's dresses and Halloween, and I spent minutes squirmy scared and hopeful that he would say or do something to reach out, and wondering if I should be the one to do or say something (terror excitement indecision), then Caleb got up despite my extremely loud psychic messages sent to him twenty times per *millisecond,* and he left.

He left.

Once I realized he was not coming back I could have gone after him but instead I held on to Georgia and curled into a tight snuffle to make a list of horrors. Caleb does not want me. My mother concealed Tori from me. I envy Evangeline and Kenyon. I'm on the run. Clever evil adults such as Caleb's father and Kenyon's grandfather are after us. Antoine is dead dead dead. (Separation from Georgia is ahead because of my disguise, and yes I know that should not be in the same ballpark only it's Georgia.) Through hiccups sobs and snot I prayed that Caleb wouldn't return to find me like this (I have my pride).

So he doesn't want me after all (mixed messages anyone?) and now on the train I am disguised as a little boy while he is dressed maternally holding me in obligatory fashion. What do I do?

I snuggle closer and fake sleep because actually? I have zero pride.

Also maybe because romance novels have rotted my brain and my independent moral fiber like my mother said—she may be a liar but that doesn't mean she is wrong about everything.

Caleb's arms tighten.

"Saralinda?" His hand gently covers my mouth, I suppose to stop me if I startle awake and scream.

I want to kiss the center of his palm. Instead I open my eyes and blink slowly, blearily (if I survive I will consider a career on the stage, no I won't I will live in a hobbit hole with Georgia who I miss desperately right now, Kenyon will keep her safe, oh Georgia on my mind).

Caleb has no idea I am fully cognizant, I do not enlighten him and he whispers, "We're still on the train. There are lots of people here now, so whisper, and keep your head down. Okay?"

I sit up and his arms fall away. I glance around, yes the subway car is now crammed.

"How do you feel?" Caleb whispers. "I mean, your blood sugar?"

I hold out one hand to show him I am not shaking, which I am not because I took no insulin but then again I might be shaking just because anxious, no insulin no insulin no insulin. "No problem yet," I say.

"I checked and there's a Duane Reade near Times Square."

I nod, this is no surprise they are everywhere.

A few minutes later the Q pulls into Times Square. I grope automatically for Georgia and find the scooter. I can't use the scooter in the subway however. Caleb holds my hand as if I really am a child. I let him, see above about zero pride. We wriggle our way onto the platform and then upward. The Times Square station is crowded so it is a good place to feel safe.

After we emerge onto Broadway and Forty-second into an incongruously fine day that feels like summer not October, our new phone buzzes. It is Kenyon and Evangeline texting from their phone as planned.

—*Are you in Times Square yet?*

Caleb texts back: At 42nd. Heading to pharmacy.

—See you Bryant Park at 11. E meeting Gabrielle Dubois there.

"What?!" Caleb explodes. He shows me the phone and then texts back asking for more details but they don't answer and he swears.

It is 8:23 a.m. We flow with the crowds on Forty-second to Sixth Avenue (it is still too crowded to use my scooter but Caleb holds my hand to help keep me steady, I like and resent it both). Then we walk north.

I have been worrying of course, I have never picked up my insulin on my own. Plus there is the AMBER Alert and what if my giving my name at the pharmacy triggers something? Caleb thinks it might and so do I.

As we pass a bakery my feet slow and I stare in the window at the muffins and croissants.

"Want something?" Caleb asks.

"You go ahead."

He shakes his head. I say, "I can't but it's stupid for you not to eat. If you're hungry."

"I'm not."

"I don't believe you."

He shrugs. We go on in silence and when we get to Forty-fourth just before the drug store I grab his arm. "Wait, I think I have to show the pharmacist an ID. Right now I'm an eleven-year-old boy. Plus my ID was in my backpack which went overboard."

We stop which annoys the stream of people until we move to stand closer to the building.

Caleb says, "Oh."

"Maybe *you* can ask for my insulin? My mother picks it up all the time."

He bites his lip. "But I just have my own ID." He looks down at his costume.

We're out of ideas. We go into the Duane Reade and buy the test kit which is to say a new slick glucose meter that I had sort of been coveting but my mother said we didn't need.

When we leave the store, Caleb touches my elbow and says, "So, I am really hungry. But it seems rude to eat in front of you."

"I can turn my back," I joke.

He doesn't smile.

I say, "Okay, once I test, I'll know what's going on and maybe then I can eat a hard-boiled egg. But now I can definitely have coffee."

Caleb nods and then his eyes widen. "Saralinda!"

"What?"

"I know how to get a new prescription that we can fill, no problem."

Chapter 43. **Caleb**

You and Saralinda speed across town, running/scooting from Times Square over to catch the Lexington Avenue Express uptown, and then running/scooting again.

The sight of you jogging along in your red coat and polyester babushka—alongside Saralinda's little boy on a scooter—would raise a few eyebrows elsewhere. In New York, nobody glances twice. Still, you are nervous once you reach your hoity-toity neighborhood, where you also have to slow down. You're not sure if this makes you more self-conscious or less. But from beneath her Yankees cap, Saralinda smiles cheerily at everyone, and even the most fashionable Upper East Side moms smile warmly back.

You're amused until you spot a redheaded woman. You stop and look after her for a second, but it's nobody you know.

Saralinda skids to a halt and turns. "Hey, what's wrong?"

You come up beside her. "Sorry."

"What is it?"

"It's not important," you say. "It's just, this is Evangeline's neighborhood too."

Saralinda connects the dots. "You're scared of bumping into Spencer Song?"

"It crossed my mind. I know it's unlikely."

"I think they live further uptown. High Eighties."

"Oh."

"Do you believe Evan's right? That her stepmother is too much of an airhead and a wimp to go after Evan's money?"

"I don't know. Maybe someone else is doing the dirty work for her. She's very pretty."

"That's kind of sexist," Saralinda complains.

You shrug. "Evangeline agrees that Spencer's manipulative. Manipulators don't have scruples. They go after what they want, however they can."

"So you think she's involved?"

"Yeah, I guess so." You shrug again. "I don't think it's a coincidence Evangeline was in the carriage house with us."

Saralinda sighs.

Or that you were, Saralinda, you think, but you don't say it because you've finally arrived at the café.

A few minutes later, you leave Saralinda—with her test kit and the rest of the money—at Chatime. You linger outside the café, looking through the glass at where she's standing on line among the uptown moms. Will they spot that she's a teenage girl? Or will they interfere, thinking that a small boy shouldn't be there alone? Will someone recognize her from the AMBER Alert?

She turns and her eyes meet yours. Her lips move, and you read them easily because she already said it on the trip uptown:

You don't have to do this.

I do, you mouth back.

You turn and jog onward. The plan is for Saralinda to go without you to Bryant Park if you don't get back for her fast enough.

Your building is on Sixty-fifth. A lucky break: The doorman has his back turned. You enter the lobby, sail confidently into the elevator, and press the button for the twelfth floor. You shed the coat and headscarf and drape them over your arm.

Don't be home, don't be home, don't be home.

Standing before your apartment door, you think of Antoine, but *your* key works. Inside, you know instantly and with enormous relief that, as you hoped, your father is not home. When he is, his presence dominates the very air. Your mother is surely here—she always is—but her room is at the other end of the apartment, off the kitchen.

With luck, she won't know you have come.

You enter your father's study, its walls lined with framed diplomas and award citations and pictures of him with minor celebrities of the intellectual variety, writers and doctors and the occasional politician.

His prescription pad is in the top desk drawer. You rip some pages off and shove them in your pocket. Each one has his medical identification information at the top.

You don't hear her come in until she speaks.

"Hello, Caleb."

Your mother stands in the doorway of the office with the toes of her shoes short of the threshold, as if she doesn't want to cross it.

She's wearing shoes, not slippers, you notice with surprise.

Also, she is fully dressed, not in pajamas. She's wearing pants and a red sweater, and has her long dark hair pulled back and twisted up in a neat bun on her head. Her brown eyes are wide. She looks her age, which is to say young. She was only seventeen when you were born.

She smiles tentatively.

Though she still couldn't go out onto the street and look like she belongs among all the self-confident moms, there is something different about her today.

Her arms move as if she wants to reach out to you but doesn't dare. They fall back down and she clasps her hands and says breathlessly, "I have news." Before you can respond, anxiety reenters her face and she looks around.

"I have to go," you say, and push past her. "Sorry."

"Wait!" she calls. "Wait, listen to me—"

You're at the apartment door.

"—listen, your father has asked me for a divorce!"

You stop. You turn.

There is so much unsaid between you—including all the things you have only just realized about her, and about her relationship with your father.

Her eyes are shining. "He says I can have custody of you—you're almost too old for anybody to have custody of you anyway—and alimony. I can start my life over. We—" She holds out her hands. "We can start over. If— if you will."

Years ago, she tried for a few weeks to fight for a divorce.

"I don't believe it," you say flatly. Your mind races. What does this mean? Is this part of his game?

"I didn't either," she says eagerly. "But he let me meet with a lawyer. And that lawyer has talked to his lawyer already."

"But why would he—" you start, and then you shake your head. Saralinda is waiting for you. She needs insulin. Then you're due downtown—Kenyon, Evangeline, Mrs. Dubois.

"I've got to go," you tell her.

"But—"

"Do whatever you want! It doesn't involve me!" you snap, and then you're gone, slamming the door behind you.

Chapter 44. **Saralinda**

Timing is tight to get to Bryant Park, and on the last leg after we leave the subway, I am glad for my scooter (which is not meant as a dis at Georgia).

When Caleb returned, he did not say a word as he gave me the prescription paper he stole from his father, *stole*. And he also did not say a word as I handed him the cookie which I bought for him. (I knew I shouldn't spend any more money, we have so little, and there was a moment when I wondered if I could get away with stealing it but I did pay.)

We have become thieves and this particular theft of the prescription paper was for my sake. I am grateful and sickened and relieved and terrified and I think queasily about everything Caleb said about his father. And about himself. His face at Johanna's when he told us what he thinks about himself.

I want I yearn I ache to make it better.

Almost 100 percent I believe what I said at Johanna's to him. He is good.

When Caleb returned with the prescription paper his eyes locked with mine and I felt for a moment like his eyes were a mirror in which I saw myself as well as him.

I don't know anything anymore, I never did know, only I didn't know I didn't know.

Also while I waited for Caleb at Chatime I talked to Evangeline, who insisted she needs to meet Gabrielle Dubois and that she will be careful and it's her risk to take and Kenyon supports her and therefore Caleb and I ought to trust her to know what she's doing. I don't actually trust her on this, not completely. Evangeline is confused about Mrs. Dubois, that is what I think.

I had some dark thoughts while I sat in the café and drank jasmine tea (an acquired taste which I have not acquired), including obsessing over how little money we have and whether we can afford my insulin anyway. I tested my blood sugar: 215 which is high but not desperate. If I eat it will go higher, so I *can't* eat until I have insulin to balance things and bring my number down. This is what it is to have a broken pancreas. Scientists are working on cures and interventions (some already exist), which makes me think of Antoine, there might have been a cure for him in time.

Bottom line I am a burden on my friends in this desperate hour. Caleb should not have to be doing this for me. If we were together as a couple he would get tired of it, like my mom is tired apparently.

Caleb and I reach Bryant Park at 11:08 a.m. *Hurry hurry hurry* we are late.

The park has a big central grassy area and chairs and tables and a fountain and random kiosks and lots of people and a carousel which is operating on this fine day. I check out every woman who has a baby carriage even those who are obviously not Kenyon. I also look for enemies who could be anyone and anywhere. I am not well disguised. As to Caleb's disguise I can't tell, when I look all I see is him.

Will Mrs. Dubois truly be alone with apologies and money and information like Evangeline claims is possible?

Finally I spot Kenyon, blond and flamboyantly pregnant. She pushes her baby carriage along on the far side of the carousel.

"Evangeline," Caleb says into my ear. "With Mrs. Dubois." He points his chin.

They're sitting on a bench by the carousel fence. Mrs. Dubois clutches a big leather satchel under one arm and holds a plastic cup in one hand, and talks rapidly with her gaze locked on Evangeline. Every now and again she drinks from her cup.

My heart thuds madly.

"Do you see anybody else?" I whisper. "Your father? Kenyon's grandfather? Police?"

"No."

This doesn't mean they're not here. We move clockwise around the carousel which as it revolves is playing the *Sleeping Beauty* waltz.

We come alongside Kenyon. I take a selfish moment to glance in her baby carriage and yes, Georgia is in there swaddled in a blanket next to a baby doll.

Mrs. Dubois pours more liquid from a thermos into her cup, drains it, and sets the cup aside. Then she takes a plastic bag from her satchel and gives it to Evangeline, who glances inside and tucks it away. Evangeline says something and rises. Mrs. Dubois gets up too and reaches as if to embrace Evangeline but Evangeline steps back. Mrs. Dubois moves her hands in a pleading motion and holds the thermos out to Evangeline. After a moment, Evangeline nods and takes it. Mrs. Dubois turns away then and there is something very sad about her figure. She starts to walk slowly north across the park toward Forty-second Street.

"Following her," Caleb says in my ear. "See you soon."

My heart thuds faster than ever in my throat now but is this going to be safe after all? Was Evangeline right?

Evangeline walks straight past me and Kenyon. We trail after her.

Nobody calls to us or stops us, and we exit the park and continue south one block to the Cordette Pharmacy exactly like Caleb and I planned. Kenyon and I duck inside together, maneuvering her baby carriage with care because it is almost too big for the aisles, and walk into the back where Evangeline is waiting.

"Gabrielle gave me five thousand dollars in cash," she whispers. "This could make all the difference for us."

Chapter 45. **Caleb**

You follow Mrs. Dubois.

Your father wants a divorce, so he can start a new life? You are incredulous, and suspicious.

Your mother's hopeful happiness hurts to remember. She's like a caged mouse being tortured with a glimpse of garden. She ought to know better!

For a moment you wish you had had time to talk to her, to tell her that you're beginning to understand now, to see the past differently. However, your priority at this moment is Saralinda's insulin.

Your father's game. You can't play if you don't know the game or the rules . . . your thoughts go round and round and round like the carousel . . .

In front of you, Mrs. Dubois goes down into the subway. She gets on a train heading across town. As soon as the train pulls out, you retreat.

You arrive at Cordette Pharmacy. The girls are there. Saralinda has written out her prescription, but in your name. Even if all the Duane Reade pharmacies are alert for Saralinda de la Flor, there's a chance that the Cordette Pharmacy will not question a prescription for Caleb Colchester Jr. A chance your father wouldn't have thought of this. A chance the AMBER Alert doesn't go to pharmacies and your name (his name) won't trigger anything.

After all, his name isn't *that* famous. Most people don't care about writers or therapists.

(You hate your name, your name which is his, you hate it.)

You take off your coat and scarf again. You approach the pharmacy clerk. She looks at the prescription, and at your ID. "About ten minutes," she says pleasantly.

You don't believe in God, but still you pray as you nod and retreat.

Two minutes later there is an announcement. "Caleb Colchester, come to the pharmacy window for a consultation. Caleb Colchester."

This is soon. Too soon? You don't know. You look at Saralinda. She seems nervous and jerks her chin sideways, toward the door. Without a word the four of you file down the diaper aisle and out onto the street, where Saralinda takes the lead on her scooter, weaving in and out of sidewalk traffic. You stride along behind Kenyon and Evangeline. Your heart pummels inside your chest.

Failure.

South on Sixth.

West on Thirty-seventh.

South on Broadway.

At last Saralinda plunges into Penn Station. On the underground concourse, which is thick with people, she pauses and Evangeline takes over the lead. Finally the four of you cram into a booth in a busy, noisy restaurant, Evangeline and Kenyon on one side, you and Saralinda on the other. The waitress arrives to offer water and menus. Saralinda drains her small water glass instantly and the waitress pours her more. The waitress disappears. You catch Saralinda glancing at your water and push it over to her. In a minute, she has drained your glass, Evangeline's, and Kenyon's.

"Sorry," she says. "Thirsty. It's a side effect."

You and Evangeline and Kenyon make eye contact.

Evangeline signals for the waitress, who pours more water and takes orders. Saralinda gets one scrambled egg. When the waitress asks her about toast and potatoes, Saralinda nearly barks her head off saying no.

When the waitress leaves, you say, "It might have been fine at the pharmacy. I panicked. We could try again at another place."

Saralinda pulls out her test kit. She uses it discreetly on her lap but the three of you watch her anyway. Finally she says, "250." She drains her water glass again. "I've been worse."

You push the other water glasses in her direction.

Kenyon leans in. "What do you mean by worse, Saralinda?"

"Once I was 653. So, I need insulin, but not urgently. Let's not worry about me. Evan, what did Mrs. Dubois—"

"What was your blood sugar before?" you ask. "When we were uptown."

She shrugs. "215."

"So it's climbing."

"But slowly. Look, food raises it. Insulin lowers it. But sometimes it does what it pleases." She drinks more slowly now, but she drains the other glasses.

"What happens to you when it's high?" asks Evangeline.

"Bad things," Saralinda says evasively. Then: "It probably *will* get higher. Stress makes it worse."

"We'll try another pharmacy," you say. You are glad you took several pieces of the prescription paper.

"Evangeline, tell us—" Saralinda starts to say, but Evangeline holds up her hand as the waitress arrives with food. Saralinda's eggs comes with the toast and potatoes that she did not order. The waitress disappears just as you open your mouth to ask for more water.

"Eat," Saralinda says. "There's no sense in everybody starving."

You wish you could say you're not hungry. But you are. The cookie Saralinda got you uptown was nowhere near enough. You begin working your way through your club sandwich.

Saralinda takes one bite of her eggs and then stops eating. "Evan?" she says. "Tell us about Mrs. Dubois."

"Well, you know about the money."

"I don't," you say.

"Five thousand dollars. More than enough to get a hotel and make our videos—except for the credit card thing, but I think we can buy a prepaid card and use that." Evangeline looks at you, one by one. "They're all in this together. I mean, we knew, but Gabrielle confirmed it. And yeah, that means Spencer too. Hahaha on me."

You look at Saralinda.

"Saralinda's mother as well," says Evangeline.

Saralinda braces her hands on the table. "But—I still can't understand *how* it would have happened. How the conversation even began."

"Well, she didn't say exactly and I forgot to ask for that detail, I'm sorry, she was already telling me so much. They met at school, I guess? They decided to help each other out. The carriage house—all five of us were supposed to die that day. What happened was, Gabrielle directed operations for the explosives, but the others helped her."

"My mother too?" Saralinda says, still processing the truth.

"Yes, your mother too, Saralinda. Gabrielle said so, and

I don't believe she's lying. Remember, I know her well."

You watch Saralinda struggle not to believe Gabrielle's story. "But she's crazy," Saralinda says.

"I know. But I still believe her." Evangeline shrugs. She looks at her empty water glass, sighs, takes out the thermos, pours from it, and drinks.

"What—" Kenyon starts.

"Oh, it's just my green smoothie. Gabrielle's peace gift. Along with the money."

Kenyon grabs the thermos. "Evangeline—"

Evangeline makes a face. "Oh, don't worry. Gabrielle drank it herself, in front of me. And it tastes fine." She laughs sharply. "Gabrielle loves me. Maybe she's the only adult woman who ever has, you know? I guess I should have been nicer to Spencer, huh?"

Firmly, Kenyon takes the thermos away from Evangeline, who tries to hold on to it, but eventually gives in with a shrug.

"Anyway, Gabrielle told me everything," Evangeline says. "Like I said, she's not herself but she still makes sense. She's glad Antoine is dead. She said she knows he's in heaven and now he won't suffer on earth, and for that she is prepared to go to hell herself. But now that she has what she wants, she doesn't see why the rest of us should die too. I asked her to go to the police. But she said no, she doesn't want to turn in the others, since they did her such a favor." Evangeline's mouth twists. "But she is okay with us defending ourselves."

Evangeline looks again at Saralinda. "So I think we're back to Saralinda's video plan. Now we have money for a hideout."

"We still need insulin," you say.

Chapter 46. **Saralinda**

I feel Caleb's gaze on me and also his leg against mine and it could be anyone's leg at that moment, that's how shocked I am.

"I'm sorry," he says. "About your mother. I know you . . . well, hoped."

"It's okay," I say.

Kenyon reaches across the table and puts both her hands over mine.

"You already knew, SL." Kenyon's eyes hold infinite compassion. "That day in the carriage house. You told me about your mom. You knew she was done with you. Just not—not *this* done."

Yes I knew only also I didn't.

I take my hands from Kenyon's.

Some minutes go by.

My scrambled egg is sitting there and ordinarily it would do me no real harm to eat it, it would not elevate my blood sugar that much. Toast isn't tempting but as for the potatoes they are hot and grilled and salted and buttered and what I really want is to stuff myself with them until I can't think or feel anymore. My mother is not here to stop me. Then I realize that maybe—no, certainly—she will never again be present to stop me because she doesn't want to be.

She wanted my neck broken in a pile of rubble.

Evangeline and Kenyon and Caleb eat. They sneak looks at me. I drink more water. "Videos," I say finally because I refuse to be sorry for myself and also frankly throwing a personal pity party is not a good survival strategy and there are other people involved here besides me and they are just as devastated in their own ways (even Evangeline about her stepmother which is weird, right?).

Crying is for when I am alone.

I say, "We need to figure out that safe place for making our videos." I think of Johanna's and wonder if we could go back there, only it's not like we know Johanna herself and as for Marcial and Troy it is crazy to think they could help us any more than they already have. We are on our own. "All we need is to make and upload one video."

"First we need your insulin," Caleb says.

I shrug. I don't believe we're going to get insulin.

He touches me. He puts his hand on my arm. "Saralinda? Do you think your mother is home now?"

"Unless she's off plotting." This comes out all bitter.

"If she's not home," Caleb says, "could you get in?"

I blink. I swivel to face him. I say, "Yes. I could."

Home, where there is insulin. Plenty of insulin. My insulin.

Because Caleb's brilliance is catchy I have a brilliant idea of my own. "I bet my mother is there, but I know how to get her to leave. Not just for ten minutes, for long enough to let us make a video and get it out in the world."

Hope hope hope, I suddenly have it.

"Give me the phone," I say to Caleb and I take it and pray that the photo backup worked like it should have so that everything from my own phone is up there in the cloud. My fingers tremble and I enter the wrong password twice, then I get it right.

Everything is there.

My stomach compresses with something like panic so it's good there is no food in it. I am going to do this. We are going to do this.

I tap the photo of Tori, and Caleb leans over my shoulder to look, she is as adorable as ever. I still want her or maybe I mean I want the universe I used to think I lived in—however in this new universe at least I have friends.

I show the phone to Evangeline and Kenyon, who sit with their shoulders actively pressed into each other and one of each of their arms out of sight under the table (I'm sure they are holding hands). I am happy for them truly but the way they look at each other gives me a lump in my throat.

"The little girl," Kenyon murmurs to Evangeline. She gives me my phone back.

Evangeline looks all sad for me.

I advance to the next photo and expand the text. "This is the adoption agency's letter," I explain. "See, there's the name of the agency and their address and phone number. So, my plan is that I call my mother and pretend to be them and ask her to come sign something. Then when she leaves we go into my apartment."

"Could work," says Kenyon.

"She'll know Saralinda's voice," Caleb says.

"I'll be the one to call," Evangeline says. "Where's the adoption agency located?"

"Fifth Avenue at East Ninety-second," I say.

Caleb says, "Great, she can't get back from there very fast. Once we know she's gone, we enter and grab the insulin. But then I think we should find some other place to make our video. I don't want to stay there that long, Saralinda."

"A hotel in Brooklyn, maybe," Evangeline says.

I think my apartment is probably the safest possible place, and also the place nobody will expect us to be. I say so.

"Fine," says Evangeline. "Compromise. We get started

there, get one thing up online, and then move on."

"Okay," I say.

We grin at one another.

We decide that we should call from near my apartment so we can watch my mother leave, so we pay and I take my food in a to-go container which Kenyon puts in the carriage with Georgia.

Once I have insulin I will eat all the potatoes.

Out again into the city we separate for the rest of the trip. It is a short walk to West Twenty-fourth. Caleb walks with me and I go slowly on the scooter. Nobody in the streaming crowd looks at us for more than a second in passing.

"What do you think your mother is doing today?" Caleb asks.

"I'm not sure. She'd be working at home if it was an ordinary day. I mean, I assume she's still home but I won't know until we call and she answers the house phone." I pause. "Wait. She won't answer an unknown number!"

"Maybe she will," Caleb says calmly. "You're missing. She'll think it might be you. If she doesn't answer, though, we should try going in."

I scoot along in silence for half a block. "Where do you think they've been getting together? You can't exactly plot death at a restaurant."

"My father's office?"

"But shouldn't it all be top secret?"

He shrugs. "My father conducts group therapy all the time."

I steal another quick glance at him. "I keep thinking, my mother has had plenty of chances to kill me all my life. All she had to do was give me an insulin overdose. She could have claimed it was an accident. Why do things this way?"

"Are you asking me, or yourself?"

"Both. The thing is, my mother is not stupid and this is stupid. Also, she's not really a group person. She doesn't have any friends, even. She doesn't hang out with people. She doesn't *like* other people."

"My father can be very persuasive," Caleb says.

I say, "Well, he's a famous doctor. She'd like that. Maybe she never would have thought of it on her own."

I halt my scooter. My building is ahead.

Home.

Chapter 47. **Caleb**

Saralinda's building is fine, but let's just say your father would look around and smile patronizingly. As far as you're concerned, the best part is that there is no doorman, which makes it easy for you and the girls to take up temporary residence in the laundry room off the lobby.

"Showtime." Evangeline sits on a dryer and calls Saralinda's mother's landline. All of you crowd around. You hold your breath as the line rings once. Twice. Three times.

"Hello?" Saralinda's mother's voice is flat and cautious.

"Ursula?" Evangeline says efficiently. "This is Carrie Macdonald from the Chaplin Center for Adoption. How are you this morning?"

"Oh! Hello. Fine. I'm fine." Still cautious, but decidedly less cold.

"I understand you normally work with Hannah Joplin, but she's out sick today."

"I'm so sorry to hear that. I hope it's nothing serious?"

"No, thanks, just a cold. But I'm covering for Hannah and it turns out we need you to sign some paperwork, and we need it today, so that you can have your first meeting with Tori as scheduled. We'd hate to have to delay that. But of course we can delay the meeting if signing today isn't convenient for you?"

You eye Evangeline approvingly and she smirks back as Ursula responds, all warm syrup.

"Of course! No problem. Just email it to me, and I'll return it right away!"

Evangeline hesitates for a second. "Sorry, we can't do that. You have to sign the papers in our office. There has to be a, um, witness."

"What do you mean? Notarized?"

Your alarmed eyes meet Kenyon's and Saralinda's but Evangeline sails on smoothly. "Yes. That's correct. We need your signature notarized. The thing is, Hannah is the one who knows all the details, not me. Sorry. All I know is that we need you to come in this morning and do it. So, can you? It's the fastest and easiest way."

Ursula pauses. "I guess I can."

Relief whooshes through your chest.

"Excellent. Can you come now? Before lunch? Because I have afternoon appointments."

"Yes. Now, what was your name again?"

Evangeline's eyes widen. She says, "See you soon," and disconnects.

The four of you, together, exhale an enormous amount of air.

"You sounded good," Saralinda says.

"But I forgot my name." Evangeline hits the side of her head.

"Carrie Macdonald," Kenyon says.

"Which is the name of my lawyer. I mean, my father's lawyer. My mind went blank for a second." Evangeline slides down from the dryer and leans against it. Absently, she wipes sweat from her forehead.

You say, "You did great. All we need to do now is wait and see if she leaves."

In the next few minutes, there is activity in the lobby, just not the activity you want. You peer out the half-closed laundry room door as a man in running clothes stretches and an old lady with a walker gets mail from her mailbox. Saralinda murmurs, "That's Ms. Pfeiffer. She's nice. She told me once she knew Gloria Steinem."

"Who's Gloria Steinem?" you ask.

All three of them glare at you.

"A really important feminist," Saralinda says. "Of historical importance."

"Oh. Sorry."

Saralinda pauses. "Okay, so I had to look her up too. My mother laughed. She said she had failed in her maternal duty." Abruptly, she blinks, closes her eyes tightly, and puts up a hand to cover them.

"SL? What is it?" asks Kenyon.

Saralinda looks up, suspiciously bright-eyed, and sighs. "It's just—that day. Her and me. We sat in the kitchen and my mother told me about Gloria Steinem, and I pretended to listen more than I *was* listening, if you know what I mean, and my mom kind of caught me and—and she laughed and hugged me. She said when I was older, I would understand." She pauses. "There were so many good times. It's just hard to believe what's happening now. Part of me . . . I can't help wondering if it's my fault."

Your stomach twists. Your fists clench. You want to shout at her, No! No, this is what being manipulated is like—you doubt *yourself* rather than your parent. At which point your brain stutters to a stop. When it restarts, your thoughts have shifted abruptly. Was Saralinda right about what she said at Johanna's about you as a little kid? *Were* you being deceived and manipulated all along? If you could write down all the times when you thought Mr. Hyde did something, and logically work out where your father was, each time . . . what would that look like?

Evangeline says to Saralinda, "I get what you're feeling. Nobody is an evil supervillain *all* the time. Listen, I even had a couple good moments with Spencer." She shrugs uncomfortably. "Which I sort of stomped on, to be honest."

"You?" Kenyon says, and Evangeline laughs.

Then Kenyon says seriously, "But I hope you're not saying that Spencer's right to go after you because of that?"

"God, no."

"Just checking."

The two of them make protracted eye contact. You look away, at Saralinda. "How are you? How's your blood sugar?"

She squirms. "Oh. I can hold out."

There is silence. You keep watching the lobby. Nobody comes. Evangeline boosts herself up on the dryer again. "It's so hot in here," she mutters. "What's taking your mother so long, SL?"

You're not hot.

Saralinda says, "My mom was probably in her pajamas when you called. Now she'll be standing in her closet trying to decide what to wear that will impress the people at the adoption agency—"

Kenyon interrupts. "Wait, is that her?"

Looking straight ahead, Ursula de la Flor strides out of the elevator, through the lobby, and out the main door.

A minute later, you and the girls are in the elevator heading up. You encounter no neighbors to recognize Saralinda or look twice at the friends accompanying her. It's great luck—even, you can't help thinking, unbelievable luck. But you'll take it.

It turns out that Saralinda keeps an apartment key inside her cane. She works a tiny mechanism located under the handle that swivels a piece of wood near the top of the cane.

"A secret compartment!" Kenyon says. "Sweet!"

Saralinda gives her cane a pat. "You can't spot the lines when it's closed."

"Is it a handmade cane?" asks Kenyon.

"Yes. Although I superglued the crystal ball-thing on it by myself." Saralinda ducks her head as if she's embarrassed. "I was younger then."

"It's very cool," says Kenyon. "Very you."

"Well, I do still like it, but it's sort of, you know . . ." Saralinda uses the key, and then you're all inside the apartment with the door shut. Inside, where the insulin is.

There's a windowless combination kitchen and sitting area. Beyond it are two closed doors. One of them is extra wide like a hospital room door, and made of a visibly heavy, thick wood. Evangeline sinks down onto one of the kitchen chairs.

Saralinda doesn't run for her insulin. Instead, she waves at the closed doors like a tour guide. "So this used to be a one-bedroom. The living room got renovated so we could each have a bedroom." She focuses on the kitchen counters. "What a mess!" She moves as if to toss Chinese food containers into the trash.

"Leave them alone!" you bark. "Insulin."

She grins at you over her shoulder. "Don't worry. I'll be fine." You start to say something and she stops you. "Okay, I'm going." She goes through the extra-wide bedroom door.

You follow. You pass through her bedroom, not noticing anything except that it is a bedroom, and lean up against the doorframe of her bathroom. It's all antiseptic white tile and stainless steel, fitted with a walk-in shower, a toilet seat with arms, and grab bars on every available wall. It's as if Saralinda's mother wanted her daughter to be in a wheelchair.

Saralinda stands before the sink with her testing stuff. She doesn't acknowledge your presence behind her as she deposits a drop of blood on her meter, but when the result is ready, she meets your eyes in the mirror and says, "315, which is high, but no problem." She takes a vial and draws the insulin up carefully into the syringe. However, instead of injecting herself as you expected, she meets your eyes in the mirror again. There's a new look on her face, half-scared, half-determined.

"Would you help?" She touches her left arm. It is covered by her hoodie. "We alternate where we do the shots.

I'm supposed to do it in the back of my arm this time, which I can't reach easily by myself."

You think briefly of Evangeline and Kenyon. Why not ask them? But she *didn't* ask them.

"Okay," you say.

Saralinda shrugs off her hoodie. There's a defiant note in her voice. "You inject directly into the back of the arm. You have to sort of pinch the skin to hold it firm and steady. You don't have to worry about finding a vein. It's pretty easy unless you hit, um, scar tissue."

Her whole body tenses as you step close to take her upper arm in your hands—

Which is when you really see. Her arm where she expects you to inject her is badly scarred from previous injections. Years of injections. A lifetime of injections. Beneath your fingertips, the skin isn't soft to the touch; the scar tissue beneath is palpable.

Instinctively, gently, you touch it.

She says, "My legs are like that too."

You search the mirror for her face, but all she lets you see is the top of her head.

"My stomach too. It's like a war zone." Her voice goes higher, thinner. "Some people scar more than others. Maybe I'm worse than other people. I don't know any other diabetics." She pauses. "Or junkies."

You say nothing.

"That was a joke." Finally, her eyes meet yours in the mirror.

You say, "Your sense of humor isn't nearly as good as you think it is."

"No?"

If laughter was what she needed now, you'd give it to her by the bucket. But she needs something else. She believes that her body is ugly. Ugly! When what it truly is, is perfect. Perfectly her.

But you have no idea how to tell her that. You don't know what to say to her, but you do know how to reassure her. You know it with the certainty of millions of years of human genetic encoding.

Only you are forbidden to do it. You forbid yourself.

You say, "Show me what to do."

She puts her hand on top of yours. Her fingers move, miming. "I need one shot of fast-acting insulin, and then another of slow."

She breathes.

You breathe.

You poise the needle. You push the syringe. When it goes in, you are the one who winces. "Did I hurt you?"

She shakes her head. She prepares the second shot.

You do that one too.

Then you put the syringe down and turn toward her, and she turns toward you.

You ask a question without any words.

For answer, slowly, experimentally, she leans in.

Suddenly you don't care that you've forbidden yourself. You reach to cradle her head, threading your fingers through her blunt shorn awkward haircut. Her face is so sweet. She turns her face up just so—you lean down to her—

When from the kitchen, Kenyon cries out, "Evangeline! Are you okay?"

Chapter 48. **Saralinda**

Caleb's hand is warm on my back and his arm is strong around my waist and his eyes are dark and wanting and his mouth is an inch from mine and his breath is on my lips and as for me I am one great big *yes* (and also to be honest a little bit *at last*)—

Then Kenyon screams *Evangeline!* Caleb jerks away from me and me from him and our faces whip in the direction of the kitchen and then Caleb races away with me and Georgia right behind him.

Evangeline sits at the kitchen table with her head resting on her arms.

"She almost fell," Kenyon tells us. "She staggered. If I hadn't caught her—"

"I'm okay," Evangeline says irritably. She raises her face which is pale and sweaty. "I got faint for a minute. I already feel better."

Kenyon narrows her eyes.

"You sure?" I say.

"Yes. Stop fussing."

The other three of us look at one another and then Caleb looks directly at me and I blush.

"Shouldn't you eat?" he says romantically, not.

Food.

Oh.

The fact is all the hunger I felt before has dissolved into wanting to kiss and be kissed, but practically speaking food is not about hunger it is about blood sugar regulation so I must force food in unfortunately.

Except nothing seems truly unfortunate at this moment.

I smile at Caleb though he doesn't smile back, he has his unreadable expression on again. "Sure," I say, and warm up my food from the restaurant (I specifically calculated the insulin so I could have the potatoes, thank you) and sit at the table opposite Evangeline, which means I'm using my mother's chair which I have never sat in before—but I won't think of her.

"Our plan," Evangeline says. "We need to get started. Our online videos or whatever. We can start planning right here while Saralinda eats." She sits up slowly and wipes sweat from her face with a paper napkin.

Kenyon kneels next to Evangeline and touches her cheek gently. "Are you better?"

"Yes, only a little nauseous. If you guys will get started? Saralinda, may I—"

I point. "Use my bathroom."

"Thanks." Evangeline walks carefully but steadily into my bedroom.

Caleb says, "So we do a short video here and now, quick and dirty, and just post it."

"We can use my tablet to record it," I say. I toss my take-out container and quickly retrieve the tablet from my bedroom, glancing at the closed bathroom door as I do. Back in the kitchen I set up the tablet and its camera reflects me and my hair (about which the less said the better).

"Come sit by me," I say to Kenyon and Caleb.

"I can't just start talking," says Kenyon. "I thought we were going to write scripts!"

"No time," I say. "Just tell the truth. Say what's going on." I pause. "Caleb, what if you start? Say something about your father?"

Caleb hesitates and then squats beside me. I can't resist bumping into him hoping he will bump me back, but he is like a piece of wood. Still I catch Kenyon's raised eyebrow and I smirk at her which pleasantly shocks me, I've never smirked before in my life. Kenyon grins crookedly back, I look away and blush, oh I hope this is real it is real for me but what about him? Anyway Caleb and I are now side by side in the camera eye and we do not look too bad together if you make allowances for my demented hair and Caleb's expression.

I start the recording.

Caleb clenches his teeth which is not attractive.

I blink compulsively, ditto.

Out of camera range, Kenyon turns toward my open bedroom door.

"Hello," I say to the camera.

"Hello," Caleb repeats. Grimly he adds, "I'm Caleb Colchester. My father is"—he chokes it out—"Dr. Caleb Colchester. I'm here with my friend Saralinda de la Flor."

I wave at the camera in a friendly way which instead looks dorky, maybe we will have time to edit.

Caleb grits on. "And also my friend Kenyon, uh, Martha McKenyon. We go to Rockland Academy."

I beckon at Kenyon, who is paying half attention. She ducks her face into camera range and then out. "I need to check on Evangeline," she says, and sprints away.

Caleb and I look at each other. I open my mouth to ask if we should stop but he continues talking to the camera.

"So we're in fear of our lives. It's our families trying to kill us. Our parents or our parental substitutes. This includes my father, Dr. Caleb Colchester. There are four of us. The other one is Evangeline Song. Fuck. I am not being coherent, Saralinda."

"At least we're recording," I say, and add for clarity, "There used to be five of us. Our friend Antoine Dubois is already dead."

Caleb says, "They want the rest of us dead too. For various reasons. Like, with me—oh, Christ, stop. Stop."

He buries his face in his hands. "We'll try again in a minute."

"We need Kenyon and Evangeline anyway." I stop the video. "Maybe we can make an outline of what we're going to say? If not an actual script?"

We turn our heads toward each other at the same instant and our eyes meet and oh dear God if this is not love then actual love will be too much it will kill me.

"I *can* do this, Saralinda," he says like a promise.

He is focused. I lost focus for a minute but he's right, the video comes first. That is our job.

Also however I want my freaking first kiss.

I lean toward him deliberately with that soft fierce powerful feeling rising through me, and his face changes it warms and I know exactly what is going to happen, I can see it like a scene in a movie. I'll be in his arms with my face turned up to his and his arms curved around my shoulders and he'll cup my face in his hands tender yet strong and bring his lips to mine. I will finally know what he tastes like and he will know what I taste like, and surely it's safe to steal a moment for a kiss a long kiss a good kiss at last—

Kenyon rushes back in. "She's throwing up! I think it was that goddamned green smoothie!"

Chapter 49. **Caleb**

You run after Kenyon and Saralinda.

In the bathroom, Evangeline is on her knees. Kenyon practically falls beside her. Sweat is now dripping down Evangeline's face. She says, "Gabrielle drank the smoothie first. I swear she did. I saw her swallow. And she drank much more of it than I did."

Kenyon grits her teeth.

"Okay, so I was stupid," moans Evangeline. "I admit it."

Saralinda wets a washcloth and hands it to Kenyon. Evangeline closes her eyes as Kenyon wipes her face. She clutches the toilet and leans over it again.

You return to the kitchen. You pick up the thermos, which Kenyon left on the counter, open it, and sniff at the green goop inside. You start to wipe your finger around inside the thermos rim but Saralinda is beside you, grabbing your wrist.

"Don't touch it!" You look at her and she adds, "Some poisons work through the skin."

You go still.

"I read it," she says, as if she fears you don't believe her.

No chance of that. You're appalled at yourself. "You read up on poisons?"

She colors. "It was in a novel about medieval nuns who are assassins."

"Really," you say.

"Which was extremely well researched." She holds her hand out for the thermos, so you give it to her and she sets it down on the counter as if it were a bomb.

"It'll have to be tested," she says. "At the hospital. So they know what to do."

She's three steps ahead of you. Your eyes meet.

"Yeah. We have to take her to the hospital. At least we have money," you add, though you're not sure what good that will do.

You return grimly to the bathroom. "I'm calling an ambulance," you say.

Evangeline raises her head. "No! Once I'm at the hospital, they'll call Spencer."

Saralinda says, "That should be okay, because she can't do anything to you with all those people there—in fact you'll be safer than ever—"

"How do you know? With Kenyon's grandfather a cop?" Evangeline's voice is weak but scathing. "Plus, they won't let you guys anywhere near me in the hospital. You're not family." She sits up. "Besides, now that I've thrown up, I'm better. It's not like I drank the entire thermos." She wipes her mouth. "Give me some water?"

Saralinda scurries for a glass.

"Evan, I think you really do need to go to the hospital," Kenyon says. "We—"

"I'll make a deal with you," Evangeline says. "First we make a video and stick it online. *Then* I go to the hospital. That way, at least we have some insurance."

It's not so much that this makes sense, although it does. It's that it sounds so much like logical Evangeline. Maybe she *is* better.

Kenyon doesn't look impressed, however. "Let me talk to her alone," she says to you.

She closes the bathroom door, leaving you and Saralinda in Saralinda's bedroom.

The walls here are faded pink, and there's a crammed bookcase beside the bed. Her bed. It's a full-size bed. It has several pillows and a yellow-and-purple quilt. It's the bed that she sleeps in, with her hair all mussed, her body under the covers in her pajamas or her nightgown or maybe with nothing on at all.

You divert your attention to the bookcase, wondering if the assassin nun book is there. You stare at the books. Will you ever finish *Dracula*? Antoine tried to take away Mr. Hyde and give you Jonathan Harker instead, but you may never know how Harker escapes the vampire's castle. For all you know, he doesn't escape. Harker is a mortal, and it's Dracula whose name everyone knows, not his.

"Saralinda," you say. "Let's try the video again, just us. While they talk."

Saralinda nods decisively and brings her tablet back into her bedroom. She has just finished setting it up on her desk when—after a quick glance at the bathroom door, which remains closed—you touch her arm.

"Saralinda?"

She turns. She leans on her cane.

"Caleb," she says.

You feel desperate. You slip your hand beneath her chin but she's already tilting it upward. Then you're leaning down—

The door to Saralinda's bedroom slams shut. From the other side a woman's voice shouts.

"Oh, come on! Did you think you could scam *me*?"

Chapter 50. **Saralinda**

Caleb and I leap apart (déjà vu anyone?).

"I knew about fake phone calls before you were born! Didn't it occur to you that I might call the adoption agency and *check*?"

No. No, it did not.

Georgia and I get to my bedroom door as fast as we can though it will do no good I am aware, and yes I am correct, my mother not only slammed the door but also locked it. A locked door—I can't help quick-checking the ceiling for water droplets gathering and plopping, they are not there but my heart hammers anyway.

"You're a fool, Saralinda," says my mother.

Yes and in so many ways.

I breathe. I told my friends this was a safe place to be and now we are locked in and my mother knows we are here which means the other parents do too or soon will which means we are trapped and Evangeline is sick maybe poisoned by Mrs. Dubois and why are we here in the first place? It was because I needed insulin I hate me.

Should we call an ambulance anyway I don't know I don't know—I look desperately at Caleb only he doesn't know what to do either I can tell.

My mother rants on. "I always know what you're thinking. Even *before* you think it. Nobody will ever know you better than I do."

Certainly not if I am dead.

"You have no idea how much I've done for you. You have no appreciation either. I'm sick of it."

Caleb is beside me checking the door as if he might be able to smash it down but I watched them install this very door and its lock and they are not flimsy, we are trapped.

"In fact I'm sick of you!" my mother says.

Yes I get it.

Despite sharing a look with Caleb just now about my mom, I am feeling personally flimsy so I lean against the wall beside the door and grip Georgia. There has got to be something I can do but I cannot think what it is besides calling the police and an ambulance and hoping they'll end up on our side.

I feel frozen.

She keeps talking. "You live in a dream world, Saralinda. I expected you to grow out of it but you never did. You read all those romantic books and you just got worse."

I wish she wouldn't criticize my reading about which

she knows nothing because she doesn't read novels, my books are excellent and some have romance yes and also they have themes and interesting people in them and so much to learn. And if I were going to die (am I going to die?) I would not care about requesting a last meal, I would request a last *book* that is how important books are.

Kenyon opens the bathroom door and looks at me compassionately and also inside the bathroom Evangeline's head turns. She is still slumped on the floor clutching the toilet but she tries to smile at me, she tries though I have let her down and Kenyon and Caleb too.

My mother has not stopped the yelling in case you wondered.

"I suppose all your *friends* are in there with you? Including that *boy*?" She says *boy* like it's a swear word, and by the way I have never known her to go on a date or to have a friend of either gender. She has no interests but me and work which is weird, right, weird?

Caleb breathes into my ear. "Don't answer. Neither confirm nor deny. Why is the lock on the *outside* of this door?"

Because of my obstructionist fairy godmother.

No. Because of my mother.

I just look at Caleb, I want to crawl into his arms but instead with Georgia's help I stand upright on my two equally good feet. He touches my cheek with one finger very gently but his expression now is as vicious as I thought he was inside, at first.

He says, "Does she lock you in here regularly?"

I almost say: *Don't be silly, she's not that bad.* I shake my head. "No. The builders made a mistake and put the door in backward, that's all."

He looks skeptical and for the first time so am I.

My mother shouts, "Saralinda! Don't ignore me!"

I wish I could. Caleb's hand cups my cheek and I curve my hand over his. At which Kenyon snorts so I look up and my eyes meet hers and she blows me an exaggerated kiss although her eyes are bleak and then she turns back to where Evangeline needs her because Evangeline is sick, oh no I have certainly not forgotten. Then to my surprise Kenyon helps Evangeline up and they come out together, Evangeline leaning on Kenyon. Caleb goes to help too and they ease Evangeline down onto my bed.

"Answer me!" yells my mother.

At this point I don't remember what she asked—oh wait, I do. That *boy.* My *friends.* Yes, they are with me.

She keeps on shouting. "Answer me! Answer me!" She pounds on the door.

I shall not confirm. However I decide to lean against the wall because Georgia can't do everything by herself when I am shaky. Evangeline tries to sit up on my bed and Kenyon supports her. Sweat breaks out again on Evangeline's face.

Caleb goes to my bedroom window and heaves it open a few inches which is as far as it will go. Then to my complete shock he heaves again and the window judders all the way up. I immediately feel the breeze and Evangeline lifts her face to it.

Meanwhile Caleb leans out with his entire head and shoulders and torso and looks down, but if he is looking for a fire escape, well there is none. We are six floors up and you are supposed to use the stairwells in case of fire. While my mother rants, I waste time imagining how great it would be if we could leave by the nonexistent fire escape.

Only we can't.

Call the ambulance?

"You thankless, self-absorbed, sullen little bitch!" my mother rages on as I check the ceiling again. "I'm sorry you were ever born. That's what you've done to me. You've ruined my life!"

I wonder if the neighbors can hear her. I wonder if they would come if they could. Probably not, probably this sounds like an ordinary mother shouting at her ordinary thankless teenage daughter. At least Georgia is with me and also the wall is behind me to lean on. Only strangely this is not enough. I am okay for insulin and I ate, but my equally good foot feels equally bad and so I slowly sink down along the wall until I'm sitting on the floor beside the door.

We used to be happy, my mom and me, I swear it—only maybe I am wrong? Because it turns out there are so many things wrong with me from her point of view and, like throwing knives, she says them all. Here is a sampling of what she says.

Passive-aggressive! Rude! Inconsiderate!

Rebellious! Caught up in a dream world!

Insubordinate! Inattentive! Scheming!

From my place on the floor I pull up my knees and hold myself. It is words not knives.

Rude! Defiant! Insensitive!

Only words, except it turns out that somewhere in me I did not believe until now that she hates me and could want me dead. Now I do.

"Also, I know *exactly* what you want to do with that boy."

No kidding, she does? Does she want a medal for insight? But actually, how could she possibly know this?

"I bet you've already done it! His father thinks you have."

I am aghast assaulted appalled and also I feel shamed, I stare at the door as if a window will appear in it so that I can see my mother, she cannot be saying these things she *cannot.*

Caleb told me not to respond.

"You know what you are? You're a slut."

I can't help it. I speak to her through the door and I am quite calm considering.

"Mom, it's none of your business what I choose to do or not do sexually."

(Of course the big irony is that I have done *nothing*.)

I imagine her reaction even though of course I can't see it. But I know her. Her eyes narrow and she puts both hands on the door and leans close.

"My daughter deigns to speak at last, and why? To spout immature rubbish. Not my business what my teenage daughter does with her body? Oh, really? *Really?*"

"Really," I say as calmly as if we were having the difficult but still okay mother-daughter conversation I used to imagine us having. "I'm sixteen," I say. "It's time for me to be in charge of my own body."

Suddenly I think about my blood sugar regulation and my equally good foot and how when normal people have chronic health problems, what they do is find a trusted doctor and stick with them. Which she never did. I hadn't thought of this before—I assumed my mother knew best. Only my mother is not normal and she *never* was, this is the proof. I thought she was taking the very best care of me but her behavior has been wrong about my body all along.

"What about me?" she continues. "What about all that I sacrificed to be your mother? How about some respect? How about a thank-you? No, none of that. You only have one thing to say, and it's to defend your right to be a teenage whore!"

I don't look at the others, especially at Caleb.

"Some children are born no good," my mother says. "There is nothing the parent can do except start over."

She is talking about Tori and I shouldn't say anything else to her now, only what my brain tells me and what my body does are not the same. I shout.

Yes now I am shouting too.

"I want to love and be loved! What's wrong with that? I want to live before I die! What's so sluttish about that? I'm different from you, that's all!"

My mother yells right back. "You want love? I loved you!"

"No, you didn't! You've—you've—you've . . ." I can't find a way to articulate what I have realized.

"Bullshit! I loved you more than my life! I gave up my whole life for you. And how did you repay me? By leaving. Don't deny it. You were leaving me every day. I knew. It was like a stab in my heart. You were twelve and you—you began to *leave* me!"

Maybe it ought not to affect me but it does, it does, her pain is real she is my mother she will always be my mother and she is right, I did leave her, I had to.

I had to.

I lay my palm flat on the door because it is as close to her as I can get and I breathe, I don't know what to think, I don't know what to do, she was killing me she is killing me still.

She says (and now her voice is quiet), "I could see it in your eyes. In every word you said. In everything you did. You didn't want me to take care of you anymore. Your diabetes. Your foot. Do you know how much that hurt me? When you didn't need me? Didn't *want* to need me? Don't you understand?"

She is keening softly.

She says, "You weren't supposed to grow up. You were supposed to always need me."

I keep my palm flat on the door—maybe she is on the other side with her hand one inch from mine. This is what I imagine.

"Are you listening? Are you listening to me, Saralinda?"

I am listening.

"Don't you *understand* everything I did for you? I chose to have you! I held you in my body while you grew! I took you home with me! I changed your diapers! I fed you by hand. I combed your hair. I dressed you and taught you to read! All the times when you were full of energy and wanted to play and I was so tired, I still played with you. All the crying you did when your foot hurt, and I held you and comforted you. I was there. I was always there for you."

I press my palm harder into the door and I imagine that on the other side she does the same thing and all I want is to take my mother in my arms and hold her and tell her—

Words spurt from me. "Mom, listen, I *am* grateful to

you! But love isn't the same thing as need, and even though I don't need you the way I did, I will always love you and always be grateful."

I plead. "Mom, open the door! Let's talk for real. Face-to-face. Holding hands. Can we do that? Can we find each other again?"

She is my *mother*. Maybe she will open the door and let us out and we can—I don't know—I can reason with her. Something.

I sense Caleb close by. I glance up and see that he is holding my tablet which makes no sense but all that matters is that this is my mother and maybe it is not too late after all. My mom is laughing now however, laughing long loud and crazy. She starts ranting again—something about Tori. Tori! No she can't be allowed to adopt her—no no no—then I can't listen to my mother anymore because—

My head snaps back to Caleb. I understand why he's holding my tablet up like that.

He's recording.

Chapter 51. **Caleb**

Saralinda sits on the floor, one arm around her knees, one hand on the locked door. Her fingers are white from the pressure, as if she's trying to push her hand through the door and touch her mother's.

She gapes up at you.

The camera captures her horror as she grasps that you are filming, filming as her mother berates her, shames her, abuses her, and disowns her . . . as she realizes *this* will be the video uploaded onto the internet.

No script. No editing. No control. No multiple takes to get it right. No friends to share the spotlight with.

No choice.

She half chokes on a whispered *no*.

It turns out that you are the kind of bastard who, despite being moved, is aware that her distress makes better drama. Which is to say, you lean in for a different angle on a close-up.

Saralinda buries her face in her hands.

You hear a distant siren. However, five seconds later the siren fades and Kenyon moves into the camera eye, kneeling beside Saralinda.

"SL." Kenyon makes a pleading movement with her hands. She whispers low, underneath the ranting that's still coming from Saralinda's mother, so you go in closer to make sure the microphone catches her voice. "Keep her talking. Get her to talk about the other parents. I've called 911 for Evangeline and they're coming. It's all up to you now."

Kenyon runs back to Evangeline and you pivot to film how Evangeline slumps across the bed, shivering, retching over the side, the cell phone beside her with—you hope and pray—emergency response still live on the other end. Because then it turns out that it doesn't need to be just the Saralinda show after all.

You keep the camera on Evangeline as she looks into the camera and says, "I've been poisoned."

You return to record Saralinda shriveling against the door. She has now fully absorbed Evangeline's deteriorating condition. Her gaze moves to the camera, to you, and she nods, a crisp movement of her head.

She doesn't look pathetic anymore.

Later, if there is a later, you will tell her about the moment of connection that you had with Kenyon and Evangeline after Saralinda's mother began ranting. There'd been a nod at the tablet, another at a cell phone, and you'd moved smoothly and silently into your individual positions; you recording, Kenyon calling for an ambulance, Evangeline grimly holding on. You would not have taken the power of consent from Saralinda if all three of you had not agreed— but you are enormously relieved she is now fully conscious of what's going on, and participating.

Saralinda raises her voice to cut into her mother's continued ranting. "Mom, listen. I know about Tori."

"You know nothing!"

"I read all the paperwork. You want a little daughter again who needs you the way I don't anymore. I want Tori in our family too. I'd love a sister. We can still make our family work."

"*Family?* You're not in this family! I told you. I'm done with you! I don't want you!"

"But see, if you were to talk with a *therapist*—if we both were to talk to a good *therapist,* someone like for example Dr. Colchester. We could make our family work again. And you like Dr. Colchester . . ."

Her mother takes the bait.

"I've already talked to him! For your information, he agrees with me about you."

Saralinda's voice goes scornful. "I don't believe you. You don't *really* know Dr. Colchester. He's *famous.* He'd never talk to *you.* I bet he doesn't know you're *alive.*"

Her mother is stung. "I do too know him."

"I doubt it. No. You don't know Dr. Colchester and you don't know—" Saralinda hesitates. "You don't know my other friends' families either. You don't know Mrs. Dubois or Kenyon's grandfather or Spencer Song."

You hold the camera steady on Saralinda's face.

Her mother says, "Actually, Dr. Colchester is my very good friend. He understands about you, Saralinda, because he has a thankless child himself. That *boy*. He's *absolutely* onto you and what kind of girl you are."

"Is he?"

"Yes, he is! After you ran away, he told me you might come here for insulin. It turned out exactly the way he said. That's why you came back, right? For insulin?"

"Yes," Saralinda says slowly. Her shocked eyes meet yours and you nod in grim acknowledgment—your father was one step ahead of you the whole time.

Then her mother says, "What's your blood sugar, any-way?" For a moment she sounds like a concerned parent. "Did you take insulin already? How much?"

This video is going to be useless, you think. Full of foot-age that could be interpreted any way the viewer wants.

Saralinda hesitates, her brow creased, and then says, "I did. My sugar was high. It was—it was 653."

"653!" It's a shriek.

"Yes." Saralinda stares grimly into midair. Didn't she tell

you something different before? A much lower number?

"I've never been sicker in my life, Mom. You're right, I came home for insulin, and before you got here, I shot myself with a whole lot of it." She mentions more numbers, which are meaningless to you. "I didn't know what to do without you helping me, so I guessed."

Her mother exclaims, "You took way too much! You're going to go too low now! I knew it! I always knew you couldn't manage without me."

"It won't be too much if I eat. You taught me that, Mom. So if you unlock the door and let me into the kitchen so I can eat, then I'll be okay. Right? I need to eat something. And then maybe go to the hospital. Right?"

You stare into the level, lying eyes of the clever girl you love.

"Please, Mom," Saralinda says softly. "I need to eat. Let me. Please. Let me out. Take me to the hospital." She pauses. "Save my life."

There is a long pause.

"Oh, no," her mother lilts. "I won't."

"But I could go into a coma. I could die."

"That's right! And you'll have done it to yourself." Saralinda's mother's voice rises in triumph. "I always said you couldn't take care of yourself, couldn't calculate insulin amounts properly, couldn't remember to eat right, not on your own, and now you're proving it. All

I have to do is keep this door locked and walk away."

"That would be murder, Mom." Saralinda's voice does not quiver, but her arms clasp themselves.

"No, it would be karma. Because you brought this on yourself. Go ahead and die, Saralinda! See if I care."

You go close in on Saralinda's face.

Outside, you hear the siren.

Kenyon leans out the open window, looks back, and mouths, *They're here!*

"Mom," Saralinda says. "You don't mean it."

"But I do," says Ursula de la Flor.

Okay, you think, okay. Your video has nothing on your father, nothing on Kenyon's grandfather, nothing on Spencer. But you have Saralinda's mother crowing over her daughter's death—and the ambulance has arrived for Evangeline.

Chapter 52. **Saralinda**

I am done I am finished there is nothing left inside me. I have tricked and betrayed my mother who is mentally ill and I never knew it, and she has betrayed me too. Only I can't fall apart and I can't be destroyed, not yet anyway, my friends need me. So I stagger up on my feet and lurch with Georgia's help to Evangeline's side. There is no time for tears, also it is selfish because look at Evangeline so sick and shaking, and oh the smell, and look at Kenyon so terrified oh God oh God, I am afraid I will sob hyperventilate hystericate which is not a word but should be, so—

I slap myself on the face.

Which works.

Never ever argue with what works.

I am calm again, okay maybe not totally calm but not crying either. The point is I can function because I am not me, I am someone else steady and clear who will do what she has to do.

Caleb is working to upload the video of me and my

mother. On the video my mother says she knows Dr. Colchester and he agrees with her about me being rotten—that's all there is, that plus her being mean to me and wanting me dead, maybe that's something although there's not even my mother herself on it, just her voice but it's all we have.

I elbow Caleb, who is working too slowly. "Let me do it! I have ideas!"

Caleb looks at my cheek where I slapped myself and he steps aside before I push him out of my way.

My fingers take wing, uploading the video and tagging or linking or emailing it to the faculty and student body and all the parents at Rockland Academy including of course our own families. Also the New York City and State police departments (who cares if Kenyon's grandfather is one of their own, he won't be able to intercept it), plus @nypost and @cnn and other news places, and I make sure to use the names of Caleb's father and Evangeline's famous dead father and Kenyon's grandfather the cop in the tags. I also make sure to say that even if nobody believes us, all of our lives are in danger and if anything happens to us, then the police must investigate. I am posting to Facebook when *at last* (how long can it seriously take them to come upstairs?) there's commotion and pounding on the outside apartment door.

"Emergency! Open up!"

My mother will have to let them in, right?

Many things happen simultaneously:

Kenyon yells, "Help! Yes! Help!"

Caleb plasters himself against the bedroom door and yells, "In here!"

Evangeline's head hangs over the side of the bed as she retches and a thin string of spittle dangles from her mouth which Kenyon wipes away with a washcloth.

I tweet the video link to @obiwankenobi adding insanely *You're our only hope.*

There is a smashing noise—the outside door—and strange voices call "Hello? Hello?" and Caleb yells again. "We're locked in! She's locked us in here!"

Evangeline looks up dazedly with glazed eyes and I go crazy on Twitter trying to tweet to people or things with many followers, @emergencykittens @beyonce @thetweetofgod @hillaryclinton @neilhimself @shakespeare @benedictcumbRP and @nfl.

My bedroom door snaps unlocked, and three men and one woman crowd in wearing emergency jackets. One look and they are at Evangeline's side.

Kenyon says frantically, "She drank something, we think it was poison and she's been vomiting but there's nothing to come up anymore and her skin's so hot and—"

"We're here," one of the men says. "Stand back, miss. Let us do our job."

Reluctantly Kenyon moves aside as two of the medics

crouch and the woman puts a hand on Evangeline's fore-head. "She's burning up."

Beside me Caleb breathes deeply. They work on Evange-line while I google for law firms. Their numbers are over-whelming so I narrow the search by criminal law. Then I send the video to the first twelve lawyers on the list, with a cover note that says simply: *Our families are trying to kill us. Can you help?* I am not happy with this but writ-ing appeals to lawyers is not the kind of thing Rockland Academy teaches. I also wish I could remember the name of Evangeline's lawyer but I just can't.

Evangeline gets an adrenaline shot.

My fingers cannot be stopped. They find the Facebook page of the adoption agency which I did not even know I was looking for. There is no evidence of the parental con-spiracy on the video but there is evidence to cast doubt on my mother's fitness to adopt.

I wonder where my mother is. Did she run away? Is she lingering out in the kitchen or hiding in her bedroom?

I send the video to the adoption agency and I think:

Tori, this video is my gift. May you find a good family may you be happy may you have a good life. Though I will never know you, I will never forget you, my sister.

Caleb's hand is on my shoulder. I do not need to look at him to know that he sees and understands what I am doing.

"Bring up the stretcher," one of the male medics says to the other two. "We'll take her in."

Kenyon crowds close again.

"Sorry, miss, we need you to stay out of our way. It's best for your friend."

"*Girlfriend!* She's my girlfriend!"

"We'll take good care of your girlfriend," the woman medic says.

Kenyon staggers back toward me and I hold her with an arm around her waist, and from Facebook I hear a beep: Evangeline's roommate Irina has shared our video along with five exclamation points.

The medics hook Evangeline up to an oxygen tank. One of Evangeline's hands flutters up to hold the oxygen mask against her nose and mouth. I pray this is a good sign and Caleb's hand tightens on my shoulder as if he hopes so too. I tilt my head to touch his hand with my cheek and I clasp Kenyon to me with my other arm. The three of us breathe in unison as the two medics do things—they straighten out Evangeline's legs, they inject something else into her arm—and the other medics come back in. They position the stretcher and lift Evangeline onto it and roll her out.

"I'm going with her. I'll force them to take me!" Kenyon wrests herself from me to run after them.

Caleb calls, "We'll follow. We'll meet you there!"

Kenyon flaps a hand behind her and disappears.

I grab for Georgia. As I stand up, my mother appears in the doorway of my bedroom.

She is beautifully put together—silk pantsuit, ankle boots and scarf, with makeup and jewelry and her hair swept up—as if she did believe it about needing to go to the adoption agency.

The air from the open window ruffles her neck scarf.

"So you're not the one who's sick?" she says.

"No," I say. "I'm not sick. I took the right amount of insulin. I ate. I'm fine."

We stare at each other.

"So you lied," she says.

I turn away from her to my tablet where there are more messages about shares which I ignore. I scroll the video ahead to near the end.

The recording fills the room with my mother's voice.

Go ahead and die, Saralinda!

My mother stares narrow-eyed at me.

I say to her, "I sent this recording to the adoption agency. So, no matter what happens to me, they won't let you have Tori."

I stand steady with Georgia. We do not need Caleb's help although he stands very near to me and I am glad.

There is a long silence.

At last my mother says, "All I ever wanted was to be a mother."

351

I clench Georgia. "That's over. I'm not your daughter anymore, and you're not my mother."

More words come lashing out of me. "Also you'll never be anyone else's mother ever again! You'll be completely alone!"

Her face. I will never forget her expression.

My mother takes two quick steps toward me but Caleb blocks her way, so she looks around the room as if for some object that she can grab and bash me with—and I hope she finds it because I want to bash back. I steady myself with one hand on the desk behind me and think about lifting Georgia—no, yes, no—I can't do that—

Then I see that my mother is crying.

What happens next happens quickly.

My mother looks past me to the window which is open wide. In a blink she has covered the distance to it and despite everything my heart leaps toward her and my muscles tense toward her—to stop her—stop—

Caleb grabs me, holds me, as my mother scrambles over the windowsill—balances there for a sickening second while I scream *Mom*—

A heartbeat later comes the smash and the shrill of the alarm from the car on which my mother has landed.

Chapter 53. **Caleb**

You sit in the hospital waiting area outside the locked intensive care unit, beside a silent Saralinda and a frantic, pacing Kenyon. It's evening by the time Spencer Merriman Song races dramatically into the waiting room. She's wearing a crisp black shirt, beige leggings, and beige heels, with her hair pulled into a disheveled ponytail. A coat slips from her clutching arms, obscuring her handbag. She spies you—it seems as if she zeroes in on *you* in particular—and alters her course to skid breathlessly up. She wears no makeup, smells of soap, and her shirt is misbuttoned.

"Caleb?" She uses your name as if she knows you, lingering on it a beat too long. This makes you decide that if you live you will change it.

"You were with her?" Spencer asks urgently. "You and—" Her distressed gaze takes in Saralinda, but she entirely misses Kenyon, who is approaching wrathfully from behind. "What happened? They just got hold of me—my phone was off—I—so sorry—oh, God, how is Evangeline now, what do they say?"

You have no clue why this woman risks marrying and

murdering her way into wealth when she could *act* her way there.

Kenyon is in her face. "Get away from us!"

Spencer takes a step back. "But—but Evangeline—"

"Don't speak her name! Not to me! Not ever!"

Spencer's hands go up and her lips part. She looks at you with great big wounded eyes. You let your own eyes drift accusingly to the second button of her shirt, which is pushed into the third buttonhole.

Her hand reaches to clutch her shirt—she stutters, "I—I—"

Saralinda stands up.

"Sorry about my friends." She speaks directly to Spencer. Each word sounds like it's rasping against her throat. "They're upset. Ignore them."

Spencer blinks rapidly. "I—I—it's true that Evangeline doesn't get along with me, but—"

"Hospital policy is that they only talk to family," Saralinda continues steadily. "So they won't tell us how Evangeline is. But you will, won't you?"

"Of course—I need to go see her . . ." She looks terrified.

Saralinda nods. "Yes. Let's go talk to the reception nurse together."

"Oh. Thank you! Thank you!"

At last you process what is happening, and why Saralinda

is being friendly to Spencer, and though you think it's a waste—the woman is the enemy, and this helpless sweet veneer is for show—you're thankful that Saralinda is suddenly fully present.

She was robotic earlier, as she described to the police how her mother dived out the window. (It was a stroke of luck that her testimony and yours were corroborated by on-street witnesses, including one of the paramedics.) Saralinda insisted on going to the hospital with you to wait for news about Evangeline—not that you'd have left her. Here at the hospital, though, she has barely moved. She clutches her cane compulsively. So now you exhale in relief and watch as she moves with Spencer to the reception desk. After a few moments it is obvious that Spencer is being given an update on Evangeline's condition—the update that the hospital personnel refused to give any of you.

Next to you, Kenyon stares at Spencer. You put an arm around her and she leans on you, trembling. You look at her vulnerable bare neck and for the first time are able to read in full the sardonic words of her tattoo. *Why be happy when you could be normal?*

Indeed.

A vulnerable expression flits over Spencer's face as she listens to the nurse at the reception desk. Her left hand clutches the back of her neck, and her ring catches the light. The nurse glances at Saralinda and then back at

Kenyon and you, obviously reporting on your vigil. Spencer nods, the nurse steps away, and then Spencer listens as Saralinda says something to her. To your surprise, Spencer walks determinedly back to Kenyon and you—with Saralinda two steps behind—and says without preamble:

"They've got her stabilized. They're going to let me see her."

You look from Spencer to Saralinda, whose eyes remain bleak, shocked, and haunted.

Kenyon asks Saralinda, "Is she breathing on her own now? They had her on oxygen in the ambulance."

Spencer is the one who answers, her jeweled hand making a compulsive movement to her throat. "They've put in a tube to help her."

"A tube?" Kenyon gasps as if she cannot breathe either. Spencer reaches out toward her, but Kenyon flinches before asking bluntly, "Is she dying?"

Spencer's beautiful eyes close. When she opens them, tears shimmer on their surface. "They don't—I don't—it's serious. But there's always hope!"

You take on all of Kenyon's weight.

"What about the thermos?" Kenyon says. "Are they checking it out? Running tests?"

Kenyon had snatched up the thermos on her way out of Saralinda's apartment and thrust it upon the medics, along with a demand that Mrs. Dubois be hunted down.

Spencer's brow wrinkles. She looks at Saralinda.

"We think Evangeline was poisoned," Saralinda says. "If they can determine what she drank, maybe they can find an antidote."

"Oh, I'm sure they're checking it out," says Spencer. "This is an excellent hospital."

"Mrs. Song?" It's a woman in pink scrubs with teddy bears on them, standing nearby. "You can come in now."

Spencer nods. Kenyon starts forward as well, wresting herself away from you. But the woman in pink scrubs makes a *stop* motion to Kenyon. "Just family."

Spencer blurts, "Oh, but she is family. She's her sister." She turns to Kenyon. "Come along."

You stand dumbfounded with Saralinda as the door to the forbidden hospital zone closes behind Spencer and Kenyon.

"What was that?" you say.

Leaning on her cane, Saralinda sinks down into a chair. You sit as well and put a hand on her shoulder, but she shakes it off and begins rocking, back and forth, back and forth. People stare, covertly. After a minute or so, somehow, Saralinda manages to stop, and then she does let you touch her. You rock her.

There is silence between you.

You think of Saralinda's mother, her body splayed and

smashed on top of a Lexus. *All I ever wanted was to be a mother,* she had said. You think of your mother, smiling, hopeful. *Your father has asked me for a divorce!* You think of Kenyon's grandfather, sneaking under Antoine's car. You think of Antoine and his mother. You think of Evangeline's money. You think of that third buttonhole on Spencer Song's shirt. Finally you think of your father's psychiatry practice, of his powerful personality, his ability to influence, to mesmerize, to lead.

You make a list in your mind of all the times Mr. Hyde—supposedly—did something, and you try for each one to figure out if it might have been a lie.

Time passes. There is no news. The nurse at the reception desk still won't respond to questions, but she shows increased compassion.

You don't think that's a good sign.

At one point, you pull out the phone. It's cheap, but it works well enough to track what's happening in cyberspace. Which—joined with the news of how Saralinda's mother jumped to her death—is not nothing. Video shares are growing steadily across all media—on Facebook alone there are 434 shares—and while the first ones were exclusively students from Rockland Academy, by now those names are greatly outnumbered by people you don't know. There's a growing list of comments on the YouTube page as well, many of them nasty. It's a good thing Saralinda isn't reading. Some of the comments say she probably pushed her mother.

Thank God there were witnesses.

You're hoping the video will perform its intended task of providing insurance. From Irina, you obtain and upload the video of Kenyon's grandfather sabotaging Antoine's car. You link the two, along with some commentary.

Saralinda doesn't ask what you're doing with the phone. You have no idea how much more time has passed when your attention is caught by Saralinda's indrawn breath.

Spencer reenters the waiting room from the ICU at last. She is alone.

She does not look at the two of you. Her face is streaked with tears, she is staggering on her heels as if she's never worn them before, and her voice is high and frantic as she speaks into her phone. "Where *are* you? I need you! Where are you, Caleb—" She elongates the name an extra beat, the same way she said it when she spoke to you earlier.

The next second, your father strides into the waiting room, using the exact center of the parting double doors, as if he needs the entire space.

Like Spencer, he has his phone at his ear. When they see each other, he stops walking. Sobbing, Spencer rushes forward to fling her arms around your father.

"Oh my God, oh my God, she's dead!"

Against his back, where Spencer clutches him, the

emerald and the diamonds on her new engagement ring catch and reflect the harsh fluorescent hospital light.

You catch your breath as suddenly, you get it.

Your father pulls Spencer close and lowers his face to whisper in her ear.

By your side, Saralinda goes still.

As for you, you turn away.

You have no idea when your father and his rich, beautiful, young fiancée leave.

Chapter 54. **Saralinda**

In the time following Evangeline's death which followed my mother's death, I speak and move and see and hear almost as if I were normal but afterward all I have bridging from there to here are some moments of disconnected memory. They keep no order when they lurch up inside me, but I present them now in chronological order for the sake of documentation.

. . .

As Caleb and I watch, Caleb's father and Evangeline's stepmother embrace like lovers because they *are* lovers engaged to be married. After they are gone Caleb presses his mouth to my ear and chokes out: *Oh my God, all along it was about Evangeline's money—he made other people kill for him, puppets every last one of them, and us too.* I don't follow all of this then (later Caleb will lay it out for me and Kenyon) but I feel its truth in my marionette bones, and as Caleb shakes, so do I.

· · ·

We wait I don't know how long for Kenyon, who finally exits intensive care slowly small shriveled. We go to her and she says starkly, *They made me leave her. They made me leave Evan. They took her away.* She doesn't cry, she is wooden in my arms. In days to come she will tell me of a dream she has one night about Evangeline disassembled into parts on an autopsy table. *Like a chicken,* she says and gags, and I recall Evangeline throwing up in my bathroom, already dying of poison only we didn't know she would die, we still thought we could win.

· · ·

Two police officers want Kenyon to come with them (something to do with her grandfather) but she throws herself to the floor of the hospital waiting room, chanting *No no, I won't go* and of course Caleb and I do it with her. There is a big scene, I try to hit an officer's knee with Georgia (only I flinch away from following through), and Caleb records everything on his phone. Kenyon tweets and then yells about a lawyer, and people come running, they mill around us but nobody dares touch us because they would have to drag us kicking and screaming, and the police freak out and call for backup— only then suddenly Dr. Lee is there.

Dr. Lee our Head of School is there.

· · ·

Later I discover that Caleb texted Dr. Lee: *Help,* he said, *please come help us.* He sent it like a prayer, like jumping off a cliff into black water. Only it turned out Dr. Lee was already on his way—he saw the video we uploaded from my apartment, he knew my mother was dead, he knew Evangeline was hospitalized, so he came. This stranger— he is not truly a stranger—this stranger came.

. . .

A fragment a quote a poem from someone somewhere: *If you can keep your head when all about you are losing theirs.* It sounds so good, so laudable, but I think it is sort of un- realistic. Because no matter how strong you are sometimes you do lose your head, you have nothing left, you don't know what to do. That's how it is. However if you are lucky there will be somebody who wants to help you. I always thought my mother was that person and Caleb told me that he never ever had that person, and how odd that now a stranger would be that person for him and me and Ken- yon. *This is my watch,* is what Dr. Lee says that night when I try lamely to express something about this.

. . .

Like orphaned ducklings we follow Dr. Lee out of the hospital after he tells the police officers that he is taking responsibility for us and we are all underage and that is that. For now. About Dr. Lee, he is a medium plump man with big ears and (I am afraid) a hairstyle perilously near a comb-over, which is to say you would never pick him out in a crowd and say: *He's the man.* Later I ask Caleb how he knew to text Dr. Lee, and he says he didn't really imagine it would help but he was throwing everything he could think of at the problem and Antoine had liked Dr. Lee.

. . .

I slump in the backseat of a car with Georgia, stuffed between Kenyon and Caleb. Dr. Lee drives the car. In the front passenger seat is a woman who says to call her Shoshanna. It seems as if Caleb already knows her. She asks many questions, mostly Caleb answers and as for me I only remember that she asks me about my blood sugar. Because my world can crack in half, my mother dead Evangeline dead Antoine dead, Kenyon devastated, my love (I call him that in my heart) tortured by his father, my foot hurting, but *still* there is the need—there will *always* be the need—*to test my blood sugar.*

. . .

We end up back at Rockland Academy at Dr. Lee's house and it turns out Shoshanna is his wife and also a social worker and Kenyon and I are going to stay in their twin sons' old room with Caleb down the hall on the living room sofa. Shoshanna says we will think about everything in the morning because now it is late and we should try to sleep. Dr. Lee makes warm milk which I force down but Kenyon and Caleb refuse. Shoshanna Lee sort of stands over me while I test my blood sugar which not uncreepily reminds me of my mother.

. . .

Mrs. Dubois is dead, the green smoothie again. She drank it in front of Evangeline. It might have been that night or it might have been the next day that we learned this, I don't remember. What I remember is Kenyon saying: *My grandfather won't give up so easily, he's not going to kill himself.*

. . .

As one by one days begin to trickle past we do not discuss Dr. Colchester. We also do not discuss Spencer Merriman Song, who is now in Bermuda "mourning" her stepdaughter's death but really we figure she is waiting for Caleb's father to get divorced and for the media attention to die down.

. . .

At night I lie flat on my back in the strange bed in the dorm room that apparently is now where I live, listing the dead and wondering if there was any possible way we could have saved Evangeline, at the very least we should have forced her to throw up that smoothie right away.

Also sometimes I wonder and I know I shouldn't she was crazy but still I wonder if I could have saved my mother—lunged across the room for her at the end—or just been a better daughter beforehand so she didn't hate me and want me dead.

In the other bed Kenyon is usually wakeful too.

Eventually comes gray light outside with an entire day ahead to get through. I often reach out a hand silently and Kenyon grabs it and holds it, then after a while we get up and get ready and finally find Caleb and try to eat some breakfast.

Chapter 55. **Caleb**

Two weeks later the media storm about the parental conspiracy still occupies a respectable portion of the national
news cycle, not to mention social media interest. On Dr.
Lee's advice, you, Saralinda, and Kenyon have refused all
interviews. So has Kenyon's grandfather, Lieutenant Kelly.
Though he hasn't yet been arrested, he awaits a grand jury
summons to testify about Antoine's death, the collapse of
the carriage house, and what he knows about Mrs. Dubois
and Ursula de la Flor. He's lawyered up, and the only communication coming from him so far is "No comment."

It's your father who largely drives the interest in this
story, and you almost feel a tiny bit sorry for Kenyon's
grandfather. He surely believed he was the one with the
power, he was the one in control. He might not fully
understand yet that his true status was Lieutenant Tool.

You don't think much of the man's chances. Your father's
spin won't hang together unless the lieutenant is responsible alongside the dead Mrs. Dubois and Ursula de la

Flor. In a face-off—Kenyon's grandfather's word versus your father's—you know who will win. Your father will have planned meticulously, and so the police lieutenant is going down. You'd bet your life on it.

Your life, which now matters to you. Which is part of *why* your father and his wealthy, lovely fiancée are going to get away with it. If you and Saralinda and Kenyon—and your mother—will be able to live without his interference, you will accept it. You will take his devil's bargain. You will sell your soul.

He is too dangerous an adversary to face. Even in your dreams, you know it. They are not dreams, actually, but nightmares. In one you were facing him, confronting him. You said, *I'm not a monster! You lied to me—there's nothing wrong with me! I never killed that squirrel, or started that fire, I've done nothing! It's all you—you're the monster!* And then, in a small voice, you added: *Why? Why did you do it?*

He didn't answer. Instead he smiled and looked down.

Saralinda was lying in a curled-up heap at his feet, trembling—and he had his foot on her neck.

That day after the nightmare, Saralinda asks you and Kenyon, "Shouldn't knowing the truth give us at least some sense of . . . something? Closure? But I don't know *what* I feel. I mean, I'm angry, but I don't have any place to put my anger. I'm sad, and I'm—I don't know what."

She makes fists in her lap. "I'm still scared. Are you guys scared? Even if Dr. Lee and Shoshanna become my guardians for the next two years, well—I can't imagine not still being scared."

You think of her in that heap on the ground with your father's foot on her neck.

Kenyon shrugs in response. It's rare for her to speak these days. But yes, she's afraid too. It's written all over her. She startles at every sound, her nostrils flaring. Also, she reaches constantly for her phone, compulsively checking Twitter and Facebook and Tumblr, though the feeds are often as vile as she once predicted they would be.

You say at last, "I've always lived scared. My mother too. You just do it."

"Um," says Saralinda, frowning.

"The point is that we get to live at all," you say urgently. "Right?"

"Only I don't actually want to," Saralinda says quietly.

"What? You don't want to *live*?" Panic fills you. She can't—

She looks directly into your eyes. "No," she says. "I mean that I don't want to live *scared*." She leans forward. "Caleb? Wouldn't you rather *do* something?"

You catch your breath.

There it is, suddenly. Your choice. To go on the way you always have, frightened, but masking it as well as you can.

Or to fight . . . which you now realize you never did before you met her.

And Antoine. And Evangeline. And Kenyon.

For a very long, very tempting moment you struggle. You imagine grabbing Saralinda by the shoulders, shaking her, yelling into her face: *You don't understand! You don't know him like I do! We can't do anything! He's smarter than us! He'll crush us! He'll crush you! But if we crawl away and hide, he might leave us alone. He'll torture somebody else, if we're lucky. If we don't make him mad.*

You swallow hard. You breathe.

You do not say those things.

"Do you have any ideas?" you say instead, and you are surprised at how steady your voice is.

Saralinda shakes her head and nods at the same time. "Well, couldn't we brainstorm? One idea I had, just to start, is that we talk to Kenyon's grandfather. Maybe he'd be willing to help us now. Join forces. Kenyon? Do you think he might?"

Kenyon is staring out the window. You aren't even certain she was paying attention just now. Without turning, she says, "It's an idea."

"So you'd try?" Saralinda prompts. "Because you'd have to be the one to go see him. You're family."

"Let me think about it, okay?"

You're relieved at the delay—which makes you angry.

At yourself. "Tell us tomorrow, Kenyon," you say. "Meanwhile, we can think about other options."

Kenyon doesn't answer. Without saying good-bye, she gets up and walks out. This is normal for her these days. Saralinda scrambles to her feet, nods at you, and heads after her.

This too is normal these days.

You bury your head in your hands for a minute, thinking about your father and what you have just implicitly promised.

You look over at the book you recently took out of the school library. It's *Dracula*.

You will read another chapter and then you will think of options, of ideas that you can run by Saralinda. You will.

You will, you will.

Chapter 56. **Saralinda**

Once upon a time, I wanted to live in a dorm room at Rockland Academy with Kenyon as my roommate. Also I wanted a boyfriend even though I didn't know then who I wanted it to be. I wanted friends too and badly, and I wanted to live a regular teenager life. Finally I wanted freedom from my overprotective mom. I believed that all these things were out of my reach, but I dreamed about them and schemed about how I might get them if I was clever and if my mother and my obstructionist fairy godmother relented.

That Saralinda is gone now and I miss her—she was vivid in a way that I am not anymore. The strange thing is that the Saralinda I am now has everything the old Saralinda dreamed of except the boyfriend and normalcy. Regarding the boyfriend, I am emotionally sort of numb these days except for being scared and wanting Caleb and Kenyon close by. I am uneasy when they are not there.

Also sometimes I am angry and then I feel more like

myself. The old Saralinda was angry although she repressed it a lot.

At the same time I am truly grateful for what I do have because it is all precious—life is precious, breath is precious, friends are precious, love is precious and so is freedom. But the price has been high, and I don't think the Saralinda I used to be would have chosen to pay that price.

If she'd had any choice which she didn't.

I chalk it all up to my fairy godmother, who it turned out was obstructionist in more bizarre ways than I could ever have imagined. Not that I ever believed in her except that in a funny double-think way maybe I did. At this point I would count her as among the dead. Not that I am counting.

That is a lie. I do count.

Antoine has been dead for twenty-five days.

Evangeline has been dead for twenty-three days.

So has my mother. So has Mrs. Dubois.

I am alive and an orphan, a Dickensian thing to be. My circumstances are better than Dickensian orphans, Dr. Lee will be assigned by the court to be my guardian along with his wife. They volunteered and they are kind to me and it was good of them, I am grateful.

Plus Georgia is with me.

These things are not nothing.

Fear is supposed to fade over time and maybe that will

happen or maybe I will get used to living with it like Caleb has. Or maybe we really will think of something we can do. I go in and out of believing that is possible.

For Evangeline's eighteenth birthday I buy Cheetos, and at midnight in our dorm room the three of us eat them. I carefully measure my insulin to account for it. Kenyon gets hysterical crying and laughing uncontrollably and the girl in the room next door bangs on the wall to get her to shut up but at first Kenyon just can't.

She also says she absolutely cannot talk to her grandfather, not yet anyway, and I cannot talk her into it, it is frustrating but how can I push her?

Dead ends everywhere.

Chapter 57. **Caleb**

You go with your mother to visit her divorce lawyer in a Midtown high-rise. The lawyer comes out to greet her with a wide smile and both hands outstretched.

"Good morning, Veronica. Lots of boring paperwork, but then we'll be done. Let's get right to it, shall we?"

Your mother squeezes your arm and then takes his, with a half-doubtful, half-happy look over her shoulder at you. As they walk down the hall, you hear the lawyer say, "This may be the best divorce settlement I've ever negotiated. It was certainly the fastest and easiest. Your soon-to-be-ex-husband said yes to almost everything."

You accept coffee from the receptionist, and slump into a corner chair of the waiting area.

You're happy for your mother. Really you are. Or at least, you would be if it were possible to be happy. If you weren't so conscious of the price paid for your mother's freedom.

You're not sure how much your mother herself understands. You haven't discussed Evangeline with her. There's no point in burdening her; she's not responsible for what happened. That she is benefitting is merely a byproduct.

These last weeks, your mother has been super-cautious about what she says. She practically hasn't breathed without asking her lawyer first. You get it. She wants what is happening. Wants a life. She says she might try for art school, her dream when she was your age.

One thing's for sure, though: Your father is not being generous with Veronica for the sake of generosity. Or because he will soon have his new wife's money. He surely has other reasons. Are you being bribed, you wonder. Bribed with the possibility of freedom? Or are you being lulled into complacency?

Your mother said something the other day. A little thing, not important, yet annoyingly, it keeps drifting back into your mind. It happened after your mother showed you your father's engagement announcement. You looked at the side-by-side pictures, your father and Spencer Merriman Song. "So?" you asked. And your mother said, "It's just . . . poor girl. She has no idea what her life will be like."

A memory comes to you of your mother and father. It's the kind of thing you never let yourself remember, before. In the memory, she begs him to let her eat a hard-boiled egg from the refrigerator. He says no. He says she must wait until morning because she has eaten enough that day and she mustn't get fat.

The refrigerator wasn't locked or anything. But your mother had retreated, hungry.

Of course, Veronica was a penniless immigrant, with no green card and no money. Spencer Merriman Song is an entirely different sort of person. Also she is a murderer. In short, she's not anybody's poor girl, and your mother is—she's wrong.

You slump down deeper in your chair and take out your phone. You have a video to watch: your father's interview with Monica Baker from FOX News, from last night. Self-assigned homework. Maybe there will be something in there, a clue of some kind, that will help you figure out how to trap him.

At first you watch with the volume off, noting the play of expression on your father's flexible face. Sadness, regret, dismay, and from time to time, guilt—a nice touch. It's best to know what he's saying, though, so you plug in your headphones.

MONICA BAKER: I'm here in the studio with Dr. Caleb Colchester, the psychiatrist, mental health expert, and distinguished author. Dr. Colchester is a critical piece of this strange story we're all following with such interest and horror, about two mothers and a grandfather who schemed together to murder their own teenage children. They suc-ceeded in killing two seventeen-year-olds before their plot was ultimately revealed about a week ago—then two of the parents committed suicide—

YOUR FATHER: Actually, Monica, it's been two weeks. Two very long weeks, and believe me, I've counted every day, every hour.

MONICA BAKER: Yes, two weeks. I apologize. Now, the third parent, Lieutenant Stewart Kelly of the New York State Police—actually a grandfather—is suspended from his job and under investigation. Dr. Colchester, this conspiracy first formed in your very own office, during a group therapy session. Can you tell us more about what happened? Give us some background?

YOUR FATHER: I certainly can, although it's difficult for me, Monica, because I have to reveal how, with all my education and experience, I somehow reached my late forties still capable of being very badly deluded by my own patients. I understood the rage these people felt against their children. But I never dreamed they would do anything about it, and I'm afraid my group therapy session was key to pushing them over that line.

MONICA BAKER: There's an element of mental illness involved, surely?

YOUR FATHER: Yes, there is. But I have to take personal responsibility too, Monica. Not only did I initiate this parents' group, but my motivation for it was not—well, I had more than one motive in starting the group. I wasn't paying the attention that I should have.

MONICA BAKER: Interesting. Go on. When you imply you were distracted, that has to do with Mrs. Spencer Song, the stepmother of the young victim Evangeline Song, correct? By the way, if the name Song sounds familiar to our viewers, I should mention that Mrs. Song's husband and Evangeline's father was the late real estate developer Kevin Song. I should also mention that Mrs. Song is not suspected of being involved in the conspiracy. She is in seclusion as she mourns her stepdaughter, I understand. That's all correct, Dr. Colchester?

YOUR FATHER: Yes. Yes, it is. Spencer is away. But before I talk any more about her, I should provide some background. This goes to my marriage. My wife, Veronica—she's not a bad person. But at the time I met Spencer, my wife was depressed and dependent on medication, and our marriage hadn't been a real one for many years. Possibly the worst part of that was how it affected our son, Caleb. He withdrew from both of us. He became—to be blunt—a sullen, isolated teenager with bad grades, no ambition, and zero interest in figuring out his future.

MONICA BAKER: In short, a fairly typical teenage boy?

YOUR FATHER: That's a valid point, Monica. But wouldn't you find parenting such a child to be frustrating? Okay, see, you're nodding. Well, so did I, and so did Veronica. I believe he contributed to her clinical depression. From childhood, our son had a—a very disturbing pattern of strange and violent behavior. I won't go into detail, but there were some serious incidents that gave rise to—to concern. There were small animals involved.

MONICA BAKER: Oh! Oh, that's terrible. But at the same time, this is the boy who saved the lives of his four friends in the carriage house collapse, and who videotaped the important evidence against one of the mothers in the case, isn't that right?

YOUR FATHER: At this point, I have only pride in him. He has matured. But last spring, when I met Mrs. Song, I was seriously worried.

MONICA BAKER: I can understand that.

YOUR FATHER: It all began at a Rockland Academy fund-raising dinner, which as usual I attended without my wife. By chance, I sat next to Mrs. Song.

380

MONICA BAKER: (Leans forward. Nods.)

YOUR FATHER: We fell into an intimate conversation. Spencer manifested a sadness and vulnerability that found an immediate echo in myself. She confided in me—people do tend to do that, Monica—that although she missed her husband, her unhappiness each day was now rooted in her difficult relationship with her stepdaughter, Evangeline.

MONICA BAKER: To remind our viewers, that's Evangeline Song, seventeen, who was poisoned by one of the other parents, Mrs. Gabrielle Dubois. The coroner has released autopsy reports on both Evangeline and Gabrielle Dubois. They both drank—Gabrielle Dubois on purpose, and Evangeline because she was murdered—a green smoothie. The recipe contained avocado, spinach, kale, cucumber, peach, apple, and last but not least, a few leaves of deadly nightshade. I did my research, and it is seriously toxic stuff, which can easily be grown in an ordinary garden. That's very frightening! Personally? I may never drink a kale smoothie again.

YOUR FATHER: Nor will I.

MONICA BAKER: Another point that I should make clear on

behalf of our viewers: Gabrielle Dubois was the mother of the very first victim, Antoine Dubois, whose car was allegedly sabotaged by Lieutenant Kelly. So, Dr. Colchester, the idea of the conspiracy was that the parents would take care of killing each other's children?

YOUR FATHER: That's what they came up with, yes. That idea—I would assume—came to them after their first attempt to kill all of our children, together, failed.

MONICA BAKER: That would be the carriage house implosion.

YOUR FATHER: Yes. I understand that Rockland Academy has managed to find videotape of the three accused parents on the roof.

MONICA BAKER: My god! Really? That's news—I didn't know that! But there's a lot here, and if our viewers are anything like me, they'll need a scorecard to keep track of this story! Anyway, please go on, Dr. Colchester. So you met Mrs. Song, and she confided in you about her relationship with her stepdaughter, Evangeline?

YOUR FATHER: Yes. The relationship was not good. Spencer felt that Evangeline hated her for having married Kevin.

For her part, Evangeline was constantly, viciously mean to Spencer. I'm sorry to speak ill of Evangeline. She's a victim here, an intelligent young woman who should have had a long and useful life. Young people's characters and personalities are very much in flux during their teen years—we discussed that very point, didn't we? About my son. So I'm sure that in time Evangeline would have grown into maturity and kindness. But the Evangeline that Spencer lived with had not reached that point, and the little—the very little—that Spencer told me upon our first meeting pressed a chord of sympathy deep inside me. I told her about my son. Then I went home to my wife.

Only I couldn't stop thinking about Spencer. So, while not letting myself be fully aware of my motives, I formed the idea of the parents' support therapy group. From the parents and perspective parents at Rockland Academy, I chose three others who it seemed to me—and it's my job to be good at reading people—were concerned for various reasons about their teenagers. But my true motive was to invite Mrs. Song, so that I could see her again.

MONICA BAKER: So the conspiracy came together somehow during these meetings?

YOUR FATHER: Yes, that is now clear. Let me explain. The group met a few times, in the summer before the new school year began. I provided my therapeutic services free of charge, telling them that we were on equal ground and that we would help and support one another. But I was distracted by Spencer's presence. I didn't pay enough attention to the character and psychology of the other parents. Then, at our final session, all five of us discussed how it would be if our children were to die. We—we laughed. To my shame, I have to admit that it all felt tremendously freeing. In my case, there would be no worry about the small animals my son killed in his youth and what that might mean about him. No worry about what I would do when he was inevitably expelled from school. And I would no longer secretly blame him for the failure of my marriage.

MONICA BAKER: I am—I'm shocked! And yet—and yet—

YOUR FATHER: I know what you're thinking, Monica. This is the dirty little secret of most or maybe all parents, isn't it? We love our children, we would never see them hurt. But sometimes, in times of deep frustration—and we all have those times—we think: What if? What if they were just—gone?

MONICA BAKER: Oh, my.

YOUR FATHER: You have children, right?

MONICA BAKER: (Embarrassed laughter.) Twin boys who are eleven, and a daughter who's fourteen. So, uh. Um. I absolutely adore them. Then what happened?

YOUR FATHER: That was that, or so I thought. I disbanded the group, and Spencer and I—we began to get to know each other better. Very soon I realized that the time had come to ask my wife for a divorce. Which she has agreed to, by the way. Veronica and I are parting on very amicable terms, and in fact, the divorce will be final in a few days.

But what I did not know was that the other three parents were continuing to meet. You mentioned mental illness before, Monica. They believed that Spencer and I, even though we were not participating explicitly, would be glad if they took care of our children for us. I wouldn't be surprised if they deluded themselves into thinking that I actually said as much. Delusions are so powerful.

MONICA BAKER: It's all extraordinary.

YOUR FATHER: It's insane, Monica. Let's say that flat out. Also, it would take insanity for anyone to think they could get away with something like this! It's unbelievable!

MONICA BAKER: I have to agree! I was saying to my husband, okay, so one parent might think they could get away with killing their kid, but how could three people possibly think they could do it together? They'd have to be out of their minds.

YOUR FATHER: Which they were. But my point is that there's blood on my hands morally, Monica. I knew nothing about what was going on—but there is a degree of moral responsibility because I allowed them the fantasy.

MONICA BAKER: Yes. I understand how you feel. Sadly—because there is so much more we could explore here—our time is about up. We'll continue to follow developments here at the station for our viewers, and we certainly appreciate your coming to talk with us today, Dr. Colchester. Do you have any last comments?

YOUR FATHER: Thank you, Monica. May I say something directly to my son? He won't talk to me in person or on the phone these days.

MONICA BAKER: Oh! Of course.

YOUR FATHER: Caleb? If you're out there, if you're watching, I love you. I am sorry. We've messed up here—I messed up, I understand that—and your friends are dead. But I hope that someday, when your wounds and mine have had time to heal, that you'll find yourself open to talking. That we can find each other again, and resume our relationship.

The interview ends with a close-up shot of your father's face, pleading. Then Monica Baker reaches out and puts her hand on his.

We'll never get him, you think. *Never.*

Chapter 58. **Saralinda**

When Antoine has been dead for thirty-three days and Evangeline (and my mother and Antoine's mother) have been dead for thirty-one, Georgia and I arrive a few minutes tardy for an early morning appointment in Dr. Lee's office. Generally I am prompt but in this case I wish I could be so late that I would never get there. I don't understand why Dr. Lee is even permitting this meeting to happen, but he is *my* guardian and not Caleb's. Caleb agreed to come, he said it was better to find out what the hell his father wants—and that maybe if we watched and listened carefully, his father would let slip something that we can use against him.

Caleb has taken to heart this idea of mine that we can somehow prevail, so I don't quite dare to tell him that deep inside I don't think there's a way. Our brainstorming so far has come to nothing, and Kenyon, well, if I didn't know better I would think she was avoiding me, I have not been able to have a real conversation with her.

Caleb is already inside Dr. Lee's office and seated.

Caleb's father is there already too. Dr. Colchester has on jeans and boots and a pale yellow button-down shirt and over it a leather jacket which is too young for him in my opinion. He arches his brows in surprise at me and for my part I do not give him the finger which showcases my growth in maturity and self-control. Or fear?

"Dennis?" says Dr. Colchester to Dr. Lee. "I thought you were mediating a meeting between my son and me."

"Caleb asked for Saralinda to be here."

"I wish you had told me in advance."

Dr. Lee raises his brows. "Would you not have come? Do you mind?"

"Oh, no. Of course not."

"Good." Dr. Lee nods professionally.

I take my seat and glance at Caleb and my stomach shrivels, because if you start with how his face looks when he so much as thinks about his father, well it is ten times worse in his father's presence.

By the way, Caleb is no longer Caleb, he is going to choose a new first name and take his mother's last name. I approve completely, he should not have the same name as his father or be "junior." But until he does pick a name I don't know what else to call him.

My seat is between Caleb and Dr. Lee and directly across from Dr. Colchester. I keep Georgia ready in my right hand so that I can stand up and walk out—stand-and-walk-out is an option that you should always keep available according to Shoshanna.

"Well, Caleb," says Dr. Colchester. "I'm glad you're willing to talk at least." He smiles at me. "You look good, Saralinda. I like the short hair, and that is a very pretty top." He checks out my breasts and Dr. Lee breathes in sharply which tells me he notices and does not like it one bit. That encourages me, and also makes me think that Dr. Colchester might be trying to offend me into leaving Caleb here without my support. So I do not respond and Georgia and I do not walk out.

Caleb speaks through gritted teeth (he noticed the look at my breasts as well, which is also exactly what his father intended): "Why did you want to see me?"

Dr. Colchester smiles charmingly. "I'd like you to spend a couple of weeks this summer with Spencer and me. We're renting a place in Provence. Spencer would like to get to know you."

I imagine Caleb hanging upside down in a giant cocoon from a tree in the French countryside. Yes I have stolen this image from *The Hobbit*.

"No, thank you," Caleb says.

"What if we invited Saralinda too? Spencer suggested that also."

I choke, and Dr. Lee says quickly, "Saralinda will be

attending summer school here on campus."

This is the first I have heard of it but I am not opposed.

Dr. Colchester puts one booted ankle on his knee. "Caleb, I expected you to say no, but I hope you'll reconsider. Spencer didn't just ask me to invite you, she asked me to come here and talk to you in person. It means that much to her, to heal this breach."

I sneak a look at Dr. Lee to try to gauge what he makes of all this but he is checking the time on his phone, he is a busy man.

"It's strange," Caleb says. "You paying attention to what the woman in your life wants."

"Stop." Dr. Colchester raises a hand. "Be fair. Your mother and I may have made a mess of our marriage, but I'm not a misogynist. My marital problems with your mother have nothing to do with Spencer. You know your mother was an illegal immigrant. She lied to me about that when we were dating. Her motive for marrying me was to get a green card. She got pregnant and—"

"That's *your* story, but she says—"

"Nevertheless, I behaved well. I supported your mother for eighteen years and never asked her to earn a dime. I have been generous with her alimony. Despite your lack of respect toward me over the years, including right now, I'm still willing to pay for your college—assuming you can get accepted somewhere—just like I'm paying your tuition here at Rockland. But your comments on my relationship with Spencer are not welcome."

"But here you are inviting me to come be a witness to that relationship."

"Not my idea. It's Spencer who asked me—" Rage and frustration flicker over Dr. Colchester's face. He looks at Dr. Lee. "Spencer wants peace. And she doesn't know my son, so . . ." He turns to Caleb. "Let's discuss this logically. Is there anything you want? Because this means a lot to Spencer."

Is Dr. Colchester trying to *bribe* Caleb? But there is no way Caleb will agree and why Dr. Colchester is still sitting there trying is beyond me.

"Yes," Caleb says. "There is. I want you to tell the truth. But I don't suppose you will."

"What truth is that?" says Dr. Colchester with a patient smile.

Caleb leans forward. "That there's nothing wrong with me. That you—that you . . ." He draws in a breath. "That you made it all up, about me—" He breaks off and I think he won't go on but then he does and it is maybe the bravest thing I have ever seen with my own eyes. "About me having psychological problems." He looks straight at his father. "There is nothing wrong with me." Only then his voice goes up a little at the end like it's a question, and I wince.

I want more than anything to go to him, to put my arms around him.

I stay where I am this is not about me.

His father smiles understandingly. "I know that you want and need to believe that, son."

Inside I am dying, why does Caleb need *anything* from this man in order to believe in himself, he will never get the truth from him I know this, and I turn to Dr. Lee hoping he will end this—*please end this!*—only again he is looking at the time—

Which is when there's a very loud knock and Dr. Lee calls, "Come in!" and the door opens—Kenyon—

Followed by Spencer Merriman Song, dressed all in soft white cashmere.

Behind her, dressed to match, is Evangeline.

Chapter 59. **Caleb**

You freeze. You wonder if you're hallucinating or dreaming or if there really might be such a thing as ghosts—but Evangeline looks alive. Her skin glows, her eyes gleam, her lips curve.

Dr. Lee looks at her calmly.

Your father's mouth opens and closes, opens and closes.

Evangeline puts her palms together. "Namaste," she says, looking directly at your father. "Motherfucker."

You have no thoughts, you have no words, but a knot dissolves inside you; a knot so deeply located that you had believed it was permanent.

Kenyon runs to Saralinda and hugs her. "Sorry, you guys." Kenyon turns to include you. "It had to be a secret until after Evangeline turned eighteen. She's been with Spencer in Bermuda this whole time."

"The rumors of my death were greatly exaggerated. I didn't drink all *that* much of the smoothie," Evangeline says merrily.

You want your father's expression on permanent loop in your memory.

Spencer says, softly, "Caleb?" Automatically you look at her, but she doesn't mean you. Your father half rises from his seat but she stops him with a lifted hand.

"Stay there."

He does. "Spencer. Please. I don't know what they've made you think—"

"Nobody made me think anything. Believe it or not, I'm capable of thinking for myself." Her mouth twists in self-mockery. "When I decide to."

"Of course you're intelligent, my darling, but—"

Again Spencer lifts her hand. This time, it's to work off her engagement ring. It hits your father mid-chest. He begins again: "But you can't possibly think that I had anything to do with this, I can't be responsible for what three insane people and several traumatized kids—understandably traumatized, of course . . . Besides, the police have cleared me of any involvement . . ."

Spencer isn't listening. She holds out her arms to Evangeline. They embrace, clinging to each other, rocking for several seconds. Spencer whispers, "Text you later."

"Yes," says Evangeline. "Love you."

"Love *you*."

Then Spencer is gone.

Your father is left surrounded by Dr. Lee, Kenyon, Evangeline, Saralinda, and you.

"Well." Dr. Lee holds up his phone. "Look at the time. I'll have to ask you to leave, Dr. Colchester. We have a busy day ahead. For one thing, Evangeline has a lot of school-work to catch up on."

"Actually not," says Evangeline chattily. "I kept up from Bermuda. All those online syllabuses come in handy."

"You haven't changed," Kenyon remarks. "Still smug."

"Is that a problem?"

"Not even slightly."

They beam at each other.

Your exhilaration is fading fast. You watch your father. You have never seen him defeated before. You can't believe it will last. He grips the arms on either side of his chair, knuckles compressing and releasing. His expression is a mask of calm, with a slight smile in the eyes. This is the same expression from your nightmare, the one with Saralinda's neck under his foot.

Dr. Lee starts to say something else about the time. Your father interrupts. He looks around the room, eyes resting one by one on each of you. He ends with Dr. Lee.

"I am a bad enemy to make."

"I am aware," says Dr. Lee quietly.

So are you.

But Evangeline chuckles. "Don't tell me. Let me guess. Your next line is going to be: *This isn't over?*"

Kenyon laughs.

You don't. Neither does Dr. Lee, and neither does Saralinda.

Saralinda. Dr. Lee. Evangeline and Kenyon, miraculously reunited. Others too. Your mother. Dr. Lee's wife, who has been so good to Saralinda. And Spencer.

Targets. All of them.

Your father smiles pleasantly. "You're right," he says mildly to Evangeline. "One should resist the temptation of melodrama. My next line is: *Good-bye for now.*"

He starts to get up—

There is no decision to make. There is just one thing you can do to save them all forever, and this one moment in which to do it. You *can* do it. Maybe you aren't Mr. Hyde, maybe Saralinda is right. But you are after all your father's son.

You are going to make damn well sure that nobody is in his power, ever again.

You launch yourself across the room at his throat.

Chapter 60. **Saralinda**

I'm not sure how I know what Caleb intends, but I am
watching him and because he is my friend he can't be allowed to kill anyone, even or maybe especially his father.
It is not really a decision as there is no time. Caleb doesn't
get to his father—because I get there first.

Georgia and I get there first.

What happens is this, I jump up and my equally good
foot twists and I plummet forward toward Dr. Colchester,
who is positioned opposite me. Georgia flies out horizon-
tally as I grip her. I scream not so much because I am falling (which frankly isn't unusual) but because of what is
happening with Georgia.

As I fall I flail for a grip on my cane and press Georgia's
mechanism, twice.

Chapter 61. **Caleb**

Four inches of sharp steel slice through your father's wind-pipe.

Chapter 62. **Saralinda**

Dr. Colchester lies on the floor with his hands on Georgia and his eyes wide. He does not utter a word because Georgia's blade has severed his trachea, the whole function of which is to conduct air to the lungs. We need air to speak we need air to breathe we need air to live.

Dr. Colchester has both hands on Georgia. Tentatively he pulls at her then stops.

As for me I am on the floor and so is my Caleb. I roll away I touch my throat, oh the human throat is delicate and from mine come sobs gasps screams. I hear them, I look wildly around—Kenyon Evangeline Dr. Lee. And Caleb.

What have I done I did it, so it is done.

Caleb is on his knees now.

His father pulls feebly at Georgia again.

Nobody goes to help him.

Bilbo and Frodo had Sting for a sword but as for me I have Georgia.

They say that when a person is dying her life flashes be-fore her eyes. As Caleb's father dies Georgia's life flashes before mine. I was twelve and out alone which was a rare thing, and the sign on the basement store in the West Vil-lage said HAND-CARVED CANES and GOING OUT OF BUSI-NESS. Bells tinkled sweetly as I entered, and inside a man short like a hobbit, short like me, whittled a wooden cane with a small sharp tool. He smiled and so did I, we were friends that very instant. We drank tea and talked about life and I told him how scared I was sometimes, and he touched my ugly metal cane and said, "Saralinda, it would give me great pleasure if you would accept a gift. It has a secret, which I know you won't use unless you have to. But you will always know that it is there."

I know as I sob on the floor of Dr. Lee's office that I am saying good-bye to Georgia forever, I will not be allowed to keep her after this. I will have to make my own feeling of safety.

I put a hand over my mouth to stop sobbing.

Dr. Lee has a hand over his mouth like me.

"Holy crap," Kenyon says.

Evangeline inhales.

Caleb is on his feet. He says to his father very calmly, "You are the defective one. You are the monster." This time there is no question mark in his voice.

His father's face contorts. He is not dead quite yet and

he transfers his gaze from his son to me for a bare instant and there is shock disbelief hate and the very beginning of fear in his face, then he looks back at his son and opens his mouth one last time.

But he cannot lie to his son anymore, because I Saralinda that would be me I have taken his voice.

Chapter 63. **Caleb**

After your father dies, Dr. Lee punches in 911 on his phone. He says, "I'm calling to report an accident."

Chapter 64. **Saralinda**

Not-sorry-not-sorry-not-sorry sounds the gong in my head. I don't know I don't know.

Caleb puts his arms around me tight, his body heaves, and I hold him and Kenyon and Evangeline, we are in a huddle together. I say Evangeline's name she is alive! I am alive too, relief and fear, fear still, what have I done what have I done.

My friends are safe now forever. "I will go to jail," I say bravely but Dr. Lee interrupts.

"You are not going to jail, Saralinda. You're a minor. It was an accident."

"But—"

"Sit down and shut up. All four of you."

We do that. Dr. Lee says he will talk to the police first and explain how this terrible accident happened. He is so calm that when he asks me about Georgia and how long I have had her and how her mechanism works, I answer calmly too, and he nods. "So you fell and you struck the mechanism as you fell. Is that right?"

"Yes," I say. "That's true." It is.

"Repeat it."

I repeat it.

"That's what you say to the police," Dr. Lee tells me, and "Just like that, SL," Kenyon says, and "Exactly, Saralinda," Evangeline (Evangeline!) says. Caleb says nothing, he holds my hand too tightly, and I get it what Dr. Lee is saying. It doesn't matter what I was thinking only what I *did*, and now I am not sure of that. Did I *aim*? I was falling, it was quick, I wanted to get between Caleb and his father.

I fell and hit Georgia's mechanism and Georgia hit Dr. Colchester.

The police come. Detectives. It turns out that when there are four eyewitnesses to an accident including someone like Dr. Lee, it is not like on TV where they put the perp (me) in a small room and make her (me) tell the story over and over while they play good cop bad cop. They do not care what I was thinking as I fell or before I fell. However I offer to go to jail (I don't mean to say it, it comes out) and the detectives look at me and one of them says, "Just stay in school."

That said, I am in some trouble because guilty of criminal possession of a concealed weapon. "You'll be charged as a minor," the detective says to me without raising his head, he is filling out a form. "You and your guardian will get a summons within thirty days."

I do not get to say good-bye to Georgia, they take her away in a plastic bag.

At one point I hear a detective call Dr. Colchester *that guy*. There is a tone in his voice which makes me think about Kenyon's grandfather, Lieutenant Kelly, and that maybe these detectives are not so very unhappy to see Dr. Colchester dead and maybe they were careful not to ask too many questions about what happened. This is a theory which I have which is mine.

It is a long day but finally, finally that night the four of us are alone in the room that I share with Kenyon.

"How how *how*?" I say to Evangeline.

She and Kenyon settle together on my bunk which is the lower one. They are entwined. I sit on the floor and Caleb takes the desk chair and reverses it to lean on the back with both arms, he does not sit with me. I try not to feel rejected—he hugged me he held my hand, maybe he doesn't love-love me but he does love me, I killed his father it is complicated I get it. It is complicated for me too, I killed his father my mother is dead. I hug my knees. It would be easy to cry, I didn't earlier today and I won't now. Later I will keep some lucky therapist (who is not a sociopathic manipulator) in business for years, maybe it will be Shoshanna.

Evangeline says, "I was so out of it at the hospital, I didn't know anything, but Kenyon talked to Spencer and then Spencer . . . God, you guys." She raises her hands with her palms out. "I have never been so wrong about a person. She's—you know, I even think she did love my father. She told me she has kind of a father complex and likes older men."

There is a tiny silence and I think of Dr. Colchester.

"She wouldn't *let* Evan die," Kenyon says. "She got more doctors in that ICU room than clowns in a clown car. Then somebody had a brainstorm about deadly nightshade, and they hauled Evan off to a private room, and *that* was when I *really* talked to Spencer. About your father." She glances at Caleb.

"She believed you?" Caleb asks. "She took your word?"

"No. But she said she didn't want to take any risks with Evan, so even though Evan was starting to recover, she arranged for it to look like she was dead. What a crazy idea, right? I don't know how she got them all to go along with it—"

"Those big eyes of hers. Plus heavy bribes about the new hospital wing," Evangeline puts in.

"—but she made it happen," Kenyon finishes. "The hospital issued a fake death certificate. The people that knew were asked to keep it secret. Then she whisked Evan to Bermuda."

"Where she didn't let me out of her sight until my birthday. We shared a room. Caleb, I listened in on her phone calls with your father. It—it was pretty painful for her as she figured out how she'd been manipulated. Also, she liked Antoine's mother." Evangeline looks guiltily at me. "Not so much your mother, though, SL."

I shrug like it doesn't matter although strangely it does. My mother never was good at making friends, I believe she was lonely her whole life except for me. It is sad along with depressing and sickening, like I said I will be in therapy for decades there is a lot to cover.

One thing I am convinced about however—I will always have friends especially these particular three friends (gratitude amazement awe).

That is when I realize that I am not afraid anymore. I am many things, but not afraid.

Thank you, Georgia.

We fill Evangeline in on everything that happened when we thought she was dead, and she tells us more about Bermuda and Spencer, and after a while we are all yawning even me even though I do not think I could possibly sleep no matter how tired. Caleb gets up, and I blurt, "Don't go!"

He looks back at me hesitating.

"Or we should both go, you and me," I say, and cringe inside because it sounds like I mean you-know-what when

I was only thinking of Kenyon and Evangeline, who have not been alone yet.

"Can't everybody stay here?" Evangeline asks. "All four of us, just for tonight?"

"But don't you two—" I start.

"There'll be time," Kenyon says. "Evan's right. I want all of us to stay here. So we can hear each other breathe."

It is exactly what I want too. I look at Caleb.

"Okay," Caleb says.

Then the lights are off except for a tiny night-light that Kenyon and I don't normally use but Caleb turns on. Evangeline and Kenyon snuggle together in the upper bunk and I lie in my own while Caleb stretches out on the floor beside me with a pillow and blanket.

We are silent and maybe Evangeline and Kenyon sleep, and after I don't know how long I reach out and touch Caleb. He takes my hand. We lie hand in hand for what seems like years before I slip down to the floor next to him. I reach out.

He puts his arms around me he buries his face in my shoulder his whole body shakes. I hold him and hold him while he cries and he holds me and holds me while I cry too.

There are times when there is no need to say anything, he is warm he is alive so am I, it is enough it is everything.

Chapter 65. **Caleb**

Weeks later, in early December, the four of you are on the train heading to Coney Island. The plan is to visit Johanna and find Marcial and Troy. You and Saralinda sit behind Kenyon and Evangeline, who have a new MacBook for Johanna.

This time, you are not dressed like a middle-aged woman, and Saralinda is not in disguise as a child.

This should happen in private, but if you wait you'll lose your nerve as you have so many times. You start to reach for her hand—

She says, "Caleb?"

Maybe kissing her on the subway isn't the right thing to do after all.

"What is it?" you say.

She looks up at you. "Remember when the carriage house roof caved in? I mean, I know you do. It's not like any of us could forget."

You nod. "Yeah."

"Well, do you also remember that you saved my cane for me?"

You go still. So much happened that day, and in the days after. You actually *had* forgotten this part. But it's true—you dug her cane out of the rubble and brought it to the hospital and restored it to Saralinda.

"I never said thank you," Saralinda says. "I meant to, but then everything happened and I didn't do it."

You are in shock, a little, as you think it over. The cane. You gave her back the cane. And if you hadn't—

"Thank you," she says. "This comes late, but my cane—Georgia—meant a lot to me."

You look down into her face and she looks up into yours.

If her cane had remained buried in the rubble.

"She meant a lot to me too," you say at last. "As it turned out."

Saralinda nods.

You put your hand on her cheek.

This is the right moment after all.

Only—you have never kissed a girl before. What if you do it wrong?

Instead of kissing her, you blurt, "I've decided on my new name. Want to know what it is?"

Chapter 66. **Saralinda**

I am so finished with hoping for things if I can do something about getting them.

"Tell me later," I say.

I put my hands up and pull his face down to mine.

I kiss him.

Sometimes in life you want something and you get it but it turns out not to be what you thought. This is not like that.

This is the opposite of that.

Epilogue

Head of School Dr. Dennis Y. Lee is almost in bed when a light flickers on over in the pool house. It lasts only momentarily but he's not fooled. "Skinny-dippers," he says to his wife, and grabs his pants. "Again."

Shoshanna laughs.

As Dennis crosses the quad, the full moon glows softly on new, white, pure snow. The semester ends tomorrow. He can't wait for the break; it's been a rough few months, worse even than his first year of teaching. He could laugh at his naïve younger self; he'd thought responsibility lay heavy *then*.

The surface of the Olympic-sized pool—a gift from alumni—lies undisturbed. Dennis unerringly follows the sound of soft voices into the spa room. He directs the beam of his cell phone flashlight at the hot tub. "You're busted," he says casually.

Lit candles flicker in a row on the perimeter of the hot tub. One kid is in the water, immersed to his shoulders. Three others, all girls, kneel fully dressed outside.

Of course it's those four.

"Hi," he says. "What are you up to? Are the candles necessary?"

"Hi, yes, I'm sorry, they are," Saralinda says.

"We're doing a renaming ceremony," Kenyon says.

Dennis raises his brows. "Usually that happens at City Hall."

"We know," says Evangeline. "He'll do that too. Listen, can't you pretend not to have seen us?"

The boy starts to get out of the tub. "No, we'll leave. Sorry."

Dennis sighs. "Stop. Okay, I'm not here. I was never here." He owes them, after all. And how deeply satisfying it is to see this boy grow into his new self. There's talk of him staying another year at Rockland before college, which Dennis believes is a great idea—and not for the same reason the boy does. The boy is making great progress with Shoshanna in figuring out exactly how it was that his father performed all the little evils that he blamed on his son, but therapy is not only about the rational side of things. There is also the spirit that must be tended. He adds, "But can you at least be quick about it?"

"Absolutely," Saralinda says. "We only need like half an hour."

This is not Dennis's idea of quick but he lets it go.

"What's the new name?" he asks the boy who used to be

Caleb Colchester Jr. "It took you a long time to decide."

"Yes, it did," says the boy. "But now I'm sure. It's Harker. Harker Antoine Silva."

"Parker?"

"Harker. It's the name of the main characters in *Dracula*. Antoine gave me the book. Have you read it?"

Dennis shakes his head. "I'm afraid not."

The boy—no, he is a young man—shrugs awkwardly. "Well, this married couple, Jonathan and Mina Harker, they fight back. They have other friends with them too." He pauses. "One dies."

Dennis can't answer. The familiar grief and anger rise in his throat. *On my watch,* he thinks, as he has so many times. *Hunted like rabbits on my watch!* But he didn't fail to fight for these four. He has that.

And they didn't fail to fight for themselves.

This time he counts the candles.

"Dr. Lee?" Harker Antoine Silva asks. "By any chance would you be willing to stay for the ceremony?"

The four wait.

Dennis clears his throat. "I would be honored," he says.

He steps forward as Saralinda hands him the fifth candle.

About the Author

NANCY WERLIN has written nine previous young adult novels, including Edgar Award winner *The Killer's Cousin*, *New York Times* best seller *Impossible*, and National Book Award finalist *The Rules of Survival*. A graduate of Yale College and part-time technical writer at a software firm, Nancy lives with her husband near Boston, Massachusetts.